**"What do you say? Want me to finish the song?"**

Her words brought the house down. Bree wrapped with a flourish, set the mike back on the stool on the corner of the stage, and dipped into a half curtsy.

She felt so good. And she wanted the feeling to last, not to turn into some sort of Cinderella moment where at midnight she transformed back to boring old Bree with her tea, half-finished sweater, and whatever was queued on her Netflix. That Bree was fine. Sometimes.

But tonight she wanted to be this vixen, wherever she'd come from. She sashayed down the stairs, and there he was.

"Hey there, handsome," she shouted over the cheers into the face of the hottest man she could remember seeing up close.

"You're freaking incredible," the sexy stranger shouted back.

No one had ever said that to her before, and in this heady moment she believed him.

And with that, she fisted his shirt. "I want to kiss you." The words came out not even a question. Who was she?

His smile was sudden, and devastating. "What are you waiting for, blondie?"

# Praise for *FRIENDS LIKE US*

"Transport yourself to a world filled with sand and sun."
—*Entertainment Weekly*

# Friends Like Us

## ALSO BY SARAH MACKENZIE

*Forever Friends*

# Friends Like Us

## SARAH MACKENZIE

FOREVER

NEW YORK   BOSTON

Copyright © 2021 by Hachette Book Group, Inc.

Cover design by Elizabeth Turner Stokes
Cover copyright © 2021 by Hachette Book Group, Inc.

Forever
Hachette Book Group
1290 Avenue of the Americas, New York, NY 10104
read-forever.com
twitter.com/readforeverpub

Originally published in trade paperback and ebook by Grand Central Publishing in January 2021

First mass market edition: June 2021

Forever is an imprint of Grand Central Publishing. The Forever name and logo are trademarks of Hachette Book Group, Inc.

The publisher is not responsible for websites (or their content) that are not owned by the publisher.

Library of Congress Cataloging-in-Publication Data

Names: Mackenzie, Sarah (Author of the Cranberry Cove series), author.
Title: Friends like us / Sarah Mackenzie.
Description: First edition. | New York : Forever, 2021. | Series: Cranberry cove
Identifiers: LCCN 2020030164 | ISBN 9781538751114 (trade paperback) | ISBN 9781538751107 (ebook)
Subjects: LCSH: Friendship—Fiction.
Classification: LCC PS3613.A27273 F75 2021 | DDC 813/.6—dc23
LC record available at https://lccn.loc.gov/2020030164

ISBNs: 978-1-5387-1890-2 (mass market), 978-1-5387-5110-7 (ebook)

Printed in the United States of America

CW

10 9 8 7 6 5 4 3 2 1

# Chapter One

The seagull swooped in low. Its long gray wings were a perfect match to the coastal fog and Bree Robinson's gloomy mood. She fingered her delicate bracelet, the one with the "You Got This" quote inscribed into the gold plating, as a ray of sunshine sliced through the stubborn clouds, dazzling the waves. A knot loosened in her lower belly. Maybe here was the sign she'd been looking for, a cosmic signal that today would have a happy ending. Her shoulders barely had time to relax before the damn bird banked, splattering poop over the top of her head.

Nope. Never mind. Today was an officially crappy day.

Sprawled a couple of feet away in an identical blue-striped beach chair, her bestie, Jill Kelly, fanned her hands, in danger of spraying wine out her pert nose. Finally, she must have choked down her chardonnay because she gasped, "I know this is a crappy situation, but, girl, come on, no need to be so literal!"

"Ugh, gross." Reaching for the off-white linen scarf she'd draped around her shoulders to protect herself from the ocean breeze, Bree gingerly swiped at her hair. "Is it gone? Tell me it's gone!"

Jill waved her hand in a suspiciously unsympathetic motion, losing the battle to hold back a giggle. "You'll need a shower later, but that's a good enough job to keep day drinking," she said pressing the wine bottle directly into Bree's hand in lieu of refilling her glass. "Anyway, isn't laughter supposed to be the best medicine? Or wait, was that wine?"

Then why didn't she feel better? Bree scowled at the pale liquid. Silly reaction. The chardonnay hadn't done anything wrong. "Unless you've got cancer," she retorted, "and then it's chemotherapy."

"Whoa, whoa, whoa, hold on!" Jill swatted Bree's arm while leveling a fierce glare. "You can't say the C word out loud. It's against the rules today!"

Bree took a long pull of wine, blotting her lips with the back of her hand. "If anyone can break a rule right now, it's me."

Any minute now she'd be getting her biopsy results.

Had it really been six weeks since that lazy Sunday afternoon, when her only plan had been to indulge in a little self-care: luxuriate in a hot shower, apply a hydrating sheet mask, paint her toes, and fantasize about the Hemsworth brothers? As she'd languidly massaged her favorite jasmine-scented bodywash across her chest, her breath had cut out.

*What. The. Hell. Was. That?*

She'd dragged her fingers back and probed the corn kernel–sized lump buried in the soft flesh near her left nipple. Despite being neck deep in hot water, her body went ice cold.

And the stupid knot didn't disappear no matter how many times she'd poked, prodded, and pleaded for it to go away. All she'd managed to do was give herself one wicked boob bruise.

Doctor visits were scheduled. Clinical breast exams done. Mammograms ordered. Results were inconclusive. Ultrasounds were conducted. That's when the radiologist recommended a biopsy, a needle that would reveal the truth, like the world's worst fortune-teller. Peer into the diagnostic crystal ball: Would she become another American Cancer Society statistic, her world shrinking to artful head wraps and days at the infusion center?

It was hard to rock an upbeat "Cancer is a word, not a sentence" attitude after losing her mom to her own breast lump. It was all terrible. The diagnosis, the treatment, the long, wretched bedside hospice vigil with her big sister, Renee, listening to the lengthening pauses between ragged breaths, watching her mother's creamy skin mottle, staring into her nonreactive eyes searching for a sign—any goddamn sign—that the woman she adored was still there. Her mom had been her rock, her go-to, the first person she'd call every morning, the one who had an answer for everything. The one who always told Bree to dream big and believe in herself.

Her death was like losing a limb. And the phantom pain never went away.

She didn't just lose her mom, she lost her biggest cheerleader.

"Oh heck no, we're not doing this." Jill pushed herself to standing, kicked off her cherry-red flip-flops, and stuck out a hand.

"What?" Bree frowned at her friend's manicure. Jill always had the cutest nail art. Today it was a soft nude shade with a simple gold stripe accent.

She glanced at her own ragged fingernails. It was time she had a manicure of her own. Past time truthfully.

"This is a brooding-free zone. My pawpaw used to say it was good luck if a bird pooped on you."

Bree allowed her friend to pull her up. "Really?"

"No." Jill poked out her tongue. "But it sounds like something he *would* have said, doesn't it?"

"I guess." Bree reached into her back pocket and removed her phone, glaring at the blank screen, willing it to ring almost as much as she dreaded the answer.

"I hate this waiting game so much. Part of me wishes I could get knocked out and be brought back to consciousness once someone can tell me what's going to happen next."

Jill picked up a fragment of smooth, green sea glass and flung it into the whitecaps. "You need more distractions. I know! Let's play a game."

Bree made a show of folding her arms and sizing her up. Jill was such a fixer, always wanting people around her to be happy, always the one with a suggestion. Usually Bree didn't mind. It was pretty darn great to have a friend willing to search out the best happy hour deals or find the greatest Airbnbs when they'd road-tripped to Boston.

But right now she didn't want to be ordered around. "What do you have in mind? If you suggest hot dog tag, I'm gonna trip you. Just like in third grade."

And in a tiny poisonous part of her heart, Bree *did* want to trip Jill, standing there all toned legs from her daily 5Ks, her golden skin radiating good health and infinite possibility. Sure, Jill had seen more than her share of loss but right now her body was so vibrant, so healthy. Bree choked down the bitter surge of envy like it was one of her sister's extra-healthy dandelion salads. Jealousy was the worst and never did a friendship good.

"Hilarious." Jill snorted, happily unaware of Bree's secret flash of evilness. "I haven't thought about hot dog tag in over twenty years."

"How weird that we've known each other for so many decades," Bree said, schooling friendliness back into her tone, unwilling to be held hostage by unwelcome feelings. "Half the time I still feel sixteen. But then I glance in the mirror and my crow's-feet say otherwise."

"Smile lines are gorgeous. They give a gal character." Jill tossed her rose-gold hair, dyed to match the frames of her glasses, her style since high school. "At least that's what I tell myself daily—so don't you dare contradict me.

And anyway I was thinking less hot dog tag and more what will you do when you find out that you're in the clear?"

"Shhhhh!" Bree wagged a finger "Don't jinx me."

"Oh give me that." Jill plucked the wine bottle from Bree's grasp and took a swig. "There's no jinxing here. Think I'd ever risk losing you, too?" A dark expression passed over her otherwise sunny expression. There and gone in a flash.

"Oh, Jilly Beans." Bree used her long-standing nickname as her friend's words unlocked something inside her, a poignant reminder that she wasn't the only one with problems. "Crap. I'm sorry if my health stuff is triggering. The last thing I want is to mope around, going 'poor me' while you—"

"Support my best friend." Jill's wide mouth might be crooked into a lopsided grin, but her gaze swung out to the sea, arms crossing in clear warning: "Don't go there."

If there was one thing that Bree had learned since Jill's husband's death three years ago, it was that if Jill wanted to talk about Simon, she would. Otherwise, it was best to leave the subject well enough alone. These days Jill seemed to expend all her energy on keeping others happy, almost as if she could use their energy to sustain her. And if that was the case, Bree would try her level best.

"Okay, okay, fine. You win." Bree studied her friend's profile, now staring wistfully at two boys in superhero shirts whooping up the beach in hot pursuit of their black labradoodle. "Let's play your little game. It's either that or watch the minutes tick by while getting more and more sloshed."

"We're already doing that." Jill toasted her, voice a little thick before clearing her throat. "So . . . what are all the things you're going to do once you get your second chance?"

"Do?" Bree blinked. "Like a bucket list?"

"An *anti*–bucket list. Because girl, you aren't allowed to kick any bucket until you hit the triple digits."

She snorted. "Is that a fact?"

Jill threw her hands on her hips. "Is the Pope Catholic?"

"Okay, okay. Calm down and let me think." Bree traced a happy face in the sand with her big toe, as if the gesture could summon lightheartedness. "I should really open an IRA. And I've never figured out how to install that dimmer light I bought for the dining room. Oh! And I haven't completed the five-thousand-piece jigsaw puzzle I got at the Met Store the last time I went to New York. That pretty replica of spring in Central Park—"

"Argh. You've killed me with boring." Jill clutched her chest, staggering backward before collapsing into a dramatic heap on the sand, still, impressively, not spilling a drop of wine.

"Oh knock it off." Bree rolled her eyes. "I'm being realistic."

"Sure, if you're ready to move into Silver Maples." Jill dropped the pointed reference to Cranberry Cove's retirement community. "But good lord, you're still in your thirties. I don't want to judge your list, but I'm gonna judge *this* list. Time for a do-over. Go deeper. Think about what you really want from life but have always been afraid to chase. Screw fear. Dream big."

Bree pursed her lips. Go deeper? It was cold and dark down deep. Monsters lurked in subterranean caverns. Who knows what other dangers? She preferred floating on life's surface, remaining in the shallows. But Jill was getting that stubborn set to her chin, the one that meant she wasn't backing down from a debate.

"Fine, what do you want me to say?" She pinched the bridge of her nose. "I long to hike the Great Wall of China? Dream of skydiving? Yearn to visit an endangered tribe in the Amazon?"

Jill flashed a thumbs-up. "Now we're talking."

"While we're at it, why don't I win the lottery and go on a date with Thor?"

"Now you've swung from boring to unrealistic. You can't control the lottery, and sadly for us mortals..." Jill shrugged. "Thor isn't actually, you know...real."

"This is a ridiculous exercise." Bree began to pace, restless and unsettled. "You know me! I work in a knitting store for Pete's sake. If you need a new cowl or a pair of fingerless mittens for fall then I'm your gal. But I'm not some hard-core adrenaline junkie with an appetite for danger. I get woozy on my porch swing and I hate sleeping in tents."

She refused to glance back up at the cliffs in the direction of Grandview Inn, the historic B and B that had stood sentinel over Cranberry Cove for more than a century. A property that had been closed for over a decade, had seen better days, but always seemed to beckon to Bree, a little insistent whisper of "What if..."

What if she could bring it back to life?

What if she could restore its former grandeur?

A silly notion.

Jill pushed back to standing and slung her arm around Bree's slouching shoulders. As always, she had to stand on tiptoe to do it. Towering over Jill's petite five-foot frame always made Bree feel like a lumbering Amazon. "I happen to think there is a happy medium between making your life goals a choice between jigsaw puzzles and trekking through China."

"I like to do puzzles." Bree nudged Jill gently in the ribs. "Boring knitter here, remember?"

"Why do you pretend that you're ordinary?" Jill asked after a long pause. "You're my person, my *favorite* person, the one who punched Leroy Reynolds when he wiped boogers on me on the school bus and the only one who kept me going after . . . well . . . after."

Bree's eyes prickled with sudden unshed tears. There was "Before Jill," happy, bubbly, head-over-heels in love with her handsome mechanic husband. And "After Jill," a widow too young, too skinny, and too lost, but quick to slap on a smile that passed for convincing if you disregarded the hollowed shadows in her gaze and brittle edge to her attitude. The Jill in front of her today was a lot like the Jill who had been married to Simon, but also vastly different. Bree knew from personal experience that there was no "right" timeline for processing grief. Still, Jill didn't need to act as if she was made of steel. She was allowed to drop the brave face and shatter now and again. But she never did.

And Bree didn't know how to make it okay. But she could be there.

She could go deep. She'd do anything for this woman.

Closing her eyes, she blurted the first wish that came to her mind. "Sex."

"Ex-squeeze me?" Jill startled. "Did you just say—"

"Sex. I miss it. You know I haven't gotten any action since Ian." Ian Doring, aka Ian *Boring*. High school boyfriend. Ex-fiancé since five years ago. Five long years without . . . ahem. "I'm growing cobwebs between my legs. But it's more than that. I don't want to just *do it*. I want to *feel it*. From the top of my head to the tips of my toes. Passion with a capital *P*. Love. Fireworks. Highs. Lows. Everything Ian wasn't."

"Ian the Actuary didn't rock your world?" Jill arched a brow. "Shocker."

"Don't be mean. Ian was fine."

*Fine.*

God, the bland, beige word sounded worse when she spoke it out loud.

Her ex-fiancé *was* fine. That had been the whole problem. And worse, she'd been content to go along with it because the relationship felt as easy and comfortable as a pair of old yoga pants. He'd had to be the one to end it, unwilling to settle for good enough even when she was.

She heard he'd left insurance behind and gotten into data science out in Silicon Valley, where he now lived in a Palo Alto mini-mansion, drove a Tesla, and was married to a former Miss Arizona.

That stung a bit, to be honest. Turned out that when

push came to shove boring ol' Ian wasn't quite so boring. Maybe she'd been the problem all along.

"And I want a dog," Bree blurted, glancing back at the labradoodle now playing fetch with the boys. "Ian was allergic so that was always off the table. But I'd love a furry friend to take down to the beach, or give me an excuse to get out of bed early on the weekends. It felt like a thing I'd wait to do until I was part of a couple, but why wait?"

"Sexy times with a passionate man and being an independent woman who adopts a dog." A slow grin spread over Jill's fine elfin features. "Now this is the stuff of anti-bucket list gold."

Bree picked up a chipped periwinkle shell and heaved it out into the water. "Hold on. I'm not done yet." She was just warming up.

"You go, girl," encouraged Jill. "What else do you want?" She also flung a shell in the water.

"I want something I call my own, you know, in the work department."

"Like your sis and Sadie have with Hester's Pie Shop?" Jill asked. Renee and her next-door neighbor, Sadie, had recently opened a pie shop in the Old Red Mill to local fanfare and rave reviews.

"Something like that." Bree's mind wandered to a sweet dream of running an old Maine inn, the white shingles, the cozy bedrooms, a place where people go to escape stress and rejuvenate themselves. She took a deep breath and danced around the topic. "As much as I love Castaway Yarns, I've never seen it as a forever job. I love knitting and it pays the bills—and thank god for the health insurance—but c'mon the place hasn't changed since Ronald Reagan was president. And anyway, it's Noreen's baby, not mine."

Bree was just the shop assistant. Noreen owned Castaway and called all the shots on displays and merchandise orders. And even though knitting was getting more and more popular as women—and men too!—yearned for a low-tech hobby to help them escape the real world, it didn't feel as if the store was keeping up with the times.

Truth be told, Bree was tired of dropping hints here and there about including more contemporary knitting patterns or getting more sustainably sourced wool or needles and being brushed off. "It would be amazing to have a business that was just mine."

Her insides twisted. There was one other thing, that little secret that she had never told anyone, about the embossed certificate sitting in the top drawer of her father's old rolltop desk, the one that read:

Bree Robinson. Bachelor of Arts. Hotel Management. University of Massachusetts Amherst.

The online degree she'd completed two years ago. The one that she couldn't tell anyone about because at the end of the day, while she spent nights poring over hotel websites and plotting design plans and breakfast menus in her journal, she didn't want to leave home. She loved Cranberry Cove's community, and knew she belonged here more than anywhere else in the world.

But there weren't exactly lots of hotels in the village.

Her gaze turned unwillingly up to the Grandview, the faded shingles, the big bay windows, the overgrown flowers.

"You're losing focus. What else?" Jill pushed.

Bree pursed her lips. There *was* something else she could share, a safer dream.

"I want to sing," she blurted. "Like in public. In front of real people. I used to love choir and gave it all up after high school."

"Wow. You're impressing me," Jill retorted, not a trace of sarcasm to be found for once. "What a great idea! You *are* a wonderful singer."

"Thank you." Bree's cheeks flushed as she smoothed back her hair, getting blown about in the strengthening off-shore gusts. "I'm impressing myself. I didn't really realize all that was in me, right below the surface. Thanks for making me go there."

The phone's ring cut through the momentary silence.

Bree turned her head to Jill, and they locked wide eyes before Bree glanced at her screen.

Southern Maine Medical Partners.

Her fingers shook so hard she could barely hit answer. Here it was. The moment of truth.

# Chapter Two

Bree stood statue still, her blond curly hair dancing in the wind gusts. "Uh-huh," she said blankly. "I see." She nodded once, as if the person on the other end of the phone could see the gesture. "Sorry, I meant yes. Got it. Thanks for the call. I'll be sure to follow up."

Jill's stomach gave a sudden retch, threatening to evacuate the grilled cheese and apple sandwich she'd eaten for lunch. Not to mention most of a bottle of wine. A follow-up? *Shit.* That couldn't be good.

Bree hung up and stared out at the cove. A lobster boat was coming around the far headland, traps stacked five feet high in the back.

It felt as if that dark cold water was rushing into Jill's lungs, the salt filling her throat. *No, no, no.* This couldn't be happening. She couldn't lose Bree. Not after Simon. Ever since her bestie confessed to finding the lump, Jill had been willing an all-clear diagnosis, as if she could control fate through sheer force of will. The universe wasn't going to take another one of her people. It simply wasn't allowed.

"So...I don't have cancer," Bree finally said in a soft whisper.

Jill startled, not trusting her own ears, especially when her blood was pulsing through her skull with Niagara-like force. "Wait, what?"

"I don't have cancer." Louder this time. Unmistakable.

Jill blinked. The dark waters receded. Her lungs filled with sweet, sweet air. "But you said 'follow up.'"

"The nurse told me to book another mammogram when I turn forty, and to make sure to schedule an MRI with it. But it's just as a precaution. Right now I'm okay. The lump was a benign cyst."

"A benign cyst." The word sounded beautiful on Jill's lips, the same as saying "summer in Paris" or "room service." "I freaking love cysts."

Bree burst out laughing. "Weirdo."

"You mean the happiest person alive." Jill kicked out her legs in a silly version of an Irish jig. An older woman, likely a tourist as she didn't look familiar, strolled by watching the show with a bemused expression. Who gave a flying fig? Bree was going to be okay and that's all that mattered.

"You don't give a hoot about what other people think, do you?" Bree asked with a giggle.

"Course I do," Jill gasped, kicking up the sand. "But I'm

so thrilled that I could streak down Main Street if Tyler wouldn't arrest me."

"Poor Officer Tyler. You'd traumatize the poor man."

Tyler Cox was one of two Cranberry Cove full-time police officers and he had been a few years ahead of them in school, a shy, sweet boy who'd grown up into a shy, sweet man.

"Wait." Jill froze as the idea struck her with the force of a lightning bolt. "Tonight is open mike night at that new alehouse."

"The Drafty Cellar?" Bree cocked her head. "Off Main Street? I haven't been there yet. I'm surprised it was able to open so soon after the hurricane. It must have escaped the worst of it." The hurricane that hit a few months ago had damaged many local downtown businesses.

"Weellll...it's supposed to have amazing burgers and lots of liquid courage," Jill said, getting more and more excited.

Bree's lashes fluttered closed as she sucked in a deep breath, holding it for a few seconds before releasing the pent-up air in a rush. "Okay. I'll probably regret it, but I'll do it."

"Yes, girl! You're amazing!" Jill clapped her hands. "I'm so so *so* proud of you." Turning to gather up their things, she asked, "How about I pick you up at eight o'clock? And wear those high-heeled boots you bought in Boston last spring. They make your butt look sexy as hell."

"The leather boots?" Bree wrinkled her nose. "Don't they give off Viking maiden vibes?"

Jill eyed her friend's curvy, tall frame. "They give off major Viking vibes. And trust me, that is a very good thing. You'll be a powerhouse. The eligible men of Cranberry Cove won't know what hit them."

"I don't know if the eligible men of Cranberry Cove will agree with that statement." She offered a wry smile. "There hasn't been a line of suitors wrapping around my block."

"Who knows." Jill waggled her brows. "Maybe tonight a tall, dark, and handsome stranger is going to whisk you off your feet."

"Fine." Bree pursed her lips even as her cheeks flushed. "I'll wear the boots, but I won't bother holding my breath."

*  *  *

Jill frowned at the red lipstick in her bathroom drawer. Simon used to love when she wore the bright color, said that it made her look like a vintage pinup girl. She hadn't bothered with it since his funeral. She reached down and reread the name on the small circular label: "Vixen." The tube was over three years old, well past the time she should toss it in the trash, but to do so would mean severing yet another fragile tether of Simon's presence in her life. First had been boxing up his side of the closet to donate to charity. Then went his motorcycles. His toothbrush. His shaving cream and razor. His contacts. His boots. The protein powder in the pantry.

And now the lipstick.

Without thinking she dropped it into the wastebasket.

She had lip gloss in the car and it wasn't like she was going to wear bright red lipstick again. She was Simon's vixen. No one else's. Sure, she'd dated here and there for the last year and a bit, but no one special. And lately it had been like what was the point? After getting to have a triple hot fudge sundae with a cherry on top, a carob-flavored cookie didn't really cut it. She'd gotten her happily-ever-after, even if the story ended after a couple of chapters.

Before flicking off the condo lights on her way out to get Bree, Jill paused to take in the modest space. She had once loved this little love nest that she and Simon had rented while they saved up for a down payment on a home of their own. One of the reasons it took so long was that her mom didn't have much in the way of financial resources and needed their help. After giving up bartending due to her tendinitis, she stumbled on a series of bad business decisions. The get-rich-quick vitamin supplement scheme. Selling leggings on Facebook and getting stuck with thousands of dollars of stock she couldn't move. Being a consultant for prepaid legal services. Every idea left her one step closer to bankruptcy.

So she and Simon had covered half of Linda's rent on a modest studio a stone's throw from Grandview Inn, a place that at one point had been the hotel gardener's workshop. Though it was only one room that included both kitchenette and bedroom, it was sun-drenched and offered enviable views of the Atlantic from almost every window.

The expense meant they'd delayed investing in a home, but Simon had pushed her to take the forgiveness and reconciliation route. His own parents were both gone and he wanted her to keep her remaining parent in her life. It was such a sweet sentiment, so typical of Simon. So they helped with her mom's rent while Linda worked off her credit card debt by cleaning vacation rentals and promised not to start any new ventures without consulting them.

These days that dream, like so many things in her life, had gone from perfect to poisoned. But the condo wasn't a tube of lipstick that she could toss away. She stepped outside and locked the door with a forceful turn of the key as if she could seal off the painful history that rose up every time she walked in the kitchen or crawled into her bed. She was haunted by memories.

A mile later, while driving through the four-way intersection near Bree's place, she made sure that her gaze didn't drift left toward Anchor Court and the cheerful yellow cottage with the white trim and red door, or linger on the For Sale sign in the front yard bearing a photo of a chic Korean-American woman—Essie Park, Cranberry Cove's go-getting real estate agent. Jill was friendly with Essie, who frequented most of the pinot-and-paint events she held at the Chickadee Studios. Essie had also helped Jill move her shop from Main Street to the Old Red Mill when her store had been condemned by the freak hurricane.

Chickadee would be back open for business in another few weeks and not a moment too soon.

Jill gripped the steering wheel and forced herself to drive past the charming home she'd once fantasized about owning with Simon.

"Someday you and I are going to sit on that front porch, babe," he used to say on their long twilight walks. They'd pause in front of the cottage and he'd plant a soft kiss on the back of her hand. "We'll watch the world go by and worry about nothing." He'd restore vintage motorcycles in the garage while she'd do watercolors in the sunroom. They'd fill the spare rooms with a child, maybe two.

Such a lovely dream.

One that was soon to be someone else's.

She gnawed the little sore inside her top lip, the spot her teeth always seemed to find when the idea of children crossed her mind. Her mom loved the saying "Life is what happens while you're busy making plans." The phrase had always struck Jill as so fatalistic and accepting. She'd wanted to dream bigger dreams than her mom, a life of thriving and creativity and hope, far away from her lonely childhood out in the woods while her mom bartended or tried yet another get-rich, multilevel marketing scheme. While her mom tried her best to raise Jill, Linda had been only a child herself, one who'd learned at a too-young age that the world was a hard place.

Her mom was the one person who didn't seem shocked by Simon's death: the hours he was missing, the frantic searching, the discovery of his body in a steep ravine up in the hills.

She never seemed shocked by anything, just took the knocks on the chin as if they were to be expected.

Maybe she was the wisest of them all.

As Jill turned up Bree's street it became clear that she

didn't have to park. Bree was standing in front of her big, rambling Victorian, fiddling with the mailbox's red flag.

"Hey, hey! Looking for a good time tonight, hot stuff?" Jill teased, pasting on her smile, and just like that her somber mood was hidden, *poof*, gone like it never happened. It's not that she *had* to put on an act for Bree. Her best friend would be there for her hell or high water. But more often than not it was easier to fake it; she didn't want to be the grieving widow. That was never the plan and it certainly wasn't what Simon would have wanted. Maybe one day she wouldn't have to fake it anymore, and she could take a full breath again.

That would be enough.

"Ready to sing your heart out?" Jill asked as Bree buckled in.

"Not at all," Bree confessed. "Honestly, I don't think I'm up for it. Baby steps. It's enough we're going out on a weeknight, right?"

"Wrong," Jill shot back as she stepped on the gas.

She might be merely existing, but that didn't mean Bree had to.

# Chapter Three

The alehouse was crowded, the dim room teeming with bodies pressed elbow to elbow. The interior decor was a bohemian blend of stained wood, vintage industrial furniture, and reclaimed lighting. From a small stage, a jazz singer in a sequined black dress crooned a Billie Holiday song.

"Good lord! Is everyone in Cranberry Cove out tonight?" Bree hollered over the din.

Julie beelined toward the bar. "Feels that way, but it's just that good ol' high-season foot traffic," she called over one shoulder. "Now pick your poison!"

"What's the point?" Bree gaped at the crowd thronging against the long bar. "It will take a year to put in an order."

As fun as it had been to get dolled up, flat-ironing her hair, using an eyelash curler, putting on the dark jeans that made her butt look good, and zipping up her heeled boots, now it seemed like a faintly silly waste of effort. It wasn't that Bree didn't like being around other people. She did. But only when she could see their faces, have a conversation.

In a knitting circle, gossiping over a new rom-com show, she was in seventh heaven. Here? She was going to be sweating into her underwire any second. Especially as the singer on the stage was good, really damn good. How could she compete with that? Spoiler: she couldn't.

"Wait, stop the press. I spy our gal Essie in a prime position," Jill shouted, grabbing Bree's wrist as if sensing her impulse to beat a retreat to the front door. "She's elbowing toward the front of the line."

"Of course she is," Bree muttered, a wry smile playing on her lips. "Is there anything Essie Park can't do when she puts her mind to it?"

The number-one Realtor in Cranberry Cove caught their gazes and lifted a hand, her diamond ring catching in the light. "What can I get you, ladies?"

"Two honey ciders!" Jill shot a peace sign up to the sky for emphasis. "The cider house that makes them is over near Sebago Lake and winning awards left and right."

It was hot in here. A cool drink did sound good. "Sounds intriguing." Bree watched as the blond bartender poured Essie three pints of golden liquid. While it sparkled and foamed, she couldn't help but fantasize about crawling into her king-sized bed with a cup of licorice tea and devouring her newest World War II novel.

"No second thoughts or cold feet allowed. You aren't leaving here without getting up on that stage and giving your vocal cords one heck of a workout," Jill announced with a wag of the finger. "I'm going to put your name on the open mike list."

"List? What list?" Essie asked, appearing suddenly, her jet-black hair cut in a blunt bob with equally blunt bangs.

"The list is for open mike." Jill relieved Essie of one of her ciders. "Bree is going to sing for us this fine evening."

"You've been holding out hidden talents on me," Essie exclaimed as she handed Bree a perfectly chilled pint glass. "A singer, you say? Color me impressed."

"Jill's exaggerating. I'm not a singer," Bree said, sipping the sweet liquid. Jill wasn't kidding, this cider was delicious, like taking a bite of a perfect apple, just after drizzling it with clover honey.

"Are too!" Jill countered.

"Not unless you count belting out Andrew Lloyd Webber's greatest hits in the shower."

"I just love *Cats*!" Essie exclaimed. "Not the movie though." She shivered. "I still get nightmares."

"I can channel my inner Madonna to do a mean Evita," Jill said, "but sadly only if no one is watching."

As Bree sipped her cider, Jill talked. In less than two minutes she had caught Essie up to speed on everything: the lump, the doctors, the waiting, the results, the anti–bucket list. It was strange to hear her life laid out in such simple, straight-forward sentences. Jill must have honed the practice after

Simon's death when everyone asked the same awful well-intentioned questions, "What happened? How are you?"

Jill had become a repetitive robot.

*Motorcycle accident up on Holloway Hill. We think he swerved to miss a deer.*

*I'm okay, taking things day by day.*

Bree had heard those three sentences so many times that she'd lost count, until they'd lost meaning, transforming into a numb cluster of consonants and vowels, held together by a confident delivery and a head held high.

Now Bree had a taste of what it was like to have a personal horror reduced to a sound bite. She didn't know how that made her feel so she took another sip, and another, and another, until...

"You pounded that pint like a frat boy with Natty Light," Jill crowed.

"And you would know," Bree shot back. Jill had studied art history at the University of Maine while Bree had waited tables at a now-defunct brunch spot near the Cranberry Cove Harbor. She'd visit Jill on the weekends, meeting her new frat flavor of the week, a seemingly endless parade of obnoxious Hawaiian shirts and khakis until one day they disappeared, replaced by a wiry, curly-haired guy from up near Moose River who seemed to live in flannel shirts, a gray knit beanie, and Doc Martens and rode a Triumph Bonneville.

Jill found Simon Kelly and that was that. Whatever restlessness was pent up inside of her seemed to settle. She was happy, as happy as any person should ever be allowed to be.

"What are you going to sing?" Essie's question broke into Bree's brooding.

"I...I...Oh god, I hadn't even gotten that far in my mind. I have no idea."

"Well you better think fast." Essie sipped her own cider and made a face. "Ew, I should have stuck with merlot."

"I'll do 'Make You Feel My Love,'" Bree blurted, "the Adele hit."

"Good choice," a voice growled behind her.

She spun in the direction of that deep rumble, threaded with amusement. Before she had even gotten a good look at his face, she was breathing in the masculine scent—cedarwood and musk.

"You don't strike me as the type to go for the usual open mike choices. Journey isn't your style, is it?"

She blinked. Looked around. Blinked again.

Yep, she wasn't hallucinating. That was a *man* talking to her, and not some toothy-grinned creep with a sweaty forehead and unearned confidence. This guy was h-o-t, with a jaw that could have been hewn from rugged coastal granite and a five-o'clock shadow that was on the right side of sexy. Despite his thick mop of dark hair—in this light it was impossible to decipher whether it was dark brown or black—his eye color could never be in doubt. The piercing blue seemed to brand her, his gaze tracing her face with a strange sort of calligraphy, as if sending a secret invitation.

Heat bloomed through her chest,

Someone, Jill or Essie, probably Essie, gave her a hard

nudge. *Crap.* She hadn't said a word, just stood there, lips half parted, ogling him like he was a hot fudge sundae and she hadn't eaten for a week.

"Where'd you come from?" she blurted. An honest question, even though it was totally stupid. It's not like he'd popped up like a sexy mushroom, coaxed to life by the IPA sloshed across the floorboards.

"You're a funny one." His grin was sudden, devastating, and did all sorts of interesting things to the corners of his eyes.

She licked her lips, hoping she didn't sound as dry as her throat felt. "I'm not trying to be."

"That's the cutest part." He took a slow sip of his beer, also dark, a porter or stout.

He was flirting. This sexy stranger with the bedroom eyes and perfect scruff was not only talking to her, but was also focused on her mouth, where she'd started absently rubbing her lips together.

"Her name is Bree." Jill stepped forward, lending a hand. One that Bree loathed and loved her for all at once.

"Bree Robinson," Jill continued. "She's a knitting goddess and is here to sing for your pleasure."

Was it Bree's imagination or did his nostrils flare slightly at the word "pleasure." She ground her knees together, grateful she'd grabbed her black lace bikini-cut underwear tonight.

"Castaway Yarn?" he drawled.

"Oh." He knew the store. That stumped her. "Do you knit?" If that was the case, she'd die of a mental orgasm right then and there.

His lips curled into that wicked smile again, as if he sensed her toes curling. "No. I just wrapped up working in your old space. Repairing the hurricane damage for the landlord."

"Oh," she murmured. "I see."

She could stand here and listen to him talk until the world ended in a puff of blue smoke.

But the fact she was staring and not speaking was apparently getting weird because Jill and Essie both stepped forward, bracketing her.

"Sorry to steal her, but she's promised to sing at open mike tonight."

"I promised to sing," Bree repeated like a drunken parrot.

Dark and Handsome raised his glass. "Looking forward to the show."

Jill steered her toward the stage while Essie hissed in her ear. "Do you act like that around all men?"

"No!" Bree moaned as her brain cells began to function again. It was as if she'd been in some drug-induced coma and was coming up for air. "I'm not sure what happened. One minute I was fine, hanging with you two, the next...I couldn't feel my legs. I couldn't breathe. I couldn't think."

"Ooooooh, you've got it bad. That blush. Those eyes. You are dick drunk," Essie replied.

"Excuse me?" Bree startled. "What did you just say?"

"Dick drunk." Essie arched a sage brow. "Usually it happens after sex, more like a pleasure coma, but in your case it's probably because it's been a while. You got a whiff of the D and got wasted. It's a lightweight move, but not unheard of."

Bree glanced around wondering if the entire bar was as shocked as she felt. But it was so loud it didn't seem like anyone heard besides her and Jill, who was currently lost in a fit of giggles.

"You know what," Bree said crisply. "I'm not even scared of singing in public anymore. Maybe it will erase the images you just put in my mind."

"You'll have to go find him afterwards." Essie winked.

Bree snorted. "Singing is enough excitement for one night. Chatting up a hot guy would probably give me a stroke."

"Or it could be two items crossed off your anti–bucket list," Jill said.

"I'll drink to that," Essie cheered, taking a huge grimacing gulp of her cider. "Seriously, Girl, do it. We got your back."

"Imagine my hand is inside you, stroking your vertebrae," Jill teased.

"Too far." Bree took a deep breath, set her drink on a round bar table beside them, and smoothed sweaty palms over her denim-clad thighs. " Okay, I'm going in."

There was only one person in front of her on the list, a man singing some sort of seventies funk. His number seemed to pass in a blur. All she knew was that her stomach was expressing a lot of interest in projecting its contents all over the floor. She took deep breaths through the nose and out of the mouth.

"Hey beautiful," another male voice said, not Dark and Dangerous, too smooth and smarmy. "You'd look better if you smiled."

"Huh?" Bree glanced over, the clearly drunk man breaking her focus.

He wore a white polo shirt and swayed a little like he'd been at sea for months. The reality was he'd probably had too many of the pale beers he was double fisting. He looked vaguely familiar, probably from the city with a vacation rental up here.

"I said give me a smile, doll."

"No thank you," Bree said, just as the MC announced her.

Stepping around Mr. Drunk and Disorderly, she took the stage. It was smaller than she anticipated, and higher too. The heels made her go a little woozy, the same way she always felt when getting too close to a ledge.

The crowd murmured, expectant, while she waited for the music to begin. It was odd just standing there so she put the microphone close to her mouth and murmured, "Hi, everyone. Hope you all are having a great night."

An earsplitting reverberation pierced the crowd, sending up wincing cries, and Bree flinched.

Great. She hadn't even started and already this was a bust.

Her inner critic whispered, "You could run away before it gets worse."

She gaped into the shadowy room, her throat tightening. Why had she let Jill push her here tonight? This felt awful. Open mike had been a fun idea in theory, but right now she could be home in her silky bathrobe with a hot beverage and a book or a mind-blowing true crime documentary.

The DJ gave her a curt nod and the spotlight intensified as the crowd fell silent. She was in for a penny now. She nodded back and lifted the mike to her mouth as the music began. Her eyes widened as the first note left her throat. Despite the fact that her knees were shaking, her voice was strong and pitch perfect. A few appreciative claps broke out. Someone whistled. She began to sway a little, letting the music, the lyrics, the whole damn last few months wash over her.

Take that, inner critic! She was alive. She was okay. And she was singing her heart out. Sure, it was an alehouse in a small town in a rural state, but who cared? It felt awesome. She was just hitting the last verse, savoring every syllable, reveling in the sense that the audience was collectively holding their breath, when it happened.

Two hands reached out and then there he was, Mr. Drunk and Disorderly, trying to haul himself up on the stage.

"That's it, doll, sing it for me, oh yeah." He collapsed at her feet, leering up at her. "And the view up here is even better than down there."

His buddies, clustered nearby, clapped and jeered him on.

She glanced over at the DJ, who seemed equally horrified but didn't turn off the sound. The piano kept playing as if they were trapped in a bad dream. The moment that felt so amazing just seconds before now felt ugly, tarnished by this sweaty guy who felt his twisted agenda was more important than her moment.

And hell no.

Hell no to this guy rolling around at her feet like an idiot and his awful friends trying to ruin her moment. It took guts to come out here tonight and she wasn't going to let this man ruin her anti–bucket list triumph.

She nudged the guy in his soft rump with the heel of her boot and he rolled over. Someone in the back cheered. One more nudge and he'd be off her stage because make no doubt about it...right now this was her damn stage.

So she did it. One more nudge—maybe technically a bit of a kick—and the guy was cast back down into the depths.

That did it. The audience lost its mind, drowning out the angry protests from his pals.

She tossed back her hair, for once proud of her height, her curves, and feeling power, pure and unadulterated coursing through her veins. She raised the mike to her lips and arched a brow. "What do you say? Want me to finish the song?"

That brought the house down. She wrapped with a flourish, set the mike back on the stool on the corner of the stage, and dipped into a half curtsy.

She felt so good. And she wanted the feeling to last, not to turn into some sort of Cinderella moment where at midnight she transformed back to boring old Bree with her tea, half-finished sweater, and whatever was queued on her Netflix. That Bree was fine. Sometimes.

But tonight she wanted to be this vixen, wherever the hell she came from. She sashayed down the stairs and there he was, the exact opposite of Mr. Drunk and Disorderly.

"Hey there, handsome," she shouted over the cheers into the face of the hottest man she could remember seeing up close.

"You're freaking incredible," the sexy stranger shouted back.

No one had ever said that to her before, and in this heady moment she believed him.

And with that, she fisted his shirt. "I want to kiss you." The words came out not even a question. Who was she?

His smile was sudden, and devastating. "What are you waiting for, blondie?"

A challenge.

She didn't even have to go on tiptoe, not in these boots.

Her mouth slanted over his and his lips were warm with just the perfect amount of firmness. His hand was over the back of her neck a moment later, an alpha hair grab that made her gasp, and when her lips parted he was ready to take everything she had. Some part of her brain registered she was French-kissing a stranger in public and this moment was going to be discussed at Shopper's Corner for the next decade, but it felt good to do this. So good she wanted more.

"What do you say we cut out of here?" she purred, as bold and sultry as a heroine in an old black-and-white movie. Guess she had him fooled. His nostrils flared and he looked ready for business.

"Lead the way," he drawled.

"Wait a sec, what's your name?" It was one thing to march boldly toward her first one-night stand. But there was also basic politeness. She couldn't cross "having a fling" off her anti–bucket list without even knowing the guy's first name.

"You sure you don't want to just use me for my body?" he teased.

Oh, she did indeed.

But she was still a lady.

"Just yanking your chain. I'm Chance," he said extending his hand.

"Bree."

He laced his fingers with hers. "I know."

And so she turned, pushing through the crowd, giving Jill a wink as she passed.

"You sure?" her friend mouthed, glancing to the man who held her hand.

Bree nodded. No time like the present to cross the next item off her anti–bucket list—one-night stand, here she came.

# Chapter Four

Radiant morning sunlight slanted through the two factory-style windows, casting shadows over the worn oak floorboards. Jill lowered the roller brush she was using to prime the yellowed mill walls into a crisp white and sniffed the air. *Holy yum.* It smelled like pie o'clock. Renee must be working. Jill hadn't eaten anything but a banana after her usual morning jog and her stomach testily reminded her of that fact.

After Bree had ditched open mike night with her tall, blue-eyed drink of water, Jill had stayed behind, living her best life, at one point getting on the stage with Essie and belting out a Taylor Swift song. Even though she was dragging this morning, she was fueled by the fact that soon she'd hear all about Bree's nighttime adventure. Fingers crossed she had her world rocked.

Meanwhile, until she got the gossip, there was plenty to keep her occupied. She dragged the back of her hand over her brow and looked around. It was coming along. Chickadee Studios was inching ever closer to its reopening here in the Old Red Mill. While she missed her former location over on Cranberry Cove's charming Main Street, the building's owner needed to do a full remodel after the hurricane, and had used the disaster as a catalyst to move forward with his long-term plans to convert the space into condos. Frustrating, but then the mill had fabulous character...and delicious smells, like the ones currently coming from Hester's Pie Shop, just down the hall.

She sniffed again. That's it. She needed a slice. Now. When it came to Renee's pies, Jill had one philosophy: eat like no one was ever going to see you naked.

After sealing the paint can, Jill followed her nose. Hester's wasn't yet open for the day, the mismatched wooden chairs and tables—painted robin's-egg blue and candy-apple red—waited for the influx of devotees eager to get their daily fix of the delicate buttery crusts and scrumptious fillings. Not only had Sadie Landry, Hester's co-owner and granddaughter of the beloved town baker who was also the shop's namesake, designed a place that felt like the extension of a Maine farmhouse kitchen, but she had also transformed it into a de facto community space of sorts. In another hour, locals and tourists alike would be rubbing elbows, the conversation filling the space and making the whole building feel alive.

And behind the big picture window that led directly into a gleaming kitchen where patrons could watch all the action, Renee was currently pulling pie tins out of the oven.

"Whatcha making?" Jill called over the light jazz playing on the sound system. "Because my stomach is growling like a bear coming out of hibernation and it's all your fault."

"Oh, hey you! I'm just trying out a new recipe," Renee said, straightening up, a smattering of flour on her right cheekbone. Only this woman could make a mess look artful. She was like Martha Stewart's twin sister minus a couple of decades. "It's an apple-maple pie with a special secret ingredient."

"Apple? Maple?" Jill groaned in appreciation as she wove around the register and walked into the kitchen. "Does it taste as good as it sounds?"

"Why don't you try it and tell me." Renee cut a generous slice and plated it on one of the sweet mismatched vintage china plates they used in the shop. "Forks are on your left."

"Don't have to tell me twice." Jill grabbed a utensil and leaned over the plate, breathing in the sweet aroma. Her mouth actually watered. "Amazing. It smells exactly like fall."

"Perfect!" Renee clapped her hands twice. "An autumn flavor is exactly what I was going for. Come September, I want to offer traditional favorites, but with a twist. Now chew slowly, I want to see if you can guess what element I snuck into the crust."

Jill pressed a fork into the buttery pastry as a whisper thin puff of steam released. Not for the first time she responded to one of Renee's creations with a hint of a feeling she couldn't quite put her finger on, maybe nostalgia for a childhood she never had.

Not that she expected her own mom to be chained to the stove, of course, but an occasional homemade treat would have been savored in a way that the gas station Twinkie on her birthday never had been. She shoved in a mouthful of the pie with extra force as if it could fill that empty part of her, still starved for the fantasy of a perfect family. It didn't quite work, but the explosion of flavors in her mouth made her eyes widen.

"Holy crap, lady, this is amazing," she sputtered, mouth full. "I'm burning my tongue to charcoal, but it's worth it. I need another bite."

Renee's eyes lit up. As much as she was praised around town for her baking prowess, Bree's big sister always acted as if it was the first compliment she'd ever received. And it was genuine too. It wasn't that Renee had false humility, but she seemed to derive genuine pleasure out of bringing happiness to the world, one sweet treat at a time.

"Let the flavors roll around on your tongue. Can you taste the mystery ingredient?" she asked, brimming with anticipation.

"What mystery ingredient?" Bree asked, entering the kitchen, Essie in hot pursuit. "And no fair that you're letting Jill eat pie when yesterday you said I couldn't."

Renee burst out laughing. "That's because you were trying to eat the special order for Dot Turner's surprise birthday party."

Bree pouted.

"And you are going to her party, right? So you'll be eating those pies in a matter of hours," Essie pointed out.

"The heart wants what the heart wants." Bree reached for Jill's fork, plucking it from her hand and shoveling in her own bite of pie. "Mmmmph, that's so hot, but so freaking good."

"Hey, gimme my fork before it's covered in cooties," Jill cried out. "I don't know where those lips have been during the last twelve hours."

"Oh, yes you do," Essie sang, her brown eyes bright with amusement. "Why do you think I'm here? I want the dirt. I'm talking *all* the dirty, dirty dirt."

"What on earth is going on?" Renee looked between them with a baffled expression. "Why do I have a sneaking suspicion that I'm missing something really important?"

"I plead the Fifth." Jill threw up her hands, feigning innocence. She'd been best friends with Bree long enough to know to stay well out of the way of Bree's relationship with her sister. Renee always meant well, but sometimes she could be an overprotective mother hen, especially when a man was involved.

"Bree took home a sexy stranger from the Drafty Cellar," Essie crowed, never one to let tact get in the way of juicy gossip.

The kitchen went quiet except for the soft whirring of the dishwasher.

"That's not like you, Bree." Renee sounded befuddled. She took off her red-checked pinafore apron and tossed it on the counter. "A one-night stand? You're joking, right?"

"Why?" Bree raised her chin a fraction, her full lips pressing into a thin line. "Is it funny to think a man might be interested in me once in a blue moon?"

"Meow," Essie said, adding a lashing of fuel to the fire.

Jill groaned inwardly. *Here we go.*

"That's not fair." Renee shook her head with such force, her newly cut bob swinging around her chin. "I'd never say you aren't desirable, don't be silly. But look at the facts. You haven't dated for a, ahem, while. And now suddenly you're taking strangers home? Bree, you're an adult and I respect you but wow. What if he was a serial killer who wanted to turn you into a pair of boots? What if he traffics in sexual slavery? What if he was an underwear-stealing pervert?"

Bree snorted. "Come on."

"I'm serious!" Renee's voice went up an octave. "What do you know about him?"

"The most important details. He's tall, dark, and handsome as sin," Essie blurted.

"Hello—so was Ted Bundy! Did you know about this?" Renee shot Jill a look that made her feel like a naughty kid.

"I already told you." Jill held up her hands again. "I plead the Fifth. I'm not making one of the all-time classic blunders—never get in the middle of a sister fight."

"And where were you last night?" Bree ignored Jill's attempt to diffuse the situation, giving Renee a pointed look while steepling her fingers. "No, wait. Let me guess. You were at home with a certain pediatrician. And I would bet my bank account balance that you weren't watching PBS and playing Jenga."

"That's entirely different." Renee flushed. "Dan and I are in a committed relationship. And we live together. He's not some random guy from who-knows-where that I escorted home from the bar."

"No, he was your former boss and that's even better," Essie crowed.

Before Renee transformed her baking hobby into a profession, she'd been the receptionist for the local pediatrician, Dr. Dan Hanlon, who had most of the mothers— and possibly some of the fathers—feeling twitterpated whenever their kids spiked a fever. Renee snapped him up a few months ago after it became clear that Dr. Dan had the prescription for her lonely, long-divorced heart.

"I don't want to argue. What's done is done." Renee sighed and turned to wipe off a spotless counter. "Tell me you used protection at least."

"Tell *me* you did it more than once," Essie added.

"Tell *me* you had fun," Jill chimed in, trying to play along even though she was starting to feel off, like her torso was too hot, her legs were too cold, and she wanted to strip off this old T-shirt with the itchy tag she'd worn for painting.

"If you must know, the answer is: yes, yes, and oh my god, yes." Bree leaned back on the table in a feigned swoon. Her eyes were bright and she looked more relaxed than she had in ages. "Honestly, I didn't even know hookups could be like that…I mean it was even better than a battery-operated boyfriend."

"No!" Essie pressed a hand to her heart. "You won the jackpot!"

"Seriously. I'd never have believed it was possible," Bree said faintly, staring into the distance as if she was still attempting to process the information. "But the things Chance did with his tongue..." She blushed. "Let's just say he was creative."

"Girl," Essie screamed, "give us the tea!" at the same time Renee clapped her hands over her ears and began singing "Jingle Bells" at the top of her lungs.

Jill froze in place, a strange feeling taking over. It wasn't quite jealousy, goodness knew she wasn't interested in anyone's creative tongue if it wasn't Simon...but this sensation *was* something.

Longing.

Strange. She frowned slightly. She'd come to terms with the fact that she'd buried her libido with Simon in the Cranberry Cove Cemetery. It wasn't a melodramatic attention-seeking idea, in fact, she'd never even discussed it with Bree. On the few dates she'd had since her husband's death, she'd never wanted to even hold the man's hand, let alone allow one into her bed.

She stubbornly forked another mouthful of pie and as the kaleidoscope of flavors burst on her tongue, the mystery ingredient revealed itself.

"Bacon," she hollered, clapping a hand over her mouth to catch any spraying crumbs. "That's what you put in the crust, isn't it?"

Renee pumped a fist in the air. "You nailed it."

"I think you mean, *you* nailed it," Jill said after swallowing, grateful to change the topic from men and beds. "Bree, I'm going to need you to knit me a giant sweater for Christmas because I plan on expanding at least four sizes this fall eating that pie."

"Hello?" Essie wasn't to be deterred. When it came to men she was like a bloodhound on the scent. "Renee, I'm sure your pie is good, no offense. I mean, it's always good. But am I the only one who is more interested in Bree's new sex life than bacon?"

"I mean, in all fairness, bacon is orgasmic," Jill quipped but she knew her hopes for a topic change were dashed. Essie loved gossip like *she* loved smoked pork. And any way, she should be happy her best friend got action. Of course, she was pleased—she'd encouraged Bree to take the leap. It wasn't like Jill could expect Bree to remain celibate just because her own libido had closed up shop.

As if hearing her thoughts, Bree glanced directly at Jill, holding her gaze a moment before shrugging. "I'm sorry. I shouldn't kiss and tell."

"Ugh." Essie rolled her eyes. "You're no fun. Tell us you're seeing him again at least."

"Nah." Bree ducked her chin. "It was just a onetime fling. I think he said he's from New York City, but truthfully we didn't do a lot of talking."

"Ah, NYC. The good ones always end up there," Essie said wistfully.

Jill and Bree exchanged amused glances before Renee cleared her throat. "So wait, then how did you end things?"

Bree shrugged, her gaze dimming a little. "My goal was a one-night stand so when I woke up I got worried about being clingy. I sent him off with a mug of coffee. It was from a Christmas white elephant, and chipped, so no loss."

"And no promise to reconnect?" Essie pried.

"Nope." Bree rumpled her already bed-tousled hair. "He didn't ask for my number or to see me again either. And like I said, my whole goal was to keep it casual. Mission accomplished."

A timer dinged and Renee turned to stir some delicious-looking strawberry sauce bubbling on the stove top. "Okay, as much as I love hearing about my baby sister's new free love outlook...*not*...I do have to get the shop ready to open. So that means all of you pervs need to scram."

"Even me?" Jill said, sneaking in a last bite.

"Okay, perverts and Jill."

"Oh, Jill." Essie whirled around and poked one of her delicate fingers into Jill's face. The diamond on her finger was blinding. "I almost forgot to mention, your sweet little cottage is for sale."

Jill's mouth went dry and it took her extra effort to swallow that last bite. "I don't have a cottage."

She wouldn't let her mind stray to the little yellow home or the bright dreams she'd once had for it.

"Of course you don't, but you can now. That place that you always loved is on the market. You know, the one on Anchor Court where the owners lived out of state. They're finally letting it go."

Jill didn't respond as the words registered. Couldn't respond. In fact, it was laughable to think she could eke out a shallow breath. Her lungs were made from concrete.

"Essie," Bree cut in, knowing where this was going.

"Come on, girl! You know which cottage I'm talking about," Essie pushed on, oblivious to the growing tension in the kitchen. "I remember you saying it was your dream house—yours and Simon— Oh . . . shit." Essie clapped her forehead. "I'm an idiot, aren't I?"

"It's okay," Jill managed. "You can say his name. And . . . and . . . I saw the For Sale sign in the yard."

"You should still go for it," Essie said. "They want a quick sale so it's priced for a song and maybe it's the change you need to get unstuck and—"

"Hang on. You think I'm stuck?" Jill asked, turning slowly to look directly into the stricken faces of her closest friends. They *all* thought she was stuck?

Oh, who was she kidding, of course they did.

"God. Leave it alone, E," Bree said firmly.

"Do you all look at me like I'm some big loser?" Jill couldn't help it, the words burbled up, hot and acidic. "Poor Jill the Tragic Widow who hosts pinot-and-paint sessions at her gallery and is stuck on the shelf in her midthirties?" That wasn't her, right? That couldn't be her.

"Jill." Bree's voice burbled into a sob. "No, that's not it. No one thinks that. Not by a long shot."

"Of course not." Jill held up a hand, warding Bree back, the bottled-up feelings would burst out of her with just a little more pressure. "Sorry. I'm fine. I actually forgot that I

have an appointment. A...uh...really important...thing."
And with that she beat a hasty retreat. Avoidance wasn't
elegant, but it worked in a pinch.

"Hang on a second!" Bree called. "Wait."

But Jill couldn't stop, because if she did she'd fall apart
and if that happened, she wasn't sure how she'd ever put
herself back together.

# Chapter Five

Jill was nowhere to be found. From the moment they froze in Hester's kitchen, immobilized in slack-jawed shock, to Bree snapping to and ordering them to give chase, Jill had managed to vanish from sight.

Bree's neck began aching, deep in the tendons that connected her head to her shoulders. The cause? Emotional whiplash. Last night she ended a five-year sexual dry spell with a deluge of touch, taste, and sensation. God, her whole body felt as if it had been brought back to life, as lush and fertile as a meadow after a long, hard rain. She hadn't just had a one-night stand; Chance was a gold medal winner in the Olympic event of the six-hour hookup.

In his exquisitely muscled arms, she'd felt beautiful for a while, sexy even. Heck, at one point she'd even let him coax her into getting on top and never once worried about any stomach rolls or weird boob angles. He'd worshipped her from her lips to the tips of her toes and it had felt incredible, if all too fleeting.

And now, though her body felt more alive than it had ever been, her heart hurt for her friend, even as she wrestled with confusion over the exact cause.

"Ugh, this is all my fault. I feel like such a doofus going on about that cottage," Essie moaned, teetering on her narrow, five-inch heels across the grassy lawn that separated the Old Red Mill from the Indigo River.

"Don't bother coming this way. She's not down here," Renee called up from her perch atop a fallen willow trunk on the soggy banks. "Although I just found the sweetest little bird nest."

Bree raked a hand through her disheveled waves before blowing out a long, frustrated breath. "Thanks for the help, sis, but you better get back inside and get ready for your adoring fans." She gestured at the cars already pulling into the parking lot, ready for their morning sugar fix. "If Jill doesn't want to be found, trust me, we aren't going to find her until she is good and ready."

Essie looked two seconds from tearing out her hair. "I didn't mean to—"

"I know. I didn't want to hurt her either." Bree took Essie's hand and gave it a soft squeeze. "But for now we need to give her space. When she's ready, she'll find us. She always does."

That was hard-won wisdom right there. In the first terrible months after Simon's death, sometimes it felt as if Jill was intent on burying herself right alongside him. Nothing

Bree said or did could shake her friend from her grief-stricken stupor. Jill wouldn't return calls. She wouldn't answer the door. Her shop remained empty.

But eventually she did come back to life, slowly, tentatively, like a snowdrop in early spring, that delicate three petal blossom unfurling from the frosty mud with surprising strength.

And as Jill began the path to healing, the path wasn't always linear. Sometimes she took a few steps back and that was okay. It was part of the journey and Bree believed from the bottom of her heart that good things were ahead for her best friend, waiting until she was ready to receive them.

"Call me later, sweet pea," Renee said, squeezing Bree's shoulder as she passed. "I still need to deliver a lecture on the dangers of taking strangers home, not to mention into your bed."

"Yes, Mom." Bree rolled her eyes. As much as she loved her big sister, sometimes she wished Renee didn't act *quite* so maternal. After all, she was hardly a nun. Dr. Dan was in the process of selling his house and moving in.

Sure, a one-night stand wasn't the same as a long-term, committed boyfriend, but Chance hadn't been an ax murderer. In fact he'd been nothing short of an attentive and giving lover, one who kept asking "Do you like this?" and "Would you like to try that?" And hot damn it was so freaking sexy to have him asking permission and then taking his pleasure. Her ex Ian's go-to had always been quickie in the missionary position without even removing his flannel pajama bottoms all the way because he complained that his butt cheeks got cold.

She shuddered at the memory. And even though Chance was a whole level up she'd meant it when she said that she couldn't go around making one-night stands a hobby. There was a reason pumpkin pie only tasted good at Thanksgiving, or she only ever ate funnel cake at the county fair—there could be too much of a good thing.

Although now that she'd scratched the itch, she found herself ready to rub up against a big, strong—

"I don't know what to do with myself now," Essie muttered. "I don't have any appointments for the rest of the morning and I left my gym bag at home."

"W-W-What were you doing here at the mill anyway?" Bree stammered, trying to focus back in on the conversation and not the feel of Chance's scruff roughing up her sensitive skin.

She shook her head and forced her toes to uncurl.

This morning, she had been coming here to kiss and tell and fill in Jill and Renee on last night's sexathon and found Essie pacing near the front door.

"I've just leased out another space here to a couple who want to open a bookshop. I came in early to take measurements of the space. After I gave them all those specs and sent off pictures of the mill, they committed verbally over the phone. Cha-ching, cha-ching!"

"Really?" Bree bounced up on her toes. "Oh my gosh, that is so exciting! Cranberry Cove is finally getting a bookshop? We're really stepping it up as a destination town. I can't wait to be one of their best customers. When will they open?"

At last she wouldn't have to drive to the big bookstore over sixty miles away. She knew she could buy books online, but it never felt right somehow. She wanted to hold the cover in her hands, let the weight of the words settle in her palm. And now she could do that right down the hall. Hopefully, the owners would stock lots of historical fiction and the page-turning thrillers that she loved.

Essie gave a very unladylike snort. "Look at you getting all excited. It's like I've said an all-male stripping review was setting up shop. Book o'Clock is meant to be in business sometime mid-fall."

"It's called Book o'Clock? That's flipping adorable. I can't wait to meet the owners, where are they coming from?"

Essie thought for a moment, a hint of a frown line between what Bree knew were carefully Botoxed brows. "Vermont. Yes, Burlington. A married couple. The woman, Ashley, seems great but the guy, Jack, is kind of a loudmouth. Anyway, I wish I could share your enthusiasm but I'm not really a reader. It's too hard for me to sit still."

Bree cocked her head and studied her friend. While Essie was a Cranberry Cove fixture—from chairing community drives to her headshot swinging from most of the For Sale signs in town—in many ways the woman was a mystery, thrumming with the nervous energy of a hummingbird. Despite knowing her for years, Bree hadn't spent a lot of one-on-one time with her.

"I'm not scheduled to work today," Bree said. "We're still waiting for the last big inventory shipment to arrive before Castaway is back in business. Want to come to my place and have a cup of tea?"

"Tea?" Essie's eyes widened a fraction with surprise. Bree had never had her over before.

"Tea," she repeated firmly. "Otherwise known as a hot beverage whereby boiling water is poured over the cured leaves of *Camellia sinensis*. And did you know herbal teas aren't actually true teas at all? They're technically tisanes, which are made from herbs, spices, or flowers."

Essie continued to gape.

"What can I say? I'm full of random facts." Bree heaved her shoulders in an unapologetic shrug. "Pick me first if you ever form a trivia team. I'm good for more than tawdry one-night stands."

"Noted," Essie mumbled before slipping back on her mask of cool amusement. "I suppose tea could be fun. Count me in."

Twenty minutes later, Bree was just taking the whistling kettle off the stove when Essie rapped at the front door and entered brimming with her usual "I just slammed a can of Red Bull" energy.

"Sorry to do this but I can't stay long. I received a surprise call on the way over here. The owner of Grandview Inn wants to talk about selling."

Bree set the pot back on the burner and turned off the gas so she didn't risk dropping the scalding liquid on her bare feet.

"Grandview Inn?" It was only at the last minute that she caught herself from saying *my* Grandview Inn, the one she'd fantasized about the entire time she worked in secret to get her degree, imagining what it would be like to own a piece of history.

The oldest hotel in Cranberry Cove had been a simple bunkhouse for workers at the local quarry at the end of the nineteenth century. It had evolved over the decades into a small but stately historical landmark, fifteen rooms all with perfect seaside views. Set on a granite cliff and surrounded by flower beds it had a lost-in-time quality, as if it wouldn't be a surprise to see women in long, white gowns promenading past under delicate parasols.

She had always loved it and as a girl—and yes, even as a grown woman—daydreamed about making it hers. Her conversation with Jill popped into her mind. *Yeah right.* As if her small inheritance from her parents would in any way secure her the right to own the most coveted coastal property in the county. She'd need to win the lottery.

Still, it hadn't stopped her from subscribing to a range of hospitality management magazines, studying trends: personalization, healthy and organic meals, local experiences, strong online presence. Heck, she'd even researched the best online reservation systems and designed a logo.

But pretending to run the Grandview was a heck of a lot different than actually doing it.

"You know," Essie said, breaking Bree's chain of thought, "this house could use some updating. No offense but this kitchen looks like it's from the set of an eighties sitcom."

"Ouch." Bree flinched, wrenching from her nineteenth-century daydream with a jerk. "Tell me what you really think." The house might be a little rough around the edges of late, but it was where she'd grown up. She'd never lived anywhere else.

"I'm serious. The bones of the house are good, but nothing I'm seeing feels like *you*. When I think of Bree Robinson, I picture cozy nooks and a natural color scheme. We all have a signature style. Take your sister, for example. Renee is whimsical and a little romantic and her home reflects that vibe. I'm more trendy and contemporary and thus have a modern home full of simple detailing devoid of decoration, because let's face it, *I'm* the ornamentation. This place here? It feels like you are living in someone else's life."

"My mom and dad's."

"Of course." Essie's features softened with understanding. "I'm sure they loved you very much and would adore knowing that you made this space your own. Hmmm. We could get Sadie Landry in but she's juggling her pregnancy and redesigning the upstairs of the mill.

"How about this?" Essie snapped her fingers. "I'll pass along the name of a new contracting company that has come to town and is drumming up business. I hear they do quality work." Her phone buzzed and she glanced at it. "Ugh."

"Bad client?"

"Bad *potential* client. He's the brother of that new bookstore owner I was telling you about. Kent Wood. I call him Awful Kent."

"That bad, huh?"

Essie wrinkled her nose. "Let's put it this way, if Satan had a love child with a chauvinist pig, he'd look and act exactly like Awful Kent."

"Sounds charming."

"Sadly one of those cases where money can't buy class. He's slobbering about the Grandview coming on the market, but the less he has a foothold in this town, the better."

"I really, really, *really* love the Grandview," Bree blurted, taking the contractor's business card from Essie. "If I could sell a kidney and buy it, I probably would."

"I thought you were happy at the yarn shop."

"I am. It's fine, but that's the problem...Being there doesn't challenge me. It's not my store, it's Noreen's baby. I just punch in, do my shift, and leave. It's been great there, and I have a lot of flexibility, but I'm starting to think that I need to push myself more. This is my one life you know, maybe I should dream bigger for a while. I mean, I sang in public and had a proper one-night stand. What's to stop me from conquering the world?"

She was kidding and yet, she was absolutely serious.

"Well, well." Essie gave her an appraising once-over. "I like what I'm hearing. Ambition is almost as attractive on a woman as the right color lipstick."

Bree giggled as Essie glanced at her smart watch. "I am sorry to go," she said. "But maybe I've underestimated you. You've got this whole new fire inside you and I gotta say, I'm loving it. Let's chat more about the inn soon.

Maybe at Dot Turner's birthday party later today. You are going, aren't you? I've arranged a big surprise."

"Of course I'm going. I wouldn't miss Dot's party, or the biscuits at the Lobster Shack," Bree said. "But don't encourage me to have false hope. I don't have money or a clue how to run a place like the Grandview. A silly pipe dream is not a business plan."

Nor were the dozens of notebooks under her bed bursting with boutique hotel color schemes, ideas over linens and textiles, design concepts, wine lists, anything to take seriously.

"I'm a firm believer that if you set an intention, the universe finds a way."

"So if I tell the universe I want a six-pack I'll lose my belly pudge?" She giggled.

"It's not quite that simple." Essie rolled her eyes. "The universe would likely suggest cutting out carbs and jogging."

"Ugh." Bree shuddered. "Never mind. I'll stick with Spanx and keep eating bagels."

"Seriously, call the contractors." Essie gave the surroundings another critical once-over. "You deserve a place that is yours. Don't box yourself in with the past."

And with that she was gone without even taking a sip of her tea.

Bree picked up the embossed business card: "Granite State Builders. Owner: Luke Elliston."

"Hmm." She leaned back on the pale pink Formica counter. Okay, so the house was a little eighties with its pastel color scheme. Contacting someone to come in and give her some ideas and a quote wouldn't hurt. After all, she'd been taking giant leaps since her all clear. What was one more?

"Granite State Builders," she said to herself, trying to imagine her childhood home transformed. With a little bit of elbow grease the space could be transformed into a cozy, boho vibe. White masonry paint would do wonders covering up the red brick and she'd love to replace the poop brown–grouted tile kitchen floor with bamboo. It could be a vibrant home that still honored its Victorian roots.

Why hadn't she made changes? Renee didn't need the house to remain a time capsule of their parents. In fact, she'd probably be the first to cheer if the powder-blue shag carpet in the upstairs bedroom came out.

Another item for the anti–bucket list. After singing in public and hooking up with a stranger, making a call like this should be a cinch.

Bree dialed the number and held her breath.

# Chapter Six

Jill absently drummed her fingers on her lap to the tune of Ed Sheeran's "Perfect" playing on her car's Bluetooth. For the past three minutes she'd been idling in a parking spot outside of the nondescript beige building. The yellow sign over the front door was bright and cheerful, with "Hospice of Cranberry County" written in ruby-red cursive.

She'd always known that the hospice existed on the outskirts of the village. A few kind-faced volunteers from the organization had even come to her condo during the first brutal weeks following Simon's death. But at that point, despite their best intentions and patient, respectful offers to listen, coherent speech wasn't possible. It was easier to stay in bed and try to pretend she'd become invisible, or better yet, never existed so she'd never have to know what it was like having your heart carved out of your chest.

And once she was strong enough to step back into the world, her feelings had always felt safer locked inside a box deep in the darkest part of her chest. After all, it hadn't done poor snooping Pandora any good to go poking inside hers, and why should Jill's actions turn out better than a Greek myth?

Truthfully, most people seemed relieved by her emotional lockdown. When folks would tilt their heads, purse their lips in sympathy asking, "How are you holding up, really?" all they needed to hear was a reassuringly plucky, "Okay. I'm getting through it."

No one wanted the awful truth behind her soft smile—that out of sight wasn't really out of *mind*. And that even though she didn't open up with her feelings she still carried them around like an invisible griefcase.

The flyer beside her on the empty passenger seat read, "Widows and Widowers Bereavement Group."

As of today she'd been a widow one thousand, two hundred and ninety-six days—sixty-three days less than she had been married.

She rocked her head back against the seat and let out a low, frustrated growl. Another few seconds and she might scream. Yet she couldn't move. It was one thing to know you were stuck, but it was another thing entirely to realize that your closest friends secretly concurred. Her griefcase wasn't as invisible as she would have liked. Maybe she wasn't getting away with anything.

Before giving up on her, the hospice volunteers had left behind a list of local counseling resources. Last year, after having a panic attack on Simon's angelversary, the day of his death, she impulsively decided to give therapy a whirl, but it was hard to find anyone with the availability she needed. One of the pitfalls of rural life was that the mental health support systems were woefully lacking.

The one person she did get in to see was named Dr. Broccoli. It would have been funny if Simon had been around to share the joke ("Who works across the hall, babe? Dr. Cauliflower?"). Instead, she perched on the edge of a leather couch, choking on the sandalwood essential oil wafting from the salt crystal diffuser as Dr. Broccoli stroked the ear of her Pomeranian, Snowball, while leading a mindfulness exercise in a monotone voice.

At one point, Jill had cracked an eyelid to see Snowball taking a dump on the World Market rug and promptly slammed it shut. It hadn't been her circus, or her monkey, and definitely *not* her dog doo.

"Snowball!" Dr. Broccoli had gasped a moment later. "No! No! No! Mommy is not happy. Not happy at all."

As Jill called it a day, rushing out of the office unsure if she was laughing, crying, or laughing *and* crying, she'd decided to give up on therapy once and for all. She had her gallery. Her memories. And the beach. Saltwater air was a tonic to the soul.

But this morning, after she'd fled Hester's—and the bitter truth that everyone who mattered saw through her smoke and mirrors and knew she was stuck like a horse in quicksand—she'd gone to Shopper's Corner to buy a pint of Ben & Jerry's for a late breakfast. Instead she spied the bereavement group flyer on the community bulletin board outside and registered that the meeting time was only an hour later.

The discovery had seemed like fate, except so far in her life fate had been nothing but a fickle bitch.

She chewed her worry spot inside her lower lip and turned off the radio. All she had left to lose was her dignity. God help her if she was asked to do anything cheesy like a trust fall.

She dropped her hand to the multitool keychain still dangling from the ignition—another little keepsake from Simon that she wasn't able to relinquish. Why put herself through this? No one was making her be here. It would be so easy to drive away, become another anonymous car on the road back downtown. She could head to the main beach, it was great vitamin D weather—a rarity for Maine, but always welcome.

The rap at her window almost gave her a heart attack.

"Oh shoot! Sorry, sorry. I didn't mean to startle you." A kind-faced man with salt-and-pepper hair leaned down, giving her a crooked smile. "I just saw you sitting here and it looked like you might be thinking about leaving. I wanted to tell you we don't bite."

"Oh. Ha. Right." Jill tried to laugh but it came out a weak snort. "I was going to come but...I don't know..."

"The idea of being surrounded by a bunch of strangers feels overwhelming? And to be in the presence of so much grief might discourage you, drag you back to the darkness?"

Jill glanced away from his too-perceptive gaze. "Maybe something like that, yeah."

"Well, what if I told you this space was a place where you wouldn't be alone? Grief is not a club anyone wants to belong to; once you're in, though, there can be a healing benefit in surrounding yourself with other members who've walked a mile in your shoes."

For a moment Jill wondered if this is what it would have been like if she'd had a dad who'd stuck around, a wise, friendly older man who seemed to have all the right words.

"I don't really like doing things like this," she said, grabbing a tissue from her purse to dab her nose.

"Like what?"

"Sharing my deepest darkest feelings. Or any feelings really. It seemed possible an hour ago but now that I'm here, I-I-I don't think I can do it." She began crying, unable to hold back the flood even for a stranger's sake. "Shoot, look at me. It's been three years. I should be so much more together by now."

"*Should* is the enemy of *do*." This guy really went all in on the eye contact. Jill found herself steadied by his warm brown gaze, so much like melted caramel or freshly boiled maple syrup, rich and comforting. He had a dapper, timeless look, like Cary Grant during Hollywood's Golden Age. "What if I suggested that you aim low? Cut the word 'should' from your vocabulary. The only thing you need to be is better than the person you were yesterday."

"You sound like you could coach Little League with

that kind of pep talk," Jill joked as she crumbled the soggy tissue into her pocket as if to hide the evidence.

"Heh. Been there, done that." The man gave a fond chuckle. "I coached my daughter all the way through. She was a crackerjack pitcher, threw a better curveball than any boy. God, it was a lot of work, but looking back I'm glad for every practice, every out-of-town game. We forged a bond through baseball and that bond carried us through the loss of her mother, my Elizabeth."

And just like that the waterworks started again. What he told her was well meant but he couldn't know how his words tore at her, how she had *nothing* left from Simon, no piece of him to carry on, no legacy.

No, that had been taken away too, just like all her hopes and dreams.

"Hey." The man crouched down so they were eye to eye. "I'm Andrew Weathers. And I'm not going to tell you coming to group will be easy but it *will* help. Plus the coffee in the conference room isn't half bad and they have real cream, not the crappy powdered stuff."

Jill closed her eyes. She saw herself pushing Bree along, urging her to get out there and embrace life with gusto. What a coward she was hiding behind her best friend so she didn't have to challenge herself.

"Okay," she said, turning to Andrew and yanking the keys out. "Hi. I'm Jill Kelly and I'm doing this thing."

And as they walked toward the front door, Jill studied a long fracture in the pavement, one of the nuances unique to living in a climate filled with frosts and thaws.

"Cracks are how the light gets in, babe."

Jill almost tripped. It was Simon's voice she heard in her ear, so clear it was almost as if he was walking beside her.

And just like that her doubt washed away. This was exactly where she needed to be.

The next hour passed in a blur of surprisingly good office coffee, introductions, some sharing, and then it was finished. Jill didn't speak, that was too much, but it was helpful to hear from a few people who were further along in their grief journey, and were finding peace and even happiness in their new normals.

One of those was Andrew Weathers, who turned out to be a cofacilitator. Afterward, they walked back to their cars together.

"I'm glad you came today. I hope you come back."

Jill shot him a covert glance but he didn't seem to have any hidden agenda. He wasn't trying to subtly hit on her; he genuinely just seemed to want to help. The realization let her drop her guard a little.

"I think I will. I can see how sharing might be helpful."

"This is me," he said, pausing to unlock a silver Honda with a giant bouquet of pink dahlias propped up in the passenger seat in a lovely glass vase.

"Those are gorgeous," she said. "Who are they for?"

Andrew gave a small, sad smile. "My Elizabeth. Our daughter Penny made the vase. I stop by Elizabeth's grave after group each time and leave her favorite flowers at her headstone."

Jill pushed away the thought of Simon's empty plot up in the Cranberry Cove Cemetery. She hadn't been able to put a marker up yet, the idea of seeing his name and birth and death dates engraved in cold marble felt too final, too awful, to face.

But, guilt still gnawed at her. He deserved tangible proof that he'd existed. And the more time passed, the worse it felt that she still hadn't given him a marker.

There was a stone-cutting company in the next town over who did good work. She'd looked them up online a few times, but always found an excuse to put it off.

God, she was so hopeless.

But maybe she deserved the pain.

After all, if she hadn't picked that stupid fight over his purchase of a few expensive tools he'd made online, then he wouldn't have stormed out in a huff, or been distracted. Maybe he'd have had better reflexes when the deer bolted in front of his motorcycle.

For a moment it was impossible to breathe, to swallow, to move.

"Hey." She finally managed to clear her throat. "Did you say your daughter made that vase?"

Andrew straightened his posture, eyes bright, chest puffed beneath his plaid shirt, the epitome of a proud papa. "Penny's an amateur glassblower. She graduated from high school last June and wants to go away for art school in the fall. Maybe fine arts is an impractical degree these days and I'm being overindulgent, but she seems to have a gift. Still, I'd prefer she stay closer to home."

"Yes, I can see she's talented." Jill's gaze traveled over the multicolored glass, a style definitely inspired by the artisans of Murano. "This is outstanding artisanship. You should bring her by my shop, I have a boutique called Chickadee Studios that will be reopening next week in the Old Red Mill over by the Indigo River."

"That's a great place." Andrew looked thoughtful. "I'm living in Bayswater myself," he said, naming a town about thirty miles up the coast. "And I don't have to ask to know that Penny would love to come by for a chat about her work. Thanks for the invitation. I'm just so proud of her. If it hadn't been for that girl's strength and courage, I might still be lost."

And just like that Jill hit her capacity to withstand the conversation. She'd taken huge strides today and now all she wanted to do was burrow in for a nap, one where she hopefully wouldn't dream of children or unmarked graves.

"Well I need to run!" she said as brightly as she could muster. "I have to go and um...feed my cat."

The lie sounded glaringly obvious.

"See you in two weeks then. Be well, Jill."

As she drove down the two-lane road, she glanced left, that way would take her to Simon and the cemetery. Her hand went to the signal and she slowed down.

But at the last minute, she slammed the accelerator, heading straight for the beach. She had her running shoes and shorts in the trunk. Time for some vitamin D, warm sand, and the waves that took away everything in the end, even memory.

A car beeped behind her, annoyed by her indecision. But she wasn't upset, she sympathized. Her indecision annoyed her too.

The trouble was she wasn't quite sure how to unstick. But, as she rolled down the windows and let the summer air into her car, breathing in the saltwater taffy and flowers on Main Street, her leg muscles felt ready to work. She had to admit while she was drained she also felt a little lighter than she had in a long time.

# Chapter Seven

"Happy birthday to you, happy birthday to you, happy birthday dear Dot, happy birthday to you," Bree sang at the top of her lungs, heartily joining the unruly cacophony of off-key voices.

In the middle of the packed locals-only crowd stuffed around an ocean-view table in the back of the Lobster Shack, Dot Turner, the beloved former Cranberry Cove gym teacher, blew out her candles. There were only eight but they represented each one of her decades. She extinguished them all on the first try—no surprise there. In her neon tank top she sported enviably defined biceps and was planning on through-hiking the Appalachian Trail from north to south come spring, the more grueling route, naturally.

While Dot was tough as nails, everyone in town loved her, which is why they were crammed elbow to elbow into the tight space while clutching fresh lobster rolls in plastic sandwich baskets. Dot claimed her remarkable stamina was due to the secret sauce in the Lobster Shack's famous rolls. As a result, Bree was stuffing one into her mouth right as Jill walked into the room, glancing around shyly as if uncertain how she'd be received.

"Jilly Beans," Bree called out, clasping a hand over her mouth so as not to spray any bread crumbs.

"And what do we have here?" Essie came through the emergency exit wheeling a suspiciously large box wrapped in gold foil paper and topped with a red velvet bow. Her tight leather miniskirt meant she could only take the smallest steps.

"Hoo doggy! That better be a male stripper," Dot cracked as she adjusted her pointy party hat.

"Oh lord, please don't let it be a male stripper," Jill whispered in Bree's ear as she sidled up beside her.

Bree reached out and squeezed her hand as they traded rueful grins. Wherever Jill had disappeared to after fleeing Hester's ... she was back, and not a moment too soon.

"I don't know," Bree muttered. "I think I'd pay a whole stack of dollar bills to see Dot get a lap dance."

Jill shuddered. "I'd pay more to miss out."

"Ta-da!" Essie cried, pulling a hidden string to open the box.

Everyone leaned forward—in equal parts anticipation and dread—but there was no hip-thrusting hunk smothered in baby oil inside. It was an architectural diorama of a basketball court.

"Huh," Dot said, appearing a trifle crestfallen not to be stuffing dollar bills into a bulging G-string. "Lookee here. You bought me a sculpture."

"No silly," Essie said, rolling her eyes. "It's a model for the new gym at the high school that's being built with the new county bond money that was approved in last year's election. The Dot Turner Memorial Gymnasium."

"Well I'll be!" Dot jolted back in her rickety wooden chair. "A memorial? But I ain't dead yet. You trying to give me a hint or something?"

All conversation cut out, as the room went quiet.

Essie looked faintly queasy, as if she couldn't stomach sticking her foot in her mouth twice in one day. "I-I-I—"

"I'm just getting your goat there, Park," Dot boomed in her raspy baritone. "My. This is something! Really something."

And if Dot could look sentimental, that's just what she did. Her bright hazel eyes even seemed to mist a moment before she cleared her throat and slammed a fist down on the red-and-white checkered plastic tablecloth.

"Well that's enough blubbing. Quick, someone look lively and order me another dang strawberry margarita! Rocks, extra salt. And see if you can get one of those local fellows to strip down to their socks." She let out a hearty chuckle and no one seemed to know if she was serious or not. Least of all the four fishermen sipping lagers at the bar who looked more suited to watching a ball game in a La-Z-Boy than executing any sexy *Magic Mike* moves.

"You okay?" Bree asked Jill quietly. "Sorry, I know

it's a dumb question, but you left so quickly this morning and I hate to think I hurt you by sticking my foot in my mouth."

"No, no. Trust me, nothing you said was bad. I'm glad you got some action. Thrilled actually. I want all good things for you. Honestly, the only one who is hurting anyone is me," Jill said after a pause. "I've had to face some hard truths about myself lately, like maybe I'm not as okay as I want to be. I am sort of stuck."

"Healing takes time," Bree said. "I know it's not the same, but after Mom and Dad died I had good days and bad days, heck I still do. But you don't have to pretend with me, okay? Ever?"

"Promise," Jill said.

"Pinkie promise?" Bree raised a crooked finger—their old challenge.

"Oooooh. Look at you! Pulling out the big guns, Robinson." But Jill hooked her finger. "I won't shut you out anymore. Actually," she dropped her voice so no one nearby could eavesdrop, "there is more I need to tell you about Simon's death and the aftermath. Things I've never had the words for before. I don't know if I have them yet, but I'm trying to, okay? Just be patient."

Bree raised a quizzical brow, curious. "Of course. Take the time you need. I love you and I'm always going to be there for you no matter what. You were there for me when I found that horrible lump, and you were there for me through losing my parents, and for every single childhood milestone. You don't need to pretend to me."

Jill cleared her throat. "I know. Thank you."

An alarm buzzed on Bree's phone. "Oh shoot, I have to go. I didn't realize it was so late. I made an appointment to talk to a contractor and they had an availability."

"Back it up. Contractor?" Now it was Jill's turn to look curious. "What for?"

"It's another item for my anti–bucket list. Essie came over this morning and convinced me to call a company that's looking for work in town. She said my house needed updating."

"Oh?" Jill didn't say anything more but her politely neutral expression said it all.

"Hey, now," Bree said, swatting at her. "Are you telling me that you have been silently judging my house?"

"Me? Judge?" Her friend's eyes went wide with mock innocence. "Never ever ever."

Bree pursed her lips. "The lady doth protest too much methinks."

"It's your family home. I know you love it, but let's be real. Shag carpet, waterbeds, oh my!" Jill buried her face in her hands while dissolving into helpless giggles. "I'm sorry. Pinkie promise and all of that. Truth is, it's an eighties time capsule, maybe a bit of an homage to the nineties as well. But Essie speaks the truth, it could use a spruce up."

Bree jokingly wagged her fingers. "Only the truth from you from now on."

"Only the truth," Jill promised.

After a quick hug with Dot, and a promise that she'd

at least try to attend one of her dawn CrossFit sessions at Whitepoint Beach, Bree was speeding back home trying not to wonder too much about what Jill had hinted to her.

Bree had been by Jill's side so much after Simon's death that it seemed impossible that she could be keeping any sort of meaningful secret from her. But then, she did have all those times she'd shut down and shut out the world. The thought kept niggling at her until she pulled into her long gravel driveway and saw a parked black pickup truck. It looked disconcertingly familiar with its "The Closer You Get, the Slower I Drive," bumper sticker.

Her heart skipped a beat, and then another.

There were lots of black trucks in the world. Surely this one wasn't driven by—

"Hey there." Chance, her one-night stand, stood up from the rocking chair on her front porch and winked, confidence personified. "My brother said we had a consultation this afternoon. I'm helping him out for the summer. He got caught up on another site and I offered to come see what you needed."

Her toes curled in her tennis shoes.

Oh, she needed a lot.

He hooked a hand around the back of his neck and maybe it was the sun in her eyes, but it seemed like there was a hint of a blush to his chiseled cheekbones.

"Wasn't till I pulled up front that I realized why the address sounded familiar."

It was hard to look at him, standing there in worn tan Carhartts that hugged his narrow waist and a black T-shirt clinging to rock-hard pecs that she may or may not have recently licked in tipsy midnight ecstasy.

Why was she so stunned? After all, he'd mentioned he was doing some casual building. And she'd felt the strength in those callused fingertips, the way his body was strong because he earned it through honest sweat and hard physical labor.

"You're my new contractor?" she squeaked, still trying to process that this was real and not some sex-starved fever dream.

"Well, that all depends." His dimples put in a devastating appearance.

"On what?" Her voice was so high she probably sounded like she'd been sucking helium.

"Whether or not you'll have me."

With that he turned on the full force of his smile, and before her brain went to mush she had one coherent thought: she was in big, *big* trouble.

# Chapter Eight

As Dot's birthday party dwindled, Jill felt a little pang of hunger tugging at her insides. She had arrived at the party too late for lobster rolls and now she wondered if she had anything dinner-worthy lurking in her fridge or if she should stop by Shopper's Corner's incredible deli for one of their cranberry-quinoa salads. It wasn't usually worth the bother to cook a meal for one so she often found herself subsisting from a motley assortment of frozen microwave dinners, Greek yogurt, bowls of granola, and the occasional orange to ward off scurvy.

Her phone buzzed inside her purse and she dug it out, wincing a little when she saw the incoming call. *Mom.*

As much as she'd like to send Linda straight to voicemail, her mother wasn't one to be ignored. She'd just hit "redial."

With a sigh, Jill extricated herself from a conversation

with one of Dot's octogenarian friends and headed out of the Lobster Shack before hitting the green "answer" button.

"Hey, Linda," she said, trying to sound like she imagined other women her age sounded when their moms called. Pleased to hear from them. Not filled with a low-grade dread. She leaned against the restaurant's brick facade. Truth was she'd stopped calling Linda mom at thirteen—right about the time she'd had to single-handedly shoo a black bear off the front porch by herself. Even before then, "mommy" or "mama" had been a big stretch.

She knew her mom had been given a heavy load, becoming a mom a few months before her eighteenth birthday. Her dad split before she was born and to Linda's credit she had kept Jill fed and housed come hell or high water. But the strain had extracted a heavy price. Linda had gotten a bartending job to make ends meet, which meant she was gone from five in the afternoon until two in the morning most nights.

Jill had grown up alone, microwaving dinner, watching television, and given they lived on the edge of the forest, dealing with the critters that came out at night, everything from raccoons to bears. Some nights she'd get so scared she'd sleep under her bed just so the house looked empty in case a bad guy ever wanted to break in.

"Jilly," Linda's husky voice sounded relieved. "Thank goodness that you picked up. I'm standing at my window trying to stay behind the curtain. There's some strange man out there nosing around my place."

Jill startled. "Like a burglar? Linda, if that's the case hang up and call 911 and I'll come straight over."

"No. It's not like that. He doesn't seem like he wants to take anything. He's walking up and down right outside my kitchen window taking pictures of the inn. It's the strangest thing."

"Okay, let's think about this logically. Have you thought about popping outside and asking him what the heck he's doing?" Jill glanced at her watch. Maybe she'd skip dinner and head to the local coffee shop. "Look, it's probably some tourist who wants to snag a postcard-perfect photo to brag to all his friends on Facebook. People love the inn. It's got that incredible view even if the place itself has seen better days."

"Hmm. Maybe." Linda didn't sound remotely assuaged. "But I don't like his energy, honey. He's got a dark aura. Very murky intentions. I'm telling you this man means trouble."

Jill rolled her eyes. This New Age obsession was a recent development and while Jill loved a pretty rose-quartz crystal as much as the next person, she wasn't about to slap one on any of her chakras. "Step away from the curtain. Quit being a nosy local and forget about him. He isn't bothering you and I'm sure he'll be gone in a flash."

Her mom sighed. "Maybe I should light some sage and do a little smudging. Clear the energy fields."

"Sure. Do that." As far as Jill was concerned the matter was settled. "Well, if there's nothing else, I've got to go and—"

"Wait!" Linda blurted. "There was one last thing."

She paused.

"What?" Jill said, perhaps a little too impatiently.

"Are applications still open for the Cranberry Cove Art Fair?" her mom asked in a very fake breezy tone.

Jill frowned. She organized Cranberry Cove's arts and crafts fair, which closed off Main Street and brought in a flurry of visitors who trolled the white tents full of pottery, photography, and whimsical wares. "Yessss," she said in slow suspicion. "Why?"

"I was wondering about having a booth."

"You?" Jill didn't bother keeping the incredulity from her voice. "What for?" As far as she knew, Linda didn't have an artistic bone in her body. "You want to do tarot cards or palm readings?"

She was kidding—sort of.

"I've taken up jewelry making," Linda said, a trifle defensively. "Hey, maybe you'd like to stop by and see if you'd want to sell any in Chickadee. I've been doing these pretty silver earrings set with tourmaline—you know—the state gemstone. They come in a raspberry-pink red and minty green."

A vague throbbing headache took root deep in Jill's left temple. She pressed two fingers to the spot and gave a slow circular massage. Great. Now her mom wanted to play artist. She didn't want to shoot her mom down, but she wasn't in a position to coddle her either. Her boutique had limited space so she had to have sky-high standards.

"Are you still there, honey? Did I lose you?"

Linda's tone intensified the pain in Jill's head. She hated that her mom annoyed her, and that she never left a conversation with her satisfied. Why did she resent Linda so much? Maybe it was due to the fact that Jill had been left home so much, watching television shows about perfect moms who were around to cook, to clean, to cuddle a child when they had a cold, to tuck them in at night with a kiss on the forehead. Linda had never been that mom, she was just the woman who was *supposed* to be her.

Jill was the one who got a work permit at fourteen and hustled side jobs all through high school and college. Jill was the one who started her own successful business that grew slow and steady. Jill was the one who paid off her bills at the end of every month, but who had to bail out her mom and delay her dreams with her husband...dreams that now would never come true.

Blood roared in her ears.

"Jill?"

She blinked. "I'm here. We can talk about it later."

"Okay, sure." Her mom's sigh was soft but she was clearly disappointed by Jill's lack of enthusiasm.

Guilt and resentment flooded Jill's stomach, roiling around and making her queasy.

"Give me some time to let it all sink in. I didn't even know you were making jewelry."

"I used to do it before I had you. A few months ago I was sorting through things and found some old tools."

Her mom used to make jewelry? "I've never seen any of your work."

"I quit when you were little. Too much going on."

Imagine having a mom who loved to shape pendants or fashion delicate earrings? Or she and her mother working together, side by side at the kitchen table, singing off-key to radio pop songs, giggling when they mixed up lyrics.

"I'm going to be straight with you." Jill's mouth hardened as the dreamy mental image popped like a soap bubble. "If you want to apply for a booth, the forms are at the library and the mayor's office. The deadline is next Friday at five sharp. You want in, you need to follow the rules just like anyone else. No special favors."

That settled that. Linda never met a deadline. Even now it was common for her to forget to pay the oil or power bill, collecting increasingly threatening municipal notices until Jill forced her to go settle things at city hall.

"Okay! I'll apply tomorrow." Linda's voice was bright with optimism, just like it had been when she talked about getting a job last month waiting tables or back in March when she said she'd file her taxes a month ahead of the deadline.

"Sure." *I'll believe it when I see it.* Jill plastered on a smile and waved as a few folks from Dot's party left the Lobster Shack.

"Oooooh. I have an update. That man outside, he's stopped taking pictures and now he has fished out some sort of handheld GPS whatchamacallit from a leather satchel. I think he's taking measurements of the property lines."

"Uh-huh." Jill was suddenly exhausted. She didn't want to eat dinner. She didn't want to talk to Linda. She just wanted to go home, crawl into bed, and say goodnight to this day. "Hey, so I have to go. Talk soon!" And she hung up before Linda could say anything else.

She dropped her phone back in her bag and stood there a moment, equal parts melancholic and annoyed.

What was the point of wishing things could be different? That Linda could make Jill feel taken care of for once, boil a pot of tea and know exactly what to say.

"Hey, lady! What are you doing out here all by your lonesome? And why the long face?"

Jill glanced over to see Essie walking briskly in her direction, dusting her hands off on her tailored pants.

"What have you been doing?" A good dodge.

"I had to load that diorama of Dot's memorial gymnasium into my trunk." She gestured at her cherry-red convertible in an awkward parallel-parking job. "That sucker was heavy."

"It was such a lovely gesture. I know Dot isn't big on emoting, but I'm quite certain that the moment made her entire year."

"Happy to help. Plus I'm finishing up my appointment on the school board so it was a nice way to go out. Dot's a role model to us all."

"Good lord yes. I think she could beat me in a five K now," Jill said. "With her hands tied together."

"I'm glad I got you alone for a minute." Essie shuffled her feet, looking uncharacteristically nervous. "About this morning, at Hester's—"

"Don't worry about it." Jill swatted the air like she was shooing off a mosquito. "I'm fine. Really."

"That's just it." Essie leveled her cool gaze, the one that didn't miss a thing. "I don't want to be a pain in the you know what, but I *really* don't think you are fine. And I know it's not my place, but I don't know who else is going to say it. You are hurting."

Jill blinked, not expecting the truth bomb to be lobbed at her with such casual force. "Of course I am. How can you or anyone else expect me to be any different? Sorry, but I'm not a cyborg. Cut me and I bleed. And sue me, I miss my husband and would do dark magic if it would bring him back, even for a day."

And there it was, the awful truth laid out in the open and yet it honestly felt good to admit. For too long she'd been trying to act like she wasn't living life without a heart, without her center. Simon, beautiful, inside and out, with those clear cornflower-blue eyes that always seemed to peer right inside her soul and love the sum of all the parts, even the uglier broken ones. She'd never believed in the idea of a soul mate until their first kiss. He'd taken her for a sunset ride on his bike, packing a picnic of turkey sandwiches, apples, and homemade cookies and when he gently pressed his lips to hers, up on that hillside with views of the sunset and the northern woods, she could taste chocolate chips and thought she would die of sweetness.

At last she wouldn't be alone. He'd protect her and walk beside her for the rest of their lives.

Except his path was cut short.

And now she walked alone—and had no idea where she was going.

"Don't take this the wrong way," Essie said softly, placing a hand on Jill's shoulder. "But I really do think that you should see the cottage—the one you wanted to live in someday with Simon."

Jill shook her head. "Thanks but no thanks. I'm not a masochist."

"You're still young and you're alive and deserving of more good things in this world," Essie dropped her voice, taking on an earnest tone. "I'm not telling you this as a real estate agent, but as your friend. Sometimes making just one change can give your whole life a makeover."

Jill huffed a laugh. "You sound like me talking to Bree."

"Don't get me wrong. You're an absolutely amazing friend to Bree, and she to you. But in that friendship you are always the fixer, the doer." She paused, leveling a penetrating look. "Sometimes I think it's easier for you to focus on fixing Bree rather than taking a good hard look in the mirror."

Hard words to hear, but not entirely off base.

Jill sniffed and Essie pulled out a small plastic pack of tissues, offering her one without a word. She blew her nose extra hard. If Essie kept going like this, she'd lose it right there on Main Street in front of all of Cranberry Cove. But Essie had that determined set to her jaw, the one that Jill knew meant she wasn't going to back down.

"Fine. You win." Jill threw up her hands in an "I surrender" gesture. "We can go have a look."

# Chapter Nine

Bree's fingers trembled so hard that her bamboo knitting needles felt like maracas in her sweaty grip. She'd taken a seat on her couch to hide the fact her legs had gone wobbly and while she pretended to work on a soft pink blanket for Sadie's upcoming baby, she was in fact making a mess of things.

It was incredibly hard to appear normal when the man you'd done a dozen dirty things with was crouched a few feet away, leaning forward with a measuring tape in a way that his T-shirt slid up a few inches revealing a tantalizing glimpse of deep olive skin.

She didn't think she'd ever see Chance again. Crap, she didn't even know his last name. He was meant to be an exhilarating item she'd crossed off her anti–bucket list, to live on in her memory as a deliciously wild night. It wasn't like she was going to make being a karaoke-singing bar babe a regular part of her schedule.

But here he was, a mere twenty-four hours later, her one and-only one-night stand back inside her house, but this time nowhere close to her bed. It was like trying to do a detox fast next to a warm chocolate cake slathered in buttercream icing.

All she wanted was to sneak a lick.

But once he strode through the front door he'd been nothing but frustratingly gentlemanly, asking questions about the history of the house, but saying nothing at all about the very big, very raunchy elephant in the room.

"Are there any views that are particularly important to you?"

"What sort of storage needs do you have?"

"What kinds of spaces do you value the most?"

"Do you entertain often?"

Throughout his very professional inquisition all she could do was ask secret questions of her own:

*Do you go to bed with a lot of women?*

*How are you not married?*

*Did I look okay naked?*

*Was last night fun for you too?*

Did he think she was some small-town floozy who laid out the welcome mat to any big-city man with some swagger? Not that it was his business, nor would he have a right to judge, but it was so annoying to have no idea how he viewed her.

"I'm not a betting man, but I wager if you removed this carpet, there is going to be original hardwood underneath. Solid oak probably." He went on in his deep calm voice, seemingly unaware that she kept knitting because if she paused she'd tear her hair out. Too bad she couldn't hit pause on the situation and call Jill. She'd give her the perfect pep talk but right now Bree was in this alone, sink or swim.

"Dramatic yet calming," he mumbled to himself. "Draw in more natural light." He sat back on his heels to scrawl a few more notes in the pocket-sized Moleskine journal he'd produced from his snug back pocket.

"What's your last name?" she blurted. He had to have one, and she'd feel a lot better knowing at least that much.

The question got his attention. He stood and tucked a pencil behind his left ear, a gesture that was equal parts dorky and dashing. "Elliston." He mimed tipping a hat and laying on a thick courtly drawl. "Chance Elliston at your service, ma'am."

It was unfair how attractive he was. "My last name is Robinson."

"Bree Robinson." He seemed to savor her name, as if it tasted decadent.

"And you work for Granite State Builders?" She inwardly frowned. What good was it to state the obvious?

"For a few months. Like I said, my brother owns it, and I don't see enough of him so I found my way up here. Nothing like honest hard work and sweat to clear the mind. I sold my firm and I'm figuring out my next steps."

"Back in New York City."

"Brooklyn technically." Two faint lines appeared between his brows. "But I had to get out of there for a while."

Oh god. Her stomach plummeted to her toes. She could hear Renee's "I told you so" already. What was the issue? Was he an on-the-run felon? Maybe a drug deal had gone bust. Or maybe he was a hit man. He seemed too good to be true so that all made sense. Yes, for sure. Look at that craggy jaw, those muscled forearms. He was definitely a gun for hire. Probably mob. Or gangs. Or a gang of mobs—

"I'm an architect." Chance offered the nugget of information with a half shrug. "One who up until very recently lived, ate, and slept work. I hadn't taken a vacation or sick day in ten years so after the sale went through it seemed like a good idea to come up here and clear my head. We dissolved the firm in March but I'm planning to bid on a project in midtown by October. Biggest one I've done to date so I want my head a hundred and ten percent in the game."

*O-kay.* So not a drug dealer or an assassin. Just a successful urban architect who designed giant buildings in one of the largest cities in the world.

And she worked in a knitting shop.

Great. Yeah, they were perfectly matched.

Her eyelid twitched. "So if you are this hotshot architect, why are you here measuring my poor old house? Shouldn't you be off on a yacht or rubbing elbows down in Kennebunkport with one of the Bushes?"

"A Bush?" He folded his arms with a chuckle.

She glared at his amused mouth, wondering if it still tasted like mint. "I'm just saying you don't have to be here."

"Is this twenty questions?"

"More like me preferring to know who is in my house." She kept her chin high, unwilling to be intimidated. "Last night—that wasn't my usual. Not the singing in public and certainly not what happened after."

"Yeah." The corner of his full mouth quirked, threatening a full-out grin. "I kinda figured that."

"What! How?" Her cheeks roasted and she resisted touching the skin in case she scalded her palm. "I wasn't good?"

Maybe she should just poke one of the knitting needles up her nose, do a personal lobotomy and forget this whole awkward conversation.

He stepped back like she'd struck him. "Shit. No. God. No! You were good. Great. Better than great. A pro. Double shit. Not a pro but..." He hooked a hand around the back of his neck. "I just meant you kept saying that last night. How you never did things like this."

She squeezed her eyes shut as memories of her tipsy ramblings flooded back. If a giant meteor was going to strike Earth this would be an optimal moment. "I did say that a lot, huh?"

"It's fine. It was cute. You're cute as hell."

She popped open one eye. "I am?"

"Yes. But I'm on the clock and you are a potential client. To answer your last question: I like working," he said simply. "And this kind of grand, old Victorian house—it's something. Got character in spades for sure."

She gave an unladylike snort. "Is that a nice way to say that it's a little worse for wear?"

He shook his head so hard that his yellow pencil slipped to the carpet. "I wouldn't say that. It's just not being allowed to shine. There's potential lurking around every corner."

And from the intense way he held her gaze, she wasn't sure if they were talking about the house at all.

"So what do you think? Should I take the plunge and renovate?"

Chance glanced around the space. "Tell you what. I could draw up some plans, just for fun. No pressure and no cost to you. And if you like what you see, my brother's company can do the work once I'm gone. It's a win-win. I dig old places like these and would love to figure out how to keep the character while bringing the interior into the twenty-first century."

"Nothing in this world comes for free."

A muscle flickered in his jaw, drawing attention to his perfect bone structure. "You could keep me company on a trip to Portland this weekend. I have to get some supplies for Luke. I could use your help."

"First question." She stalled, buying time while she processed what he just offered. "Who is Luke?"

"My little bro. Two years younger. The owner of Granite State Builders."

"Gotcha." She toyed with the knitting in her lap, remembering the name on the business card Essie had given her.

He cocked a wry brow. "The strange thing is that my folks also named their new dog Luke as well. He's an all-white French bulldog."

"I'm sorry, what?" She paused, searching his face for a tell that he was playing a trick but he returned her gaze without expression. Shoot. He'd make an expert poker player. "You can't be serious."

He held up a three-fingered salute. "Scout's honor."

"Wow, guess your parents know what they like."

"No one's ever accused them of creativity. Dad's a civil engineer, retired, and Mom did patent law. They retired down to the Gulf of Mexico a while back. How about you?"

"My dad owned a hardware store and Mom was a homemaker." Bree adjusted the elastic cuff of her flowy coral-colored top. "They're both gone. This was their house actually. I inherited it—my sister has her own place in town and I ended up staying here. But I guess I never really made it my own."

"I see. So there's history here." He gave a thoughtful frown. "This isn't just a house, it's a home."

"Yes. Now for my second question: Why do you need my help in Portland?"

"I'd like you to come because way I see it, you're kinda the cutest person I've met in a long time. I'm not in a getting-tied-down mode at present and you've been clear how you're in the same boat so what can go wrong?"

He spoke easily—too easily—as if he was holding back a long story. What would Renee say? Probably to be careful. To wait. To slow down.

What would Jill say?

Probably to remember that it wasn't long ago that she

wasn't sure if she'd be in the fight for her life, so it was time to fight to have a life.

"Okay, what the heck," she said impulsively, deciding to err on the side of the imaginary Jill. "When do we go?"

"Tomorrow. When are you off work?"

"Five."

"I was thinking we could spend the night there, I know a cool B and B. And there are some great historic houses in the area that might give you some ideas for what we could do here."

"B and B?" Her skin tingled all over, suddenly the old denim over her thighs, the soft lace of her bra—it was too much sensation. "What are the sleeping arrangements?"

Good lord, he could power the eastern seaboard with the heat of his gaze. "As fun as last night was, I'd like to just be friends. That cool with you?"

Friends?

She went cold, like he'd just taken a bucket of ice water and dumped it over her head. Good lord, how had she blown this? Was she so out of practice that she was misreading all the signs? Had he really just friend-zoned her?

"Of course. Yes. Perfect. Friends! That sounds nice," she heard herself say. *Nice.* Vanilla ice cream was nice. Getting a prime parking spot out the front of Shopper's Corner was nice. Folding a towel still warm from the drier was nice.

A weekend away with the only guy to ever give her back-to-back orgasms shouldn't be nice. And yet here they were.

"Great," he said before clearing his throat. "It's a date. Well, not a date, but you know what I mean."

"Of course. Buddy!" She grinned before playfully bopping his shoulder. Liar. She had no idea what he meant.

"Cool. Cool. Now if you don't mind, I'd like to walk around and take a few photos, just so I don't forget any details."

"That's fine." She tried for a casual tone. "Fair warning though, my bed is unmade, but seeing as we're just friends...guess there's no need to impress?"

"I like your style." He winked as he disappeared in the direction of the kitchen.

Bree returned to the baby blanket, but dropped a stitch in no time. Good lord, she was useless. Down the hall came the unfamiliar sound of men's work boots striding across the kitchen tiles, solid, heavy, and reassuring.

She smiled despite herself, kicking off her sandals and pressing her toes into the worn, old carpet. Friend zone or not, it was nice to have a man in the house—this man, anyway. A warm breeze blew in from the open windows carrying with it the sweet smell of roses blooming in the front yard and the crisp, briny tang of the sea.

For a moment, life was good—the question was, how long would it stay that way?

# Chapter Ten

Essie dialed in the password combination for the lock-box, pulled out the brass key, and handed it to Jill. "Would you like to do the honors?"

Jill turned the handle on 108 Anchor Court's candy apple–red front door and sucked in a deep breath before stepping over the threshold. She'd never been inside the little house that she and Simon had once pretended might be theirs for the taking. And now here she was, in another life, in many ways another woman, and yet somehow this moment felt like a homecoming.

The interior of the cottage was even better than she'd ever imagined. The whitewashed open ceilings made the small space more bright and airy than it had any right to be. Outside the double French doors that faced quaint, English-style gardens, were two Adirondack chairs, perfectly positioned to soak up the fleeting heat of a Maine summer while savoring a French roast coffee in the morning or a glass of wine after work. The antique nautical chart hanging on the wall that separated the living room from the little farmhouse-style kitchen showed Cranberry Cove and the surrounding coastline. She peeked into the alcove and couldn't help but squeal at the built-in bookcases and the cozy window seat begging for a reader on a rainy afternoon.

"There's no place like home, am I right?" Essie said.

But hearing her friend's innocent question broke the spell.

A home is a place where there is love, family, people. Jill had nothing but a strained relationship with her mother.

Her vision went blurry with unshed tears. It was time to step out of the daydream and back into real life. "I think I've seen enough. This house isn't for me."

"What?" Essie looked genuinely surprised. "How can you say that?"

"I know you mean well. I do. But it was a bad idea to come here. This cottage has what...three bedrooms? Essie, it's just me. I don't have a husband or the two-point-five kids. All this would be wasted on me."

"Speak for yourself." Essie bristled. "I'm not married, nor do I ever plan on having children, and I feel like I'm deserving of nice things. We, as women, are enough just as we are."

Jill's heart sank. Talk about sticking her foot in her mouth. "That came out all wrong. Of course a woman doesn't need a man or to reproduce to be of value. It's just that I *did* want both of those things, and I was close, so close to having it all. And if I bought this house I feel as if I'd just live alongside ghosts of a future that I'm never going to have."

"You're still young, girl." Essie arched a perfectly threaded brow while giving her a slow once-over. "You can still have everything you want, you just need to stop hiding in the shadows and grab life by the tail. Refuse to take no for an answer."

"Oh come on. I'm not exactly a hide-away-in-the-shadows type of gal."

Essie leveled a hard gaze. "Not to most. But from where I sit, I see a woman who is trying to make herself small, not living the bold, big life she was born to."

Jill wanted to believe her friend's words so bad she could taste it. And yet, to want such a thing, what would that do to the memory of Simon, of what he meant to her? She felt as if something was tearing inside her heart, almost as if she was being ripped in two.

"I'm too busy and overwhelmed." She fiddled with the long ceramic beads she wore on a thin leather string around her neck. "I have a lot of work to do for the art fair, all the table logistics and contracts to review. Not to mention I should get to bed early because I need to finish painting the gallery if I'm ever going to open on time."

Essie snorted. "I never knew you were such a ballerina."

Jill wrinkled her nose. "What are you talking about?"

"You keep dancing around the truth." Essie's face was serious; she wasn't messing around. "Stop making excuses."

"Look." Jill tucked a loose lock of hair behind her ear, taking off her glasses to give them a shamefaced polish with the hem of her tunic. "You're right. I can't say no to this house. But I also can't just jump in and say yes. My guess is that while I decide what to do someone else will snap it up and that will be that. It's better to be realistic."

Essie cocked her head. "Is that a chance you really want to take?"

Yes. No. For Pete's sake, she didn't know! She was so spun out that north felt like south, and east could be west. She could see herself in that other perfect life from the corner of her eye. She and Simon slow dancing barefoot in the living room or cozied up on the couch making faces at the swaddled baby they were cuddling.

She pressed the heels of her hands into her eye sockets so hard she saw stars.

Essie seemed to sense her inner turmoil and finally relented. "Before you go," she said softly, "mind if I show you one thing?"

Jill hesitated, then dropped her hands, blinked until she could focus again, and then gave a hesitant nod.

Essie led her through the kitchen and opened a glass door that led to the side of the house. "It's right out here." The flower beds were bright purple with echinacea, but Essie was pointing through the stems and leaves at the foundation.

Jill adjusted her glasses. There was something carved into the cornerstone. "'Max Loves Martha.' Huh. Who are they?"

"I can't say I know," Essie said quietly. "But I want to believe they were the original owners, and that they built the house on love. Open up and feel it. I don't want to be cheesy but it's like you can still sense their love suffused into every nook and cranny. It's just such a special place and it deserves a special owner."

Essie went statue still, tilting her chin to face the impossibly blue sky, not a single cloud around to mar the perfect unbroken color. Somewhere in the distance, a seagull cried while low down in a nearby hydrangea hedge a yellow-throat sang its happy *wichatee-wichatee-wichatee*.

Jill turned and tiptoed over the granite pavers to a bed of beach roses, their sweet smell mingling with the sea air. The yard was a perfect mix of an English cottage garden and the hardy Maine landscape...Many of the lichen, blueberries, bayberry, and moss looked as if they'd always grown there, and the towering spruce spread its blue-green branches over the faded yellow shingles, protecting the roof like an old friend.

"I love it here so much that I can barely breathe," she heard herself say. "But like I said, I'm really not in the market. It's nothing I've planned for."

Thank goodness Bree wasn't around to overhear her being a giant hypocrite. Her shoulders tensed from the realization. Turned out that it was easier to encourage a friend to step out of *her* comfort zone than to follow suit.

"This place is you through and through," Essie replied, hand planted on one narrow hip. "Tell you what, why don't you go home, have a cup of tea, work on your plans for the art fair, and clear your head. I'll check back in a few days."

Jill nodded, unable to speak around the knot in her throat. She could see Simon taking one look at the back porch and claiming he'd screen it in, knowing how the mosquitoes loved to hunt her down like evil little vampires, addicted to the flavor of her blood. There was the ideal spot for a child's swing near the back fence, with the perfect amount of dappled light and a thick carpet of grass underfoot.

She pressed a hand to her lower belly, feeling a pulse beneath her palm. It wasn't another life, safe and curled inside, just her own blood, whooshing its lonely way through her body

"Please. Let's go," she said at last, simultaneously enchanted and haunted.

Jill and Essie got back to their cars in the front of the cottage just as a couple approached from down the adjacent street, swinging a little boy between them who howled in delight while kicking his short legs into the air.

Sadie and Ethan Landry and their son, Lincoln.

As much as Jill wanted to escape, she didn't want to be rude to Sadie. She was a genuinely great person, a force, full of endless energy and a smile that could light up a room.

A smile she gave Jill now, even though it was tinged with third-trimester weariness. Her baby bump was showed off to perfection by her formfitting polka-dot jersey dress.

"Jill!" Sadie stepped forward and wrapped Jill in a big hug, giggling as her belly shoved Jill back. "Sorry,

sorry, oh jeez, I'm sorry, Watermelon here likes to get in the way."

"Watermelon?"

Sadie giggled. "That's what I'm calling the baby these days. Mostly because of my shape. Thank god for thick elastic waistbands."

"No complaints here, honey, you're perfect just as you are," Ethan said with a rumbling chuckle as he affectionately wrapped his arm around her shoulder and planted a kiss on the top of her head. "She's glowing, isn't she?"

The love in his eyes shone clear and bright and he gazed down in unabashed adoration.

"Mommy glow?" Lincoln scrunched up his freckled nose, adorably perplexed. "Like one of those fireflyers?"

"Brighter, lil' bud," Ethan said with a grin, ruffling his son's hair. "Mommy shines so much we should all be wearing sunglasses."

"Oh stop you, before you make me blush and embarrass my friends. What are you doing here anyway?" Sadie asked at the exact same time that Jill said, "Essie was just giving me a sneak peek of her newest property."

"This your house now?" Lincoln looked between them, incredulity stamped into his chubby features.

"Hey, want to race me to the playground?" Ethan slapped his hands together, getting Lincoln's attention. "We should let the ladies talk for a bit."

Lincoln rubbed his round chin looking wise beyond his years. "Them ladies sure like talkin'."

They all burst out laughing.

"We certainly do," Essie said once she caught her breath. "Oh my, I don't know how you stand all that cuteness."

"You know what they say about kids." Sadie gave a good-natured shrug. "Darndest things and all that."

"One...two...three...," Ethan shouted and off they went, father and son, in matching white polo shirts, their tousled brown hair going a warm caramel in the sun.

"Sorry about all that," Sadie said, although her face was filled with love. "Lincoln's of an age where the world revolves around him. He butts into every conversation. I should be more strict with him but he's just so funny. I never know what he'll come up with next!"

"Aw." Jill smiled so hard it felt as if her teeth might crumble to dust from the pressure. "You must be so excited for another."

"Thrilled, but feeling a little spoiled. People keep dropping off sweet board books or clothes. I mean I have so much from Lincoln still. I don't want to be greedy or anything."

"We know that," Essie said, "but you are not allowed to stand in the way of all of us filling your drawers with adorable little dresses. I found one that came with a matching diaper cover stitched with dainty ruffles on the butt. It's so sweet that it might give me a cavity."

"That sounds adorable," Jill said with as much enthusiasm as she could muster, which meant that she ended up sounding like the captain of the cheer team during the homecoming parade, brimming with too much pep and perkiness.

She feigned a glance at her watch. "Oh gosh, the time is getting on. I have to run. It was great to see you, Sadie, we need to have coffee soon."

"Coffee with you could almost make drinking decaf bearable."

Jill gave her a quick hug and jumped into her car before Sadie could come back to her question over what they had been doing there.

But she didn't drive home.

She did the same thing she always did when she felt adrift. She drove to her safe harbor.

She went to find Bree.

# Chapter Eleven

Red or white?" Bree called out to Jill from her kitchen. Jill had turned up unannounced a half hour ago. She hadn't said much but didn't need to. They were the kind of friends who could read each other with a single look. And her first glance at Jill when she opened the door was that her frazzled-looking friend needed to be tucked in on the couch with one of her mother's cozy old afghans and a thick slice of Renee's lemon meringue pie.

Now it was impromptu happy hour.

"Something sweet, I think," Jill answered back a little sheepishly. "To go with this crazy delicious lemony filling. How does it taste so fresh? There isn't a citrus tree for a thousand miles and yet it feels like Renee just plucked them."

"I know, I know, everything that woman touches turns to magic." The fact didn't even make her jealous...much.

"Sorry for barging in without a text."

Bree's heart swelled at the hint of quavering vulnerability in Jill's voice. "Stop it. You are my sister from another mother. We don't need to make advanced plans ever. Ooooh. I know just the wine for this evening." She released a big internal sigh of determination as she removed an elegant long-necked bottle from the top of her fridge. Jill needed cheering up and she was going to be up for the task. "Myles talked me into trying a new Riesling they got in stock at Shopper's Corner." The owner of Shopper's Corner, the local town grocery store, had impeccable taste in wine.

Silence from Jill.

She babbled on, forcing cheer into every syllable. "He also got this new display in the beauty and wellness section, these amazing scented candles that Daphne is making." The cork came off with a satisfying pop. "You know Daphne—the one who owns the cute little dress shop just off Main Street?"

This time she got a weak "Uh-huh."

"Anyway, you should ask her if she wants to sell any at Chickadee. I bought the Cranberry Punch flavor, it's on the coffee table. Take a sniff. It's addictive."

From the corner of her eye she watched Jill extract a hand from the afghan and reach out to lift up the candle. "Oh wow," Jill said after a pause. "That's amazing. Are there others?"

Bree's shoulders relaxed a little. Score one for the candles!

"I think six so far." Bree came out and handed her a stemless wine goblet. "Aside from this one, which is my favorite, there's a balsam fir that's not too overpowering. Ooooh, and a lovely one called 'Morning by the Sea.'" She closed her eyes in exaggerated Zen bliss. "It's serene."

Jill took a sip of wine and let out an appreciative moan, visibly relaxing. "Wooooow, that is crisp. Gosh, Miles really knows his stuff."

Bree suddenly reached over and grabbed Jill's shoulder. "And guess what?"

"What?" said Jill, laughing at Bree's sudden burst of excitement.

"There's an independent bookshop coming to the Old Red Mill with some really adorable name that escapes me at the moment."

"What?" Jill gasped. "You must be thrilled. No more treks to Portland to feed your fix."

"I know! It's like a Christmas miracle in the middle of summer." Bree let go of Jill's shoulder and returned to rocking. "Although it also might be dangerous." She nodded a chin at her overflowing bookshelves. Not only were her favorites there, meticulously arranged by author, but so were all her mom's cozy mysteries and her dad's collection of seafaring fiction. She should really donate them but they'd always been in this room—as long as she could remember.

Jill burrowed under the cream blanket, color returning to her cheeks in slow degrees. "I hope they stock a wide range of memoirs because I plan on becoming a loyal customer."

"Me too. But I'm hoping for heavy on the historical fiction and true crime, of course. You know me, I can't get enough of crowns and killers!"

Jill choked on her sip, removing her glasses to dab at her eyes. "Maybe we can finally start that book club. Otherwise someday they will find my body buried under a giant stack of paperbacks that I never made the time to start."

"Yes, I'd love that." Bree picked back up the blanket for Sadie's baby and waggled the needles. "Or we make it a book club, knitting club."

Jill toasted her. "Or a book club, knitting club, wine-drinking club."

"Let's be real. What we need is a book club, knitting club, wine-drinking club, *pie-eating* club."

They both dissolved into giggles that eventually petered into silence. A subtle sense of melancholy returned to the room.

Bree spoke first. "Jilly Beans, what's going on? I can tell something's bothering you."

"Funny girl." Jill smirked. "I was just about to ask you the same thing."

Bree set down her glass on the coffee table and laid a cool hand on the sudden blush that bloomed on her cheek. "You may be right about that. I'll rock, paper, scissors you over who dishes first."

"Dork." Jill rolled her eyes. "You're on."

"Rock, paper, scissors!" they cried in unison.

Jill made scissors while Bree challenged with paper.

"You win," Bree crowed. "That means it's time to spill the beans."

Jill wrinkled her nose but went ahead anyway. "Fine. Essie took me for a walk-through at the Anchor Court cottage." She fell back on the couch. "Oh Bree, it's perfect. Bright. Cheerful. A little whimsical."

"That's fantastic!" But Jill didn't seem happy, in fact she looked miserable. The skin under her eyes was tinged a pale purple and she was doing that habitual lip-biting thing she did whenever she got stressed.

"Essie thinks I should snap it up." Jill continued in a small, plaintive voice. "But the cottage is too big for someone like me. I mean what am I going to do with three bedrooms?"

"The house is pretty modest," Bree pointed out gently, trying to get to the real reason behind Jill's feelings. "The bedrooms must be the size of shoeboxes."

The observation didn't conjure any reaction from her friend.

Bree forged on. Jill was usually the one trying to fix Bree's life so here was a perfect opportunity to try and pay her back. "What about a roommate to help offset the mortgage? Or you could Airbnb one of the rooms. A few other people in town do that and sometimes they get really fascinating people from all over the world." These weren't the most ideal suggestions, but where there was a will, there was a way. Jill had been the one to teach her that.

"Heck no!" Jill bolted upright, the blanket falling to the side. "You know me, Bree. I value my personal space way too much. But I don't know…Being there…it felt right." She covered her face with her hands. "And that feels wrong."

Bree's eyes widened as she had a private a-ha moment. "Because Simon isn't there to share it with you?"

Jill's lower lip quivered—just once but it was enough of a tell. "It just feels so monumentally unfair to take that step without him."

Bree's heart was so full it almost hurt. She leaned over and took her friend's hand, the skin was cool and clammy to the touch. "Honey, I know this is so hard. But I also know he'd want you to be happy. Simon worshipped the ground you walked on and he'd want you to chase your dreams. And remember that anything is possible if you have friends to support you, and, honey, you have that in spades. I'm always here to share in your happiness. But I'm also equally here to help ease your pain."

"I know, and I love you for that. You can't know how much your friendship means to me. And I understand Simon's gone and that no amount of wishful thinking is ever going to make him come back and that being a martyr isn't going to change anything about this whole sucky situation." Jill withdrew her hand and flung herself to standing, striding to the living room windows and looking like a lost little girl. "But I gotta tell you, B. It's so *so* hard to imagine myself living in my dream home without my dream man."

That made sense—and yet, Bree wanted only good things for her friend. And Simon really would hate to see Jill this adrift. Sympathy flooded her. "So what are you going to do?" Bree asked after a pause once it became clear her friend wasn't going to say anything else.

"No clue." Jill wiped her eyes. "Guess I need to do a lot of thinking. Now what's your news?"

"Are you sure you don't want to process your situation more? There is a lot there to go over." She didn't say the rest of her sentence out loud, the helpless feeling she always held back from her best friend: *...and you never open up about Simon. I know you are hurting but I don't know how to help fix what's broken. And there seemed to be more, hiding right below the surface.*

"Ugh, trust me, I know, but I'm so exhausted by my stuff. I need to escape my own drama. Please do me a favor and share yours."

Behind her rose-gold frames, Jill's eyes seemed to plead with her to change the subject.

So Bree picked her drink up and recalibrated. This was definitely a story that required alcohol. "So Essie came here for tea and was pretty persuasive about a remodel, as I mentioned earlier. And I don't want to bug Sadie with interior design ideas when she's juggling the Old Red Mill renovation and the impending baby."

"Makes sense."

"Essie suggested a new contracting company and I decided to let them come out and work on a quote. But the builder who came was...well...*him!*"

"Who?" Jill blinked, clearly missing the innuendo.

"*Him!* The dark and handsome guy from The Drafty Cellar. My anti–bucket list fling! His name is Chance Elliston."

"Holy guacamole with a side of chips." Jill's lips made a perfect O. "That's nuts!"

"That's Cranberry Cove." Bree threw up her hands in exasperation. "We all know how it is in this town. There is zero anonymity here. Might as well embrace it." Bree filled Jill in on the little she knew of Chance's career in New York City and how he was helping out his brother, but when she got to the part about how he invited her to Portland she realized she couldn't say it. Because she wasn't going to go. The realization hit her with the force of a lightning bolt.

No way could she run off and leave town when Jill looked as if she was one hard wind from blowing away. Plus, to be honest, the more it festered in her mind, she had to admit a trip to Portland as Chance's friend sucked rocks. Big pointy ones.

"Hey," she said, getting up to grab the bottle to refill their glasses. "Want to sleep over tonight?"

"Really?" Jill clapped her hands. "We haven't done that in forever."

Bree warmed to the tip of her toes. It felt so good to be the one helping Jill for a change.

"And it's your lucky night because I've got a box of Korean sheet masks that arrived yesterday. Plus the new drama about the British monarchy just dropped on one of my streaming sites. We can do some serious binging and ooh and ahh over the gowns."

"That sounds absolutely smashing, old chum," Jill said with a mock British accent. "But first," she said, getting serious, "are you thinking of taking things further with this Chance character?" Her eyes narrowed. "Because I can do some digging. Check him out. See where the bodies are buried."

"Gosh, between you and Renee I don't think I ever have to worry about ending up with anyone nefarious."

Bree ducked into the kitchen for a bag of popcorn. "Besides," she said, mustering brightness into her tone. "That's never going to work. It was just a one-time thing for my list. From now on our relationship is going to be strictly professional." Maybe if she kept saying it, her words would become true. They'd exchanged numbers before he'd finally taken off and she could simply text him before bed to call the trip off.

Yes. Perfect. Quality time with Jill would be much better than heading out of town with a manly drool magnet who seemed to have a PhD in female pleasure but only wanted to be friends.

As she fought back the turbulent roiling in her tummy, her gaze caught a flyer she'd impulsively stuck on her fridge this morning. The picture of a corgi posed next to a rosebush steadied her. "Anyway, I'm thinking about getting a new man in my life."

She grabbed the flyer, in addition to the SmartPop!, and brought it into the living room, handing the flyer over while setting the popcorn between them.

"What's this? 'Second Chance Friends Adoption Weekend'?" Jill murmured, reading the header.

"Second Chance Friends is this great animal rescue group that rehomes dogs and cats if their owners pass away or get too sick to care for them. I also had getting a fur baby on my anti-bucket list, so figured I should go see if I can find a friend. A lapdog would be a sweet companion while I knit and if he is well behaved, Noreen will probably let him hang out at Castaway during my shifts."

"This is incredible. You are taking lots of *chances* lately," Jill said with a teasing emphasis. "I like to see you come out of your shell."

Bree ducked her head, pleased at the compliment.

"Before you know it you probably will be off trekking the Great Wall of China or heck, maybe even Kilimanjaro! No wait, I know, you can hike the Appalachian Trail with Dot Turner."

"Yeah right." She flung one of her mom's hand-embroidered throw pillows at Jill before grabbing the remote. "You know I couldn't keep up with her."

"Ha!" Jill said. "And sadly true. Dot will outlive us all."

"Truth."

And as they settled in on the couch, ready to escape into the behind-the-scenes dramas of Buckingham Palace, Bree glanced at her phone on the table and reassured herself that she was doing the right thing.

Needing a cuddle, she scooched down the couch, resting her head in Jill's lap. As the opening scenes rolled, she wasn't seeing the sumptuous throne room with the red velvet curtains and golden wallpaper flashing on the flat screen. She was imagining Chance's adorable dimples and perceptive eyes...and then strangely Grandview Inn—had somebody snapped it up already? Not that it mattered, she had no business or ability to do anything about either of those things. Jill's musings on the little red-door cottage probably just meant she had real estate on the brain.

Essie Park would be so proud.

Jill absently stroked Bree's hair, using the same reassuring rhythm she'd used since they were in kindergarten and Bree had fallen on the playground concrete and scraped a knee.

Her lips curled into a faint smile. A best friend and a dog—that was all she needed to live her best life.

# Chapter Twelve

After a pot of French-pressed coffee so strong that Jill swore she could hear buzzing in her ears—*and* polishing off Renee's lemon meringue pie with a scoop of strawberry sorbet for good measure—it was time to leave Bree's house and seize the day.

"Don't forget to text me pics of cute fluffy dogs," she ordered Bree while tying a knot in the old Cranberry Cove High volleyball shirt her friend had loaned her. Not exactly flattering high fashion but she needed to do some heavy cleaning over at Chickadee's so it suited the agenda.

"Will do." Bree gave her a squeeze. "Good luck today."

As she drove off, Jill found herself smiling. It was hard not to on such a beautiful Maine morning. The ocean glimpses between the charming beachside cottages filled her heart to bursting. Birds sang, fishing boats churned through the calm waters of the cove, and pale golden light snuck through the pine trees causing the bowers to glow.

But her good mood evaporated faster than a drop of water in a cast-iron pan when she spotted the woman up ahead, walking down the sidewalk while carrying a plastic caddy loaded with cleaning supplies. Jill recognized the mass of hair, the dark blond streaks that were the same shade as her own natural color mixed with thick coils of silver. The woman wore a long brightly colored Indian-print skirt and a black linen tank top.

*Linda.*

Jill didn't feel like engaging this morning, but what was the alternative, lead-footing it past at ten miles over the limit? Not an option, especially as Linda had been forced to sell her sedan to avoid bankruptcy five years ago.

Jill pulled over to the curb and rolled down the passenger-side window. "Hey. Need a ride?"

"Jill." Linda offered a genuine smile. "Now this is a happy surprise. I'm just coming back from a cleaning job, but the gig was so easy that I finished an hour ahead of schedule. The visitors left the place immaculate so I just had to do a quick mop and wipe down—I love when that happens. What are you up to?"

"I'm heading out to the Old Red Mill to work on sprucing up the gallery. It's almost ready for the grand reopening but is still sort of a mess. I don't want to bring out my inventory until it's spotless."

"Want some company?" Linda shyly raised her cleaning caddy. "I'd love to help."

Jill could tell by the way her mom's shoulders deflated that her expression wasn't exactly overjoyed. *Crud.* She needed to try harder. Linda was doing her best to be friendly and helpful.

As much as her childhood memories stung, what was the point of causing more pain now? Simon had always encouraged her to repair her relationship with Linda, especially given the fact his own parents died in a car crash when he was eighteen. He knew there was a lot of pain there—and didn't push her to rush—but she had to admit that she stopped trying to let her mom back into her heart when she'd buried Simon. It was far easier to build a wall and keep Linda on the other side. A person could only hold so much hurt in their heart before they had to compartmentalize to make it through the day. She couldn't put all her emotions on hold forever, but if she let them all out, she'd risk being overrun, and she had a business to get back on track and a life to live.

But it wouldn't kill her to make more of an effort with Linda. After all, in so many ways, she was a victim of circumstances. It wasn't her fault that she hadn't been able to be around, and that she'd financially stumbled because she wanted to improve her lot in life. But that didn't change the fact that deep down Jill felt like she'd been forced to raise herself, and then bail her mom out.

It would have been nice to be the child sometimes, rather than the responsible one.

But longing for a perfect childhood or a mom who was wise and a go-to for sensible advice wasn't the reality.

And maybe if she accepted that, she could move on.

"Help would be great," Jill said, praying she sounded like she meant it, and that Simon, wherever he was, might be proud of her.

The ruse must have worked because Linda's face brightened. "Really? You mean it?"

"Don't get so excited," Jill said as her mom opened up the passenger door and got herself situated. "It's literally cleaning. Nothing glamorous."

"This is your *store*, your baby. I want to be there for you," Linda said, seemingly unaware at how Jill flinched at the word "baby."

A few hours later and even Jill had to admit that her mom's presence was a godsend. While she finished painting the walls, getting them ready to receive the brightly colored canvases she sold in the shop, Linda scrubbed and dusted and organized. It would have taken Jill at least two full days to finish that amount of work on her own.

"Have you had enough yet?" Jill asked after her mom finished wiping down the windows with vinegar and water. It turned out that Linda made all her cleaning products from environmentally friendly ingredients and now the old space smelled like eucalyptus and lemongrass. "You're allowed to cry uncle at any time. There is no obligation or expectation to stay all day."

"Are you kidding?" Linda paused to wipe her brow, sweat sheening her top lip. "I'm having a blast. It's great to be with you. We never seem to find the time."

Yep, that was pain in her mother's voice. Pain Jill knew

she had an active role in putting there. She wasn't the little girl hiding under the bed at midnight wishing for her mommy anymore. But neither was Linda that harried too-young mom expecting her lonely kid to be a mini-adult.

"Look." Jill took a deep breath. It was high time she said a few things to try to break down that wall between them. "I know that I'm pretty distant at the best of times, but I don't want to be a jerk. It's just hard for me to know what I want from you..." She let the words trail off. It would be so great to have a mother-daughter relationship. She'd watched enough *Gilmore Girls* to crave that easy connection, a friendship with an older, wiser woman who was there to show you how to buy a bra that fits and serve up life advice alongside a homemade dinner.

But her life wasn't a picture-perfect small-town television show.

Still...she wanted something more than what they currently had. It was starting to become evident that she couldn't continue through life as a one-woman island, she needed to start building a few bridges.

Linda suddenly noticed another splotch on a window ledge and went after it a little too vigorously. After another minute of strained silence, she spoke again, scrunching her rag in her hand. "Thank you for letting me spruce up your shop. It felt good."

"To clean?" Jill arched a brow.

"To help you, baby. I see the woman you've blossomed into and I can't tell you how happy that makes me. I wish I could have been the mom who made cookies, or knew how to roast a turkey, or cook anything that didn't go in the microwave. I wish that I had put your hair in pigtails in the morning before school, and been there at dinner to hear about your day. I know I was tired too much, and loving too little. I can't tell you how much I wish we had taken more time to run out into the night barefoot to catch fireflies. To build snowmen and, you know, stuff like that." Her voice cracked, as tears flooded her eyes. "You and I are the only family we have left and please believe me that I want to spend the rest of my time on this planet putting things right. No more regrets."

Jill stood in stunned silence. This was the most her mom had ever acknowledged the pain of her youth. And as the words sunk in, something started to heal in her broken heart. Not a full repair, but a few strong stitches.

"Can I…" Her voice hitched too. "Can I give you a hug? Please?"

"Of course." Linda's lower lip quivered. "Baby, I thought you'd never ask."

They embraced for what felt like forever, and even though Jill wasn't small anymore, she slotted perfectly into her mom's arms, and for just a moment she felt safe—protected—loved, even.

"Oh dear!" A female voice piped from the open door. "I'm sorry. I can come back later."

Jill stepped back, wiping her eyes before taking in a pretty, curly-haired thirty-something woman with freckles and the greenest eyes she'd ever seen, shifting nervously in the Chickadee entrance.

"Hello," Jill said, clearing her throat. "Are you looking for Hester's Pie Shop?"

The woman chuckled, patting her stomach, hidden beneath a baggy lilac T-shirt and corduroy cutoffs. "Don't worry, I found that and I've already had a slice of blueberry pie. I wanted to introduce myself. I'm Ashley Wood. I'm going to be opening a store here on the second floor of the mill. It's a bookshop. Book o'Clock."

"Oh, I heard about you." Jill perked up, remembering Bree's excitement last night. "Goodness, I hope you are ready for a stampede," she said with a grin. "Because this town has never had a bookshop and locals love to spend our long winters curled up with a juicy read."

"Cha-ching, cha-ching!" A handsome man in a hipster T-shirt with a carefully groomed, blond goatee strode in, slapping Ashley on the rump. "Love it, ladies! Tell me more about all this money we're going to be making."

Jill and Linda exchanged a troubled look as Ashley suddenly became interested in studying her pale pink pedicure peeking out from her Birkenstock sandals.

"I'm Jack. Jack Wood. Ashley's better half," he said, sticking out a hand.

Hopefully karma slapped this jerk in the face before she had to.

"Jill Kelly," she said reluctantly. His hand was warm and sweaty and gave her the heebie-jeebies.

"We're coming up from Burlington," he continued in his booming voice. "My brother Kent is a big-time developer and has been doing research, looking for an area in New

England that could be classified as a 'diamond in the rough.' Cranberry Cove has the kind of growth potential that gets my motor going."

"What my husband means," Ashely said softly, "is that Cranberry Cove is still quiet, charming, the kind of place where all the locals seem to have created a real sense of community."

"Yes, and that's the way we like it," Linda added.

"Of course," Ashley hastily agreed. "We want to add to the place's character, not change it."

"Speak for yourself," a muscular man who was an identical copy of Jack—except with dark brown hair— swaggered in. And "swaggered" was the exact right word for it. He entered Chickadee wearing head-to-toe branded outdoor clothing, sunglasses propped up on his forehead, and an attitude like he was honoring them all with his presence.

"You guys don't know what you've got here in this town. Easy commuting distance to Boston. A fantastic bay with access to quality local seafood. It's just waiting for someone to see the potential."

"No offense, but we locals sort of like it just how it is," Jill ventured. "It's great for our small businesses to get a tourist boom in summer and then the rest of the year we mostly have the place to ourselves."

He gave a dismissive snort. "That's nothing but lost revenue."

"This is Jack's brother, Kent," Ashley offered.

Jill wished they would leave.

It didn't seem fair that she was finally having a long-overdue moment of reconnection with Linda only to have it interrupted by two out-of-town asshats who were utterly full of themselves.

On the edge of her peripheral vision, Linda gave a sudden jerk. Jill glanced over but was unable to read whatever mental message her mom was shooting her with that intense gaze.

"Anyway, I'd love to connect more," Ashley said haltingly. "Coffee sometime? Wine on the beach?"

"Sounds fabulous. We love it all. Pie too."

"It's going to be dangerous working so close to Hester's." Ashley sighed, throwing up her hands. "I'm going to have a problem controlling myself around all that buttery goodness."

"Well, you better learn to," Jack said twisting half his mouth into an amused leer. "You don't want to turn into your mother." He mimed a curvaceous silhouette before his brother Kent high-fived him. Ashley looked like she wanted to disappear beneath the floorboards.

That was it. Jill officially hated these men. "We *all* love Renee's pies," she said staunchly. "And while you might not be from around here, let me give you a hot tip. The women of Cranberry Cove don't take kindly to body-shamers."

"Or snoopers," Linda piped up randomly.

"Hey, hey, hey." Jack held up his hands. "No harm, no foul. I was just joking around with my wife. Let's not get off on the wrong foot. We're all going to be working in each other's pockets."

Jill glanced between his smarmy face and Ashley's

distraught expression and decided it was best to leave it there. She'd said her piece and she didn't want to cause that poor woman any more discomfort.

"I really should get back to work. I'm trying to open up next week and have a lot to do."

"What sort of venture is this going to be?" Kent asked.

She didn't like the calculating way his gaze slid over her shop.

"It's an art boutique. I relocated from Main Street after the big hurricane a few months ago and sell paintings and artisan wares from Maine artists and craftspeople."

"I like it," Kent said, sidling closer, bringing with him the intense scent of some type of overtly masculine cologne. "You ever think of opening up a second location, say a hotel gift shop?"

Jill frowned, practically gagging on the sandalwood and musk, as it took her a few seconds to process his question. "I—I don't know. No one has ever asked me about that."

"Well, let's just say that I plan on getting into the hotel business here in town. So maybe you and I should have a talk."

"He wants Grandview Inn," Jack shared. "That old dump is sitting on prime real estate. If he razes the place it could be a game changer for Cranberry Cove. An ultramodern luxury spa retreat."

"A steel-and-glass tower that is a futuristic rendering of a lighthouse, but instead of a lamp, picture an LED reflector that radiates a rainbow of color that can be seen up to a mile from the coast."

"That sounds like an amusement park, not a hotel," Jill said, appalled. Was he on some sort of substance? Because this sounded like the worst idea she'd heard of since cheese in a can.

"Exactly." Kent looked smug, not picking up on her disgust. In fact, the Wood brothers didn't seem to notice anything except their own internalized sense of awesome. "So keep an eye out for a message from me. We can do business."

And with that, he literally turned on his heel and swaggered out.

"Is he serious?" she asked, gaping at his brother. "A modern hotel designed like a futuristic lighthouse?"

"I know." Kent seemed oblivious to her horror. "He is a genius when it comes to real estate. Anyway, I gotta run too, need to grease some palms, but I'm sure we'll be seeing a lot of each other here."

Ashley lingered, her gaze darting to the far corners of the room. "I'm sorry about all of that. Jack has a real inferiority complex when it comes to his big brother. He's jealous of Kent's financial success although he'd never say so." She fiddled with her wedding ring. "I know Jack can come on strong, but once you get to know him he's a good guy."

"I see." Jill didn't want to argue with the woman who was clearly stuck in a crappy relationship. Jill's heart hurt for Ashley seeing what a tool her husband was. Simon had been such a lovely, supportive husband she forgot sometimes that not all men were like that.

"I...I...really would like to hang out sometime," Ashley continued. "We're moving here permanently next week. I've never lived outside of Vermont and could use some community. All this change is pretty overwhelming. Plus I've always been a mountain girl. I'm not used to the sea."

"Of course." Jill stepped forward and took her hand. "Also my best friend Bree and I want to start a book club, wine club, pie-eating club. You can be a founding member."

Ashley's laugh was surprisingly infectious. "Sign me up."

No sooner had she left the room than Linda huffed out a disgusted breath. "Kent Wood. That's the suspicious man I saw prowling around my house taking pictures," Linda said. "The one with the dark aura."

Jill turned around. "Well, heck. Turns out you called that one right."

"He can't do it though—right? What he was describing sounded like something from the Las Vegas strip."

"I don't know." Jill's stomach lurched as she looked around her shop. The Old Red Mill was steeped in Cranberry Cove history. Main Street was peppered with brick-front buildings that were erected in the nineteenth century. Now some out-of-town joker plotted to erect a monstrosity on the site of the beloved Grandview Inn? She wanted to believe it was an impossible plot, but who knew what money could buy? Indignation flowed through her as she spun to face Linda. "All I know is this—we won't let those guys win."

# Chapter Thirteen

B ree texted Chance to cancel plans right after Jill left from their impromptu sleepover.

***Bree:*** Hey! About Portland. I have to bow out, sorry. Something came up.

He responded immediately.

Well—not exactly a response. Just those maddening three dots that meant someone was hard at work composing a message. She watched it for a good two minutes before it felt ridiculous.

What on earth was he sending her back. A sonnet? A five-paragraph essay?

When her phone finally buzzed she forced herself to count to five before diving to pick it up.

***Chance:*** Okay! No worries.

Wait—that was it? She shoved the phone in her purse with a huff and headed out the front door. If it took him two minutes to write three words then she had clearly made the right choice. She didn't want to waste time with a guy who couldn't string two coherent sentences together.

Even more proof that she was making the correct decision in letting that situation fizzle out.

She drove to the Cranberry Cove community center where the Second Chance Friends adoptions were being held. As she walked through the front door, she was greeted by two friendly volunteers in yellow vests embroidered with the nonprofit's logo.

"Good morning! Are you here to make a furry friend?" the older woman with the chic white bob asked, handing her a clipboard to register her information.

"I hope so," Bree answered. "I'm looking for a lapdog, well behaved and mellow."

"We have a few that fit that bill just perfectly," the other volunteer said, "along the far left wall. You are welcome to take a few dog treats to help with introductions."

As Jill grabbed a few mini Milk-Bones, her gaze sought out the adoptable small dogs: Chihuahuas, a dachshund mix, a bulldog mutt with a friendly face. He noticed her watching and gave a few very measured tail wags. After that he curled up in a tight little ball, gave an adorable yawn, and promptly appeared to fall asleep.

Oh, yes. Mr. Bulldog seemed like the perfect candidate, a dog that ticked all the needs on her list.

"Hello!" She started walking toward him. "Hey little fell— Ahhhhhhhhhh!" One minute she was on her feet, the next she was flat on her back being face-slurped from chin to forehead by a very large, very enthusiastic golden retriever.

"Finn! No! Down boy, down. Sit! Sit!"

Bree's whole world distilled to a hot tongue and breath that smelled vaguely of meat sticks.

She pushed at that thick soft fur and fought her way to sitting.

"I'm so sorry, ma'am," said a frazzled-looking volunteer. "Finn is uh . . . a big personality."

"He's a big everything," Bree said breathlessly as she stood back up and took a better look at her assailant.

Finn was a giant golden retriever, more red than gold, with happy black eyes and a tail that looked as if it could take out everything in a three-foot radius.

"My goodness." Bree wiped her face. "What's this fellow's story?"

"Poor boy. His owner died in a car accident up in Kennebec County. His owner's parents are too elderly to take care of him and the sister has four kids."

Simon's friendly, handsome face flashed in Bree's mind's eye. "How terrible. Finn looks like a happy boy."

"Oh yes, he has a lot of love to give. He's just anxious. Pets can sense things, you know. He senses his owner is gone and is confused and sad. He acts out but that doesn't mean he's a bad dog. He just needs an understanding owner. Are you looking to give one of our animals a forever home today?"

The volunteer's wheedling tone was unmistakable. She wanted to make a love match between Bree and Finn. But no dice. He was adorable, but she wasn't looking for a big dog. She meant to bring home a lapdog.

"He's much bigger than I'm looking for, sorry," she said.

"It's okay. I've been hearing that all day. You need to go with your gut."

"Exactly," Bree said, glancing back at the sleeping French bulldog. That's the kind of dog she pictured owning. Not a wriggly ninety-pound mass of hair and tongue.

That would be a crazy choice. It didn't make any sense.

She glanced back at the volunteer who was leading Finn over to an area populated by other big dogs. He was resisting her efforts, digging his heels in and glancing back at Bree with a pleading expression that melted her reserves.

"Damn it," she muttered with a chuckle. "Excuse me? Can I spend some time with Finn?"

The volunteer spun around quickly "Are you sure?"

*Heck no.*

"He's nothing like I pictured coming here...and yet..." Bree waved her hand in a helpless gesture.

The volunteer clicked her tongue in understanding. "Sometimes the dog chooses you, not the other way around."

"Can I take him outside?"

"Of course! But if you want him, you'll need to go up to the front desk and fill out all the requisite forms."

She took Finn out into the green lawn outside of the community center. He followed her obediently to the big flower display in the middle, the one that surrounded the town fountain. "So...uh...hello?"

She'd never owned a dog. Her dad had been allergic so all she'd ever owned growing up was a goldfish named Gill that she'd won at the county fair by throwing a ping-pong ball in a bowl.

Finn stared up at her, mouth open, panting slightly.

"You are way bigger than I was looking for. Maybe you'd be happier living out on a big farm? Somewhere where you could chase chickens and barnyard cats and throw your weight around?"

Finn curled up and rested his head on her foot.

Okay, she could get behind that attitude.

"You are cute," she admitted rucfully, scratching him behind the ears. "I'll give you that. You just aren't what I expected."

Finn whined.

She sat down at the edge of the fountain, dipping her fingers into the water, the pennies reflecting in the sunlight.

"Maybe this is par for the course," she murmured, half to herself and half to Finn. "Everything I try since I've started the anti–bucket list hasn't gone quite to plan, but that also doesn't mean that it's been wrong. Maybe the whole point of trying something new is to end up in a place you never knew you needed to go."

Finn settled against her leg, resting his chin on her knee and gazing up in open adoration.

"Such a flirt." She huffed a small laugh and took out her phone, snapping a photo of his handsome face and texting it to Jill.

*Bree:* Meet Finn. Not quite a lapdog, but I think he is adopting me . . . not vice versa

Jill responded immediately.

*Jill:* Yes! I love him. Welcome to the gang, Finny Boy. Also once you get settled with your handsome new addition give me a call. I had a REALLY weird morning—met a guy who wants to buy Grandview Inn. Not good. Need to discuss.

Bree lowered her phone as her core temperature dropped. Grandview Inn had a potential buyer already?

*Her* Grandview Inn?

She reread Jill's cryptic message as if every word mattered, because suddenly it felt like it did. She hadn't realized how much her fanciful little pipe dream of running that historic, old inn had lit a fire inside of her until Jill indicated it might already be gone.

But the buyer only wants the inn. That doesn't mean they have it.

Finn gave a low growl as if reading her thoughts.

"Are you thinking what I'm thinking?" She stood up and started walking back to the community center. She never pictured herself owning a great big dog and here she was ready to sign the adoption papers. She'd never pictured herself actually having the guts to own her dream hotel, but maybe it was time to fight for that too.

Maybe all these little actions she'd been taking since getting the all clear from the medical clinic weren't an anti-anything . . . maybe they were all pro-Bree. What if everything she ever wanted was waiting for her to just have the courage to reach out and take it?

# Chapter Fourteen

Thanks for coming to this emergency meeting," Jill announced to the group assembled around a corner table at Hester's. "I know I gave you zero notice, but this is an important subject for all of us. For the community. For the very heart of Cranberry Cove as we know it."

Bree, Renee, Essie, and Sadie frowned from one side of the big farmhouse table while she and Linda sat opposite. Tansy, Renee's daughter, perched on a stool at the end of the table.

"No problem, but you're kind of freaking me out here. What's all this about?" Concern shaded Renee's eyes. She was never one to love surprises.

Jill exchanged a quick, troubled glance with Linda.

"Go on, honey," her mom prompted, resting a hand on her shoulder. "Tell them about what happened."

Surprisingly, the brief gesture felt reassuring—anchoring

even—which was a welcome sensation after the frantic hours she'd spent since the troubling encounter with the Wood brothers.

She took a deep breath. "Grandview Inn is coming up for sale."

Essie and Bree both exclaimed, "I know," at the same time before glancing at each other with rueful smiles.

Jill's heart tightened. "So you know a guy named Kent Wood?"

"Awful Kent?" Essie paled, her skin going a faint hue of green. "Ugh, he's the worst. He's been annoying me ever since he came into town a few weeks ago. I know he's been asking about the inn but it's hard to tell if he's serious or just wasting time playing at big-shot dealmaker."

"Oh, he's serious all right. He wants to buy the Grandview," Jill replied hoarsely. "And not only that, he wants to knock down most of the structure and then turn it into some sort of ultramodern steel-and-glass luxury hotel." With curt efficiency she laid out Kent's abominable plans for the lighthouse theme—all the way down to the LED rainbow lights.

When she finished her update, Sadie looked as queasy as Essie. Renee had gone white-lipped. And Bree...poor Bree looked as if she were two seconds from bursting into angry tears.

"That's...that's...impossible!" Sadie choked out, looking around as if someone would interrupt the awful conversation to say this was all just a bad dream.

"I don't know." Essie's gaze was troubled. "Kent Wood

has money, and more important, influence. He has connections around the state, especially with the governor," she added meaningfully. "Apparently they were roommates in college."

Jill fell back against her chair, her stomach queasy. Kent on his own was bad news; Kent with connections to high places?

Not good. Not good at all.

"This is a fine kettle of fish," Renee said, leaping to her feet and beelining to the refrigerated pie case. "We need fortification. Pick your poison. Brown sugar pecan or coconut banana cream, ladies?"

"Both," Bree shot back. "We need a heck of a lot of fuel for this fight." She glanced at her phone. "And I only have about fifteen more minutes here." She turned the screen around to show a baleful-looking golden retriever pacing in her laundry room. "Puppy cam," she said. "It feels weird to have left him alone, so I picked one up downtown."

"Maybe we can train him to sic our enemies," Essie said.

Bree snorted. "Finn would be just as liable to lick someone to death."

Jill made a mental note to meet her furry godchild. She'd forgotten about Finn with all the Wood brothers drama. He looked like a good friend, the kind of companion that would fill Bree's heart.

"But what can *we* do?" Sadie asked, rubbing the sides of her expansive belly in a worried rhythm. "I hate this as much as anyone here, but let's be realistic. If there is a developer with deep pockets and the right influence—how can we stop him? Chain ourselves to the hotel and refuse to move?"

"Heck yeah. I'll do that!" Tansy thrust a fist in the air. "No justice, no peace. Power to the people. Time to take a stand."

Jill sighed. Tansy's bold words sounded good but maybe Sadie was right.

Bree pushed back her chair and leapt to her feet so fast she almost fell over. "What about the Coastal Trust for Historic Preservation? The president is one of our customers at Castaway—a total yarn snob. If she even looks at acrylic she practically convulses. Their whole mission is protecting historic buildings along the Maine coast and Grandview Inn certainly falls into that category."

"You have a point," Essie said excitedly. "That might just be the angle that we need."

"And in the meantime I can draft up a petition," Jill announced. "Make sure that it's displayed here at the entrance of the mill, and also Shopper's Corner, the library, and at the craft fair. We get lots of visitors from around the state there and none of them are going to want to see a modern monstrosity thrown up on our coast. I mean, I don't know what good it will do, but it's worth a shot, right?"

"Right." Renee passed out the plates with generous pie slices. "Eat up, everyone. It sounds like we all have a lot to do and this requires energy."

"I'm sorry I won't be here to help more," Tansy said, taking a plate. "Wait! I know. I can make a website. 'Save the Grandview Inn.' I can still help from California."

"Oh honey," Renee said, clasping her shoulder, obviously brimming with pride. "That would be lovely."

"I know it's hard for you to have me live so far away," Tansy continued, "and I miss home too. But this seems like a win-win, right?"

"It certainly does." It was an open secret Renee wished her only daughter lived closer to home, but she'd been doing a great job trying to be understanding and supportive with her decision to study at the University of Southern California.

Jill looked over at Bree, who had a determined set to her jaw, the one she got when she was thinking extra hard about a job that needed to be done.

"What's on your mind, B?" she asked.

Bree forked a big piece of pie and regarded it thoughtfully. "I can't shake the feeling that this development debacle might be my wake-up call. Like—I love the Grandview Inn. I have since I was a little girl. It's always seemed so magical to me. A place where dreams can come true. And if it's really for sale, and really in danger, maybe this is the universe telling me to get over my self-doubt and try to get it."

"What do you mean?" Renee raised a brow. "You want to *buy* the Grandview Inn? How?"

"I don't know." Bree huffed a sigh, twisting her thick hair into a low ponytail with the hair elastic around her wrist. "I just have been thinking that I can't work at Castaway Yarn for the rest of my life ... that I can do bigger things."

"Of course you can," Tansy exclaimed. "You are a badass."

Bree snorted. "I don't know about that, but I do know I'd regret not giving this a shot."

"Honey." Renee furrowed her brow. "I love to see this passion but this is a big undertaking. You just adopted a dog. And after what you went through with the breast cancer scare, don't you think you should take things a bit easier?"

"Absolutely not." Two bright patches of color flamed on Bree's round cheeks. "That's been my whole problem. I've been taking it easy for years. It took that scare to make me realize that I haven't been stuck in my comfort zone, I've been in a rut."

"Well, I think this kicks butt!" Tansy clapped her hands. "This is a really cool idea. What could go wrong?"

A million ideas of things that could go wrong flashed through Jill's mind. Must be nice to be an optimistic member of Generation Z, but reality wasn't quite so carefree. There could be some sort of lawsuit, just to punish anyone who got in Kent's way. Or Bree could get in over her head and go bankrupt. But just as quickly she thought of all the things that could go *right*. Bree cutting a ribbon on the front of a lovingly restored inn. Her best friend happy and fulfilled and living her best life.

"There is a risk in going up against this Wood guy," Jill announced as everyone turned to look at her. "But look at the power we have sitting around this table. We're strong, smart, savvy women who lift each other up and have each other's backs no matter what. So I say we support Bree and if we have to go to war, we devise a winning strategy because failure is not an option."

"Dang girl." Sadie's eyes were wide. "Can I keep you in my pocket and pull you out whenever I need a kick-in-the-pants pep talk?"

Linda took Jill's hand and squeezed. "You can count on my support. I might not have a lot in the way of business sense but I don't mind if I admit to being one scrappy broad."

Jill squeezed her mom's fingers back. While it was wild that some out-of-towner wanted to bring the razzle-dazzle of Las Vegas to their quiet corner of the woods, it was almost as wild as loving that Linda was here among her dearest friends.

The little bridge she'd made to her mom was standing strong, the foundations seeming to support the weight of her hope.

Jill said as much to Simon an hour and a half later as she sat cross-legged at his grave. The grass grew thick and green as luxurious carpet and here and there sprouted the lemon-yellow tufts of dandelions. She popped the head off one and shredded the petals as she talked about Kent Wood's and Bree's competing big dreams for the Grandview Inn.

"Is it silly that I came *here* to talk to you?" she asked. "I mean, after all you could be anywhere or nowhere or everywhere." Her fingers trailed through the blades of grass and she closed her eyes remembering how she'd loved to stroke Simon's thick hair, how she never realized at the time that such a simple gesture would be something that haunted her a few short years later.

"I know I need to put up a headstone for you, babe," she said abruptly. "People talk about it down in town. Not to my face, of course, but I know it's a thing. I'm sorry. I promise I will get it done before Thanksgiving. If not, you have full permission to come and haunt me." Hot tears pricked in her eyes. "Actually, I wish you would. You could haunt me every damn day and I'd count myself lucky."

She hadn't had a single sign since his death. She knew sometimes other people reported a feeling of comfort after the passing of a loved one. The idea that they were being looked after or a subtle indication was sent from the other side that the person was thriving.

She laid down and rested her cheek against the earth, but it felt cool and remote, not warm and inviting, the way his chest used to serve as a pillow during their movie marathons.

"Talk to me," she whispered. "Please. You know I hate to beg for anything, but I'm begging now. I need to know you're somewhere. That you aren't just gone forever."

An ant crawled over a blade of grass that was right under her nose, its six legs carrying it along with brisk efficiency. It moved with purpose, knowing instinctively that it had a job to do and how best to achieve results. But it also had no idea that any moment a big boot could squash its industrious existence into oblivion. She didn't know if she envied or pitied the creature.

She stayed in that spot until her hip began to ache. Pushing herself back up to sitting, she rolled away the small rock that had been beneath her, pressing into her bones.

No sign.

No nothing.

It was just her. Alone. Her soul mate—her other half—gone. And how do you live, how do you muster up the courage to keep getting out of bed every day, when your soul has been cut out, when your better self has been excised?

She didn't know.

Once, she'd been a girl who had nothing but answers. She'd go to college. She'd study art history. Someday she'd open up a gallery. She'd make good, sensible choices and only ever have a happy life. And she'd done those things. All of them. But they hadn't mattered. She still suffered.

A tear dropped off the edge of her nose. She hadn't even known she was crying.

And that's when she saw it.

The deer stared directly at her from across the cemetery, half hidden under the shade of a broad, ancient pine. She didn't move. She didn't dare to breathe. She'd seen plenty of deer during her lifetime, but never one with such big, velvety antlers.

His gaze was calm and steady, just like Simon's had always been. He had always been able to say "I got your back, babe" with just a glance.

She took a step forward and then another. Every nerve in her body activated and it was impossible to take a full breath.

The buck's ear twitched but he didn't run away.

Peace flooded her.

Afterward she couldn't explain the how or the why. All she knew was that her heart was fuller than it had been since her husband died.

And when at last, the deer turned to vanish back into the forest, she felt a sense of renewed inner strength as she walked back to her car. She was ready to fight for her friends, her town, and most of all herself.

# Chapter Fifteen

Bree knelt on the laundry room floor, silently cursing the hard linoleum while Finn gave his stainless steel dog bowl a disgruntled look.

"You need to eat, buddy boy," she repeated, giving him another encouraging scratch behind the left ear. "Come on now, chomp that kibble. Nom. Nom. Nom. So delicious. You know what? I'm super jealous that wasn't my dinner."

Finn cast her a baleful eye, clearly thinking, *Yeah. Right, lady.*

She cocked a brow in mental response, *Hey, it's no filet mignon but this isn't the Four Seasons, bub.*

Nudging the bowl closer to his wet, black nose, he responded with a less-than-enthusiastic huff before resting his snout between his two front paws.

What a drama dog.

Bree raked a hand through her hair, half annoyed and half impressed by his diva posturing. "Good lord," she muttered. "Fine. I guess his highness prefers wet food. Got the message loud and clear." She glanced at the pink plastic wall clock and stifled a yawn. It was inching toward eleven at night. Not only had Finn been on a hunger strike since his evening walk, but she'd also been as busy as a bee in Renee's summer garden.

First she'd sent Ronnie Lowe, the President of the Coastal Trust for Historic Preservation, an email inviting her to pop in to Castaway during her next trip through town to check out the store's new shipment of New Zealand merino wool—the perfect lure to make the case for Grandview and why it should never be permitted to be torn down. Then she spent an hour poring over her finances just in case she summoned up the guts to go to the bank and talk to a loan officer about trying to buy the hotel. The idea of going up against someone like Kent Wood— who her online searching had revealed as a thoroughly unlikable fellow with a jerky Twitter feed and a propensity for Facebook rants—wasn't exactly exciting.

More to the point, while she had a modest inheritance squirreled away from her parents, that number was going to look a lot lower once she signed on the dotted line for her house renovations. But it wasn't a big hotel, only a fifteen-room inn. Maybe, just maybe she could swing it if the bank would trust her, a local resident with roots in the community stretching back over a hundred years.

A nice fairy tale, but never going to happen in real life.

And fine—maybe after that disheartening realization she did a *leeeetle* Internet nosing around for a certain Chance Elliston, but he turned out to be an Internet cipher. No social media. No tweets. No likes. Nothing. How very nineties of him. To her best guess he was either a guy who valued his privacy...or a serial killer on the FBI's Most Wanted list.

She'd been hunched above her keyboard, fingers twitching, debating on whether or not to search for his architecture company when her better angel popped up on one shoulder and ordered her to back away slowly.

Nothing good ever came from Internet stalking.

Now it was past her bedtime and her dog needed to end his hunger strike.

"The only place open is going to be the 7-Eleven," she informed him with a yawn. "And that's outside the town limits so you'll have to be patient."

Finn thumped his tail twice as his stomach rumbled.

*Stubborn.*

She rolled her eyes. "Remind me again why I adopted you?"

He rolled over and offered his round belly for a pat, tongue lolling, caramel-colored eyes warm with trust, and just like that her heart melted into a puddle.

"Fine." She rubbed the spot that made his hind leg twitch. "You want to be spoiled? Be spoiled. I can't say no to you."

Ten minutes later she was in the convenience store loading canned dog food into her straw shopping basket.

The place was deserted except for the disinterested cashier entranced by an obnoxious-sounding video game on his phone and a delicate red-haired woman in a green, bell-sleeved top, baggy boyfriend jeans, and espadrille sneakers. She was studying the ice cream in the freezer section as if the pints contained the meaning of life.

*Oooh.* Bree looked past the woman to the glass doors, blurry with condensation, and cocked her head considering. It was hard to say from where she stood, but it looked like there was a decent variety of Ben & Jerry's in stock.

"What's your favorite?" she asked the redhead, ambling up and silently cheering after spotting Chocolate Fudge Brownie. Having sex with Chance was definitely the most orgasmic moment in her life to date, but a few spoonfuls of that decadent flavor ranked a darn close second.

The woman glanced over, a little startled to be addressed. It was obvious from her bloodshot eyes and crimson nose that she'd been crying. "Oh...well...I'm not sure. If I'm going to be honest, I've never had any of these flavors."

"I must have heard you wrong. Are you telling me that you've never tried Ben & Jerry's?" Bree's jaw dropped somewhere near her knees. "That's unacceptable!"

"Especially being that I'm from Vermont. It's my deepest, darkest secret—or one of them anyway." The woman grabbed a pint of Chocolate Chip Cookie Dough with sudden determination. "My parents were vegan and my husband has a thing about sugar, namely that we shouldn't eat it."

Bree arched a brow. "Like ever?"

"Ever," the woman replied. "He's a health nut and sometimes it feels a little, I dunno, controlling."

"Ya think?" Bree clapped a hand over her mouth and set down her shopping basket. "I have a huge problem with my foot. Namely the fact that I stick it in my mouth when facing sensitive situations. Look, I don't know you and it's not my place to judge your marriage."

"I'm Ashley Wood." The woman tugged a crumpled tissue out of the back of her jeans with one hand and gave her nose a honking blow. "Now you know me. And I don't mind what you just said. I mean, you aren't wrong. We had a fight tonight and I stormed out. After driving around listening to everything from Taylor Swift, to Alanis Morissette, ice cream sounded like the perfect treat."

*Wood?* Bree's knees went wobbly, as if her bones had been rendered into Jell-O. "Wood as in Kent Wood?"

"Why?" Ashley's expression turned cautious. "He's my brother-in-law."

"I see." *Oh shizznit.* This tragic-looking woman played on the enemy's team. Bree needed to grab her treat, Finn's food, and get the heck out of dodge, stat.

But something urged her to take a closer look. The woman was thin, not just slender, but skinny as if something ate at her from the inside out. Her jawline was too sharp and underneath her fashionably billowy top, her clavicle bones jutted out in sharp relief.

No. She couldn't walk away. Not when her gut was screaming that this woman needed help.

"I'm not trying to imply that my husband is a monster."

Ashley's words came quickly as if realizing she'd over-shared. "But a healthy lifestyle is important to him. He has a very high standard. But it's not like he would divorce me over ice cream or anything."

It hurt how forced her laugh sounded, like someone doing their best to imitate humor.

"We're just getting familiar with Cranberry Cove," she said hastily, as if wanting to end the conversation. "We're opening up a bookstore at the Old Red Mill."

"Of course!" Bree smacked her forehead. "You met my best friend Jill Kelly. She has an art gallery there."

"Chickadee Studios." Ashley's eyes lit up. "Yes, I remember. She was lovely."

Anyone who liked Jill couldn't be bad. "I work in the mill too."

"What business do you own?" Ashley seemed less skittish when the topic moved away from her husband and brother-in-law.

"Um, well. None actually." Bree cleared her throat. "I'm a sales associate at Castaway Yarn—the only sales associate." It wasn't that she minded being a shop assistant, but it did reinforce how much she'd love to be a business owner.

"That's so fabulous. I've never been able to figure out how to knit." Ashley gave a helpless shrug. "It always looks so relaxing but whenever I've tried I just create something lumpy and tragic and get totally stressed out."

"You have to stop by the shop. I can get you going on scarves and beanies in no time."

"Gosh." Ashley gave her head a wondering shake. "Everyone is so friendly here. Is it always like this?"

"Pretty much. Although being such a close-knit community means we're up in each other's business all of the time as well. Double-edged sword, but I wouldn't have it any other way." Ashley seemed not only sweet but also a decent human being so Bree decided to take the opportunity to press. "I heard a rumor, actually, that your brother-in-law wants to buy the Grandview."

Ashley frowned, her mouth twisting in a patently wary gesture. "That gorgeous old inn up on the bluff?"

Bree snapped her fingers. "That's the one."

"He...has plans for it."

"I've heard something to that effect. But here's the thing. I have plans too. And my plans don't include letting one of our beloved historic landmarks be turned into a circus sideshow."

"Kent is determined." Ashley took a step back. "He doesn't let much stop him once he's on a roll." She was all but pleading.

Who the heck was this bogeyman?

Bree set her shoulders, summoning up the strength she'd gained from her cancer scare. "He hasn't met me." In reality, the blustering tone came with a heaping side of bravado because the panic on Ashley's face made her heart race like a snowshoe hare.

Ashley turned on her heel, opened up the freezer door, and placed the ice cream back on the shelf. "You know what? I'm not hungry. Jack and I had a silly little argument tonight so I thought I'd come here and do something he'd hate, but it's not worth it." She glanced around as if the bags of potato chips and rows of candy bars might hide surveillance equipment. "Please be careful. You don't go up against the Wood brothers and win, trust me." And with that she fled the convenience store as if being chased by a pack of wild dogs.

Bree's goose bumps didn't subside the whole drive home, not even when she cranked up the radio and tried belting along to Dolly Parton's "Jolene."

After getting home and feeding Finn (who decided wet dog food was delicious, thank you very much), she decided she wasn't hungry for ice cream either and crawled into bed. Ashley Wood's haunted expression kept her tossing and turning until she finally turned the white noise app on her phone to top volume and drifted off into a troubled sleep.

She woke up the next morning to a hot tongue slurping her face, from chin to forehead.

"Yech," she squealed, fumbling for a pillow to beat Finn back to a manageable distance. Outside the sun was high. Crud, what time was it? She'd slept in.

That's when she registered the persistent knocking at her front door—if someone trying to bang her door off the hinges qualified as a knock.

She groaned her annoyance. "Easy, Renee. Keep your panties on." She gathered her tangled hair into a messy topknot and tied her track pants up around her waist as she stumbled down the stairs. Finn pranced underfoot as if having unannounced visitors was akin to a Christmas surprise.

Bree preferred company after coffee.

When she threw open the front door she wished she'd reached for her silky kimono or even bothered wiping the sleep from her eyes.

Turned out it wasn't Renee after all.

"Morning." Chance slouched in her doorway looking as if he'd already gone for a brisk six-mile run, followed by a long hot shower and a triple-shot espresso. His hair was damp and his olive skin glowed. "Sorry to wake you. It's nine o'clock. I'm an early riser and sometimes forget not everyone's on my biological clock."

"Late night," she mumbled, stepping aside to let him in, all too aware of the flush breaking out at the base of her throat.

"Got company?" He glanced around at the empty couches, the coffee table with the lone wineglass. His tone was cool but she thought she picked up an edginess to his undertone. Did he wonder if she had another man over? Was he jealous?

Did she want him to be?

*Nope, down girl!* That line of thinking was a dead end. She needed to get her head on straight.

"Just my—"

Finn bounded forward, placing paws on Chance's broad chest and offering up an excited woof.

"—new dog," she concluded, lunging forward to seize Finn's collar. "Off, boy! Sit! I'm so sorry. I just got him and he doesn't have the best manners."

"Don't worry, I had a dog almost identical to him when I was a kid." Chance dropped down to a crouch, flipped Finn onto his back and began play wrestling. "Old Jesse. Best friend there ever was. I still think about him every damn day. Congrats on the new addition."

"I'm afraid that I might have bitten off more than I can chew." The zing of awareness she always felt in Chance's presence was really throwing her. Frazzled, she knew she should look anywhere else in the room. The end table next to the La-Z-Boy half buried in books. The old television. The wilting bouquet of yellow peace roses that she had treated herself to last week. *Anything* but the sight of Chance, cheeks flushed and eyes bright, rolling around with Finn, his navy T-shirt riding up his hard abs to reveal the dark happy trail that disappeared beneath his thick leather belt.

She tried to break the trance, swallowed hard and choked, coughing into her hand.

Chance froze. "You okay up there? Can I grab you a glass of water?"

"Just allergies," she wheezed. "Probably a high-pollen day. What are you doing here?" She stiffened belatedly, realizing how rude that question sounded out loud.

Good lord, when this guy was in her vicinity north turned into south, and her brain mushed to the consistency of Play-Doh.

He kicked out his legs and was back on his feet before her next blink.

"Jujitsu," he drawled at the sound of her gasp. "You learn how to fall and get back up again. I'm a brown belt."

She straightened her posture, telling herself that she didn't smell him, all clean and soapy, from a few feet away. "Sounds handy."

"It's a great sport." His thick lips curved in the corners. "You should try it. I'd love to roll with you on the mat some time."

She shivered at the double entendre, the exact same time he seemed to realize what he'd said. Despite her goose bumps, the room's temperature must have risen ten degrees. "So," she said after clearing her throat. "How was Portland? That was a fast trip."

"Decided not to stay. Wasn't the same without you."

Her brain froze even as her insides melted faster than butter in the summer sun. "Really? I find that hard to believe."

"The drive was quiet, for a start. It would have been a hell of a lot better if I had company. I found that I kept wanting to hear your take on things. Like have you ever been to the International Cryptozoology Museum there?"

She clapped her hands. "Oh my god, that place gives me the creeps! It's so weird. Did you actually go?"

"Of course. How could I miss the Dover Demon?

"Yes! I guess people in Massachusetts claimed to have seen that creepy ghoul multiple times in the 1970s."

"While I don't believe that, I do think its stupid red teeth will give me nightmares."

"I can't believe you went there." She put her hands on her hips. "What about the Umbrella Cover Museum? You didn't see that, did you?"

Mirth lit his eyes. "You mean the world's largest collection of umbrella sheaths? I checked it out online but it was closed."

"Too bad. You missed out. Most people don't think to look for the weird and quirky when visiting a town."

"Guess I'm not most people."

"Guess not."

The air seemed to thin between them. It was hard to tell if the rhythmic crash and ebb echoing in her ears was the ocean or her own heart.

He tipped his head to the side and gave her a long, unfathomable look. "I missed you, blondie."

She almost tripped standing still.

He cleared his throat and glanced away. "I also got a lot of ideas for your renovation, took some photos. It's all on a flash drive if you wanna see?"

"Love to." She offered up a silent prayer to the universe that what she really wanted to see at that moment wasn't stamped all over her features. Her fingers twitched, aching to reach out and peel off that T-shirt, trace his hard muscles before licking the clean taste of his skin.

Her cheeks began to heat. Why couldn't she be within a ten-foot radius of this guy without having a kaleidoscope of perverted thoughts?

He looked around. "Where's your computer?"

An innocent enough question.

Her cheeks officially flamed to wildfire intensity. "Upstairs in my . . . um . . . bedroom."

He lowered his chin, the energy in the room subtly

shifting, moving from friendly chitchat to something infinitely more dangerous and exciting.

Blood thundered in her ears.

"I'm game if you are."

He wasn't talking about the renovation anymore.

Neither was she.

She held out a hand, gasping as his thumb caressed the soft pad of her palm. "Follow me."

# Chapter Sixteen

Jill yawned, deep and loud. She had stayed up late last night going through her finances to figure out if she could even afford to make an offer on the cottage. Verdict: She could...but only if she used Simon's life insurance policy.

The realization had left her tossing and turning for the rest of the night. On one hand it seemed like the exact thing Simon would encourage her to do, on the other hand, it seemed so monumentally unfair to use his accident to take that step toward their dream without him.

Every hour she seemed to have her mind made up. Yes! She'd do it. Only to be hit by a wave of crippling doubt. No...what was she thinking?

The teeter-totter of emotions was making her feel vaguely nauseated, and the jittery slosh of coffee in her stomach wasn't helping.

· She needed something to do, simple and practical, to switch off her monkey mind. Maybe hitting "pause" would let the right answer percolate back up to the surface. The pile of applications for the Cranberry Cove Art Fair rivaled the Leaning Tower of Pisa. Jill approached it warily. Administrative duties were never fun, but they could be mindless. She released a soft sigh and rubbed her eyes. Like it or not, this was the perfect time to distract herself with busywork. It was that or stew until her mind boiled over. Jill trudged to the dining table and grabbed the top application.

She raised a brow as she saw the check mark tick in the top box. A first-timer. Those were always exciting.

She took a seat and settled in. Her goal was to grow the Cranberry Cove Art Fair to one of the preeminent artisan events in New England. She adjusted her glasses and read the name: Cooper Haynes. Hmmm. That sounded vaguely familiar—but why?

She glanced over his brief profile—woodworker, specializing in custom furniture, looms, and spinning wheels using reclaimed wood. A light bulb went on. She'd recently spotted this guy's work at a gallery in Portland. He wasn't just good—he was great. In fact, she'd even grabbed his business card but then came the hurricane and the destruction of her shop and insurance claims and blah, blah, blah life crisis.

He'd requested one of the small booths on a side street. She snorted. *Heck no!* Someone with his talent deserved a placement front and center near city hall. She could put him next to Castaway Yarn. The owner, Noreen, knew how to spin wool. She glanced at Cooper's email address and made a spontaneous decision to reach out to see if he'd like to be moved into a higher profile location. She'd waive the extra cost if he'd allow Noreen to use one of his spinning wheels. The demonstration would be a hit with visitors.

She pulled out her phone and dashed off a quick email. Then she took a peek at a web page she'd saved in her favorites, the one she kept sneaking furtive glances at throughout the day. The cottage at Anchor Court.

It was still for sale. She had the money.

*Do it.*

*Don't do it.*

Ugh. Her emotions were still on that stupid teeter-totter.

Mindless admin tasks hadn't given her clarity, so she did the one thing that always did, changed into her running clothes and laced up her sneakers extra tight. Outside, with the sun on her face, breathing hard, her tangled thoughts had a habit of unknotting. Stress faded. Dilemmas felt less overwhelming.

A horn beeped. She lifted a hand in greeting as Dot waved through the windshield, flashing her an approving thumbs-up.

Jill turned onto the river trail and spent half a mile focusing on the sound of water on rocks, the wind in the trees, the little dippers flitting along the shore, hunting insects. Her shoulders felt looser, her jaw less tense.

Time to ask herself some hard questions.

Would she regret it if the house sold to someone else?

*Yes.*

The word hit her like a bolt of lightning.

What was she afraid of?

Moving on. Getting to live the life Simon was denied. Using his life insurance to fund their shared dream.

She bent over bracing her hands on her knees, sucking in deep gulps of air.

What did her heart tell her?

She stood slowly, closing her eyes, shutting out the world and listening to the quiet voice deep inside.

Do it. Do it. Do it.

He'd want her to buy this house.

The truth beat like a quiet, insistent heartbeat.

She texted Essie before she could talk herself out of it.

Hey! Hope all is well. Just wanted to see if you've gotten any offers on that little cottage yet.

She'd barely hit "send" before Essie responded.

Hey girl, I don't have your offer!!!!!!!!

Do it.

Do it.

Do it.

About that…what if I was interested in making one. Hypothetically speaking.

Her phone rang. "Are you sure?"

Jill held out the phone with a frown before putting it back against her ear. "What the heck! You have been bothering me to take the leap and go for this house since you heard I had a smidge of interest."

"I know, I *know*." Essie paused for so long that Jill

wondered if the call had dropped out. "I just want this to be *your* decision. Not mine. Not Bree's. Not what you think you should want. Buying a home is a big life experience, and it's my job to make sure the process goes as seamlessly as possible. But I want you to be in the state of mind where you welcome this next step. It will be huge."

"I mean I did have to close my store a few months ago," Jill quipped. "The stock wasn't damaged, thank the old gods and new—but it wasn't exactly a stress-free process to relocate to the Old Red Mill."

"No, definitely not," Essie agreed. "But this is about you and Simon and your identity in moving forward without him by your side. Stepping back into life on your own, okay with being alone."

The truth of Essie's words hit Jill square in the center of her broken heart. They were tough but true. Simon was never coming back, but she was alive and the one thing she could do was embrace that fact and make the most of it.

"If I waited to move from this condo until I felt one hundred percent ready, then they would have to cart me out as an old lady. I'm never not going to have doubts about leaving, but I can promise you that I know I need to take this step. Once upon a time that cottage seemed like a fairy tale. Maybe my story has changed but it doesn't mean I need to do a complete rewrite of my hopes and dreams."

"No," Essie agreed firmly. "The only thing you need to do is to be a little bit braver than you were yesterday, and the day before that. Sometimes you might even take a few steps backwards but it's the journey that matters."

Jill took a mental step back, the phone sweaty in her hand. If you really looked, past the high-maintenance veneer, the threaded brows, the perfectly contoured makeup, the hair that saw the inside of the salon on a monthly basis, Essie was pretty darn deep. And a flipping awesome friend.

"Jeez, lady. When did you get so wise?"

"Oh honey, didn't you know? I was born wise." The old, familiar sass returned to Essie's tone. Then she went into full businesslike mode with whiplash speed. "You need to go to your bank and see what kind of an offer you can realistically make."

"I have enough money." She squeezed her eyes shut and plopped into a chair, head spinning. "I have Simon's life insurance money."

"Oh. I see." Essie took a deep breath.

Jill raised her chin, jaw tight. "I've thought about using it."

"I'm sure you have," Essie said hurriedly. "Sorry if my sigh gave the wrong impression. Just the opposite. I think it's a beautiful way to use his legacy, if you're sure you can handle moving and the store and the art festival. It's a lot."

Jill shrugged. "I'm good at being busy."

"I get that. I'm the same way. But there is effective busy and then there is throwing yourself in a deep end where you can barely keep your head above water," Essie said with a chuckle. "Baby steps. That's all you need to think. You don't need to change your life one hundred percent. But imagine a five percent change. Even a one percent change. Every little bit counts."

Jill placed a hand over her empty womb. *Baby steps.* Not a phrase that cheered her up.

"Here's my offer," she said, giving the listing price. "I can pay cash."

"I'll draw up the paperwork and take it to the seller," Essie said. "Stay tuned, and keep breathing."

Jill lowered the phone and did just that. No feeling of regret washed over her, only peace. This felt like a good choice. A slow smile crept over her face as an email notification buzzed. There. She glanced down. It was from Cooper Haynes, the woodworker whose talent she'd admired.

"Well, well, that was fast," she muttered, opening his reply. As she did she conjured up an image of a kindly man in his mid-to-late fifties, a sensitive soul who enjoyed tea and crafts.

Hey Jill,

Great to get your email. Thanks for the offer—and appreciate your flattering words about my work. I'm on my way to a sea-kayaking trip and then will make my way over to the festival. Appreciate your offer for a more prominent space.

Looking forward to meeting in person.

Best,

C.

She pursed her lips and wrote back.

> Hey Cooper...Sea-kayaking trip? Huh. Sounds inter-
> esting except I get sick on the ocean. Hope you have
> fun and see a puffin or two. Looking forward to meet-
> ing you as well.

She hit "send" before she could overthink it.

He sure didn't sound like a kindly older man a few years past sixty with a propensity for plaid and whittling. Interesting.

But not *that* interesting. Giving her head a half shake, she stuck her phone back in her pocket and started off toward home.

As she hit her stride, she reminded herself it wasn't worth getting curious about a man.

She'd tried online dating twice. It had taken her over a year to even contemplate seeing anyone, to admit she had the desire for companionship.

There was Troy the firefighter from two villages over who had zero sense of humor. Eric, a dentist she met on Tinder who had been addicted to sparkling water and acted like he coined the catchphrase "Yeah, baby," using it at every possible moment until it felt like her eyes might get stuck rolled up inside her head.

Both men might not have been perfect but they were attractive, attentive, and definitely interested in her. But if given the choice, a medium ham and pineapple pizza with a side of ranch dressing and staying in won every time. That or hanging out with her girlfriends.

There was no zing.

No point.

No thank you.

And worse, it felt like cheating. She hadn't been able to get through a dinner without feeling like she was betraying her vows. It was one thing to know she wasn't, that she'd promised to love until "death do us part," but try telling that to her heart. Or her stomach, which tightened at the idea of lying naked beside another man, of whispering in the dark, of drifting to sleep listening to their rhythmic breaths.

But was there any point to navel gazing?

She turned up her quiet tree-lined street, passing brightly colored Victorian apartments and sun-dappled homes with Volvos parked alongside tidy gardens.

Nope. Introspection was for the birds. She needed action. The only way she was going to get out of this funk was through good old-fashioned elbow grease.

Bounding back into her condo, without even bothering to take a shower, she marched down the hall to the closet by the front door and threw it open. Did she really need three different winter coats, and who knows what hid in those shoeboxes stuffed on the top shelf? It was time for clarity. She was going to find everything in her condo that sparked joy and purge the rest. She'd enter her new life ready to attract amazing things from the universe.

She was filling up her fourth box, blasting music and feeling productive when her door buzzed.

It was Linda.

Her mom pulled up short and looked around the growing

mess with blatant bewilderment. "What on earth are you doing?"

"I've decided it's time to move," she said, dragging a hand over her forehead to mop off the sweat. Hopefully the new house had central air. "Want to help me purge? You can start in the kitchen, there's so much mismatched Tupperware. Or maybe the board games. Simon loved Monopoly but I'll never play it. We could see if Essie or Renee would want it. Or maybe just make a pile of things for the thrift store."

"Honey..." Her mom's voice trailed off as her brows furrowed. "Don't take this the wrong way but you seem a little manic?"

Was there a *right* way to take that?

"What are you talking about?" Jill huffed a laugh. "I got this." She plucked up a loose sheet of paper on the table. The flyer for the monthly grief group. She stared at it a moment remembering Andrew and his flowers and his kindly empathy. The next meeting wasn't for another two weeks, but did talking about feelings really fix anything?

Would it take away the weird, fluttering guilt in the pit of her stomach that had been there since she responded to Cooper Hayne's email?

"Look. I need to *do*." She marched to the recycling box and tossed the flyer in. "Doing is what helps me. I've always helped everyone else—including you, if I might add. It's time I help myself. If you don't want to help clutter bust, that's fine, but this is the plan."

Her heart was beating fast, she felt good—better than

good—adrenaline was spiking. Plans were good. Plans meant order, purpose, and, most of all, control. She yanked the garbage bag from out of the can. "I'm going to toss this in the dumpster. Back in a second." But as she took the stairs two at a time, she missed one.

The world suspended for a moment as her feet left the ground.

And then gravity had the final word as she crashed hard— back to earth, her ankle erupting into searing pain.

# Chapter Seventeen

"This is crazy. What are we doing?" Bree gasped as Chance gently eased her onto her bed, his hungry lips traveling the geography of her neck. Jolts of pleasure coursed through her as he lingered on the sensitive spot where her pulse madly fluttered, planting wet, open-mouth kisses until she worried about going into sensory overload.

"Just bein' friendly." He groaned against her hot skin, the vibration making her wilt. "Isn't that what you do in these small towns?"

"I don't know about you, but this isn't exactly what I do with friends." She tilted her pelvis so that it teased the intriguing bulge encased in his worn blue jeans. His throat worked as he swallowed, hard. His deep blue eyes were hazy with pleasure.

A thrilling sense of power commingled with the lust coursing through her body. Looked like two could play in this game.

She pushed up on her elbows and nipped the edge of his mouth, lazily kissing his dimple as his breath grew shallow. The bristle of his scruff was soft, and she wanted to memorize the sensation. Her fingers locked on to the thick muscle of his biceps and gripped as if she needed to stay afloat.

"Blondie." He grabbed her hips and rolled over so she was on top, straddling him. "I can't make you any promise but this—if we do this again, I'll make damn sure that you enjoy the hell outta every moment. I want to make this all about you."

Her heart gave a painful little clench. What guy had ever been so interested in her pleasure; what was his deal? Still, it was hard not to swoon at such a wicked promise. She forced brow arch instead. "Hmm. I suppose that doesn't sound so bad."

"Nope." His gaze traveled her body as if he was starving and she were a hot fudge sundae. She could get used to that adoration. When he reached out and palmed her breasts, she arched into his touch, taking the pleasure, reveling in it. No more were her boobs dangerous death traps, body parts she feared would betray her, they could make her feel good, and god she wanted to feel good so badly. "I know I said I don't want anything serious right now, but I can't be within five feet of you and keep my hands to myself."

"So we keep this a summer fling. Friends with benefits?" She'd put the idea away, but now that she took it out again, there was a lot of merit to the plan. Why not have her fun with Chance and then say farewell in a month when he took off back to the Big Apple. A perfect scenario really—what single woman didn't crave a little summer delight? And Chance was the definition of delightful.

Didn't she deserve to treat herself?

"Friends with benefits. Okay. Sounds good. 'Cause what you are doing is beneficial all right." His breath hitched as she teased his thick leather belt, slowly freeing it from the brass buckle.

"Truth or dare," she asked playfully. Goodness, who was she? She was practically purring. Flings have gotten a bad rap. This could give her the space to clear her head, get rid of the cobwebs, and get used to having sex without all the emotional, complicated stuff that comes with a serious relationship.

His smile widened even as his nostrils flared. "Truth."

"Did you come here for this?" She undid the top button of his jeans for emphasis.

"I really do have your house plans. But I can't pretend that I haven't thought about you every hour on the hour, imagining all the things I'd like to do to you. I've never had a woman get under my skin like this."

"Mmmm." She skated her hands up under his shirt, rocking her pelvis down hard on his bulge and grinning as he hissed his appreciation. This was one heck of a confidence boost. "I guess I have to dare you to show me."

And he did, again, and again, and good god, again.

Bree cracked her eyes open a slit. It must be late afternoon, the warm rays from the sun dappled her carpet as a cool breeze blew in from the ocean.

For a moment she gazed at the roses on her wallpaper in sleepy disorientation, a calm that was destroyed a few seconds later as she realized a few important facts at the exact same time.

One: She was splayed butt naked across the sheets.

Two: A strong male arm was clasped around her middle, his big palm over the soft pooch of her stomach.

Three: This very moment she was meant to be working at Castaway.

What was she going to do? She needed to modestly cover up her bits, gracefully untangle herself from Chance, and call Noreen to beg for forgiveness all at the same moment.

Instead she reached for her phone, lost her balance, and fell out of bed landing bare on the carpet, legs wide open.

"Hullo there." Chance leaned over, his dark hair wild, his smile lazy, and his eyes sinful. "The bed worked fine for me, but if you want to take things to the floor, I'm game."

"Oh shush," she snapped, pushing herself up as he chuckled. Might as well forget modesty. With any other guy, she'd always made sure to make love with the lights out and would never be caught dead parading around naked in the harsh light of day. Her curves always seemed too much for anyone to handle, too bold, too round. But for some reason she didn't overly care to ponder, she didn't feel self-conscious around Chance. She didn't mind being exposed to his discerning gaze—in part because he seemed to make it clear that he appreciated what he saw and maybe because she felt so strangely comfortable around him.

But probably because this thing between them had an expiration date.

"I was supposed to be at work a few hours ago." She paced back and forth, frazzled, unsure what to do next. "But instead I got dick drunk."

His brows shot up. "Come again?"

She froze, realizing she was blabbering. "That's my friend Essie's expression. You got naked and I lost all common sense."

"Are you going to be in trouble?" The lazy smile faded as honest concern etched a deep furrow between his brows. "Shoot, Bree. I'm sorry. This is supposed to be fun, not complicated."

"I mean, I'm a grown-up and so is Noreen. She is probably more worried than anything. I'm not usually such a flake." She picked up her phone and sat down beside him on the bed as she hit "send." "Time to face the music."

"Bree, honey? Everything okay?" Just as Bree predicted, Noreen was more worried than upset. She told the truth—that she had slept through the start of her shift—while omitting the reason... Chance had taken her three times in as many hours and in the end her body had cried uncle and passed right out.

"It's been a quiet day but I'll need you tomorrow, okay?"

"Of course!" Bree reassured her. "And thanks for not being mad even though I totally deserved it."

"You can pay me back by telling me the real story tomorrow," Noreen said drily, making it clear that she didn't buy Bree's excuse she just happened to oversleep.

"We'll see," Bree muttered. Noreen took blood pressure

medication. She didn't want to be responsible for her early demise due to scandalous stories of wild sex.

After she hung up, she turned around to face Chance, who was lounging across her Laura Ashley Coral Coast quilt like he lived there.

The idea of a real live man here in her room after so long—and a casually undressed one at that—gave her some kind of feeling, one she forced back down into the dark recesses of her mind because that's not what this was. Fun wasn't forever. She had to keep telling herself that.

"So…" That delicious dimple put in an appearance. "Sounds to me like you don't have to rush off."

"No. I feel like a naughty teenager playing hooky."

"I'd love to have seen you as a naughty teenager."

"Trust me"—she rolled her eyes—"I was less 'Hit me, baby, one more time' and more super nerd who brought her knitting to class."

"Gotta like a gal who is nimble with her hands," he said with a mischievous grin.

She gave a laughing groan. "What am I going to do with you?"

"I was gonna say much the same thing." He reached out and caressed her cheek. "You have a free afternoon. I have a free afternoon. Damn, this time last year this would have seemed impossible."

"Why?"

"I didn't take a vacation for ten years." His lighthearted smile faded as his eyes went sad. "My work was my life, my life was my work."

"What changed?"

"Everything." He scrubbed a hand over his face as if to erase some unpleasant memory.

Bree had a thousand questions and no right to ask a single one. That wasn't what this was.

"I owned an architecture firm with my wife."

*Wife? What the...?* The bottom dropped out of Bree's stomach.

He must have noticed the look on her face because he hastened to modify the statement. "*Ex*-wife," he amended. "Very, very much ex. Our divorce was finalized right before I left to come here, to Cranberry Cove. But we'd been legally separated two years before that and things hadn't been good since almost the start of our marriage."

"Why?" She wasn't sure if she should ask, if she should care, but she had to know more. Her gaze fell to the ring finger of his left hand. The tan was deep and unbroken, not marred by so much as a thin telltale band of pale white skin. He hadn't worn a wedding ring in some time then.

Her shoulders relaxed a fraction as her stomach returned to its regular location.

"We both loved our work. I think we confused that passion for love for each other. But it wasn't. Karen is brilliant at what she does, and was an excellent business partner, but we made a mistake." He paused with a grimace. "You sure you want to hear all this?"

She nodded, hoping she didn't look as insatiably curious as she felt.

He took a deep breath before continuing. "Just because

we loved to build amazing buildings didn't mean we could build an amazing life together. And if the foundation isn't solid, the structure can't hold. Eventually . . . we just crumbled. One day I came home and realized she was nothing but a stranger. And she felt the same way."

He fell quiet, a faraway look on his face, and she did her best to wait patiently.

"We divided up our assets," he said at last. "And got two new apartments, I let her keep our dog, and we tried to see what it was like keeping the business part of the marriage going." He exhaled a slow sigh. "It wasn't horrible. We were adults. We didn't despise each other or anything. But we wanted to go in different directions there too. I wanted to focus more on transforming existing buildings, merging the past and the present in a creative new way that honored the passage of time and yet looked to the future.

"She only wanted to take on projects that went from the ground up. So when we decided to divorce it seemed like a good time to break up the business too. I let her buy me out. She kept the office and her upcoming deals, I made good money and walked away with the freedom to focus on figuring out what I really want."

"I get that," Bree said softly. "Not the whole divorce thing as I never tied the knot—although I did come wicked close to marrying the wrong guy, so no judgment. But I recently found a lump—"

"Oh shit." His eyes went wide, just as the bedroom door nudged open and Finn bounded over to them, jumping on the bed, tail thumping the mattress.

Bree reached out and scratched her dog in his favorite spot, just behind the ear, grinning as he gave her hand an appreciative slurp and jumped back down to the floor, wrestling a squeaky toy.

Her furry friend had wanted to check up on her, and she loved him for it.

"The lump was benign—thank god," she continued. "But it also got me thinking. Maybe I should dream bigger. Take a chance." She glanced at him, cringing. "Pardon the pun."

He reached out and pulled her against him, letting her rest her cheek on the hard expanse of his warm chest, the small patch of soft, dark hair between his pecs tickling her. "You can take Chance any day of the week."

"Dork." She giggled before pushing up to look at him. "Hey, have you heard of a developer named Kent Wood?"

He thought a moment. "Sort of rings a bell but I can't quite place the name. Why?"

Bree filled him in on Kent Wood's space-age hotel plan.

"The very idea makes me sick," he growled. "We can honor the past and stay current, you know? But his ideas are just bonkers, especially for a landmark like the Grandview Inn."

"I know," Bree said. "I wish I could figure out a way to stop him. I met his sister-in-law Ashley the other night and she seemed genuinely terrified of him. My gut tells me we don't want him in this town for a lot of reasons, not just the fact he wants to build a monstrosity."

"Kent Wood." Chance repeated the name before shaking

his head. "Tell you what, I'll do some digging with a couple of contacts and see what I can unearth. I'm sure there's something because his name is familiar. But I can't put my finger on why."

She scrunched her nose. "You don't think I'm crazy to want to stop him?"

"I think you're as beautiful as you are brave." His voice dropped lower, silky and full of promise.

She rested her cheek back on his chest, her heart full. How could so much change this summer? It wasn't that long ago that she was in the throes of dread over an impending cancer diagnosis.

Now she was in the throes of something completely different.

"I want to spoil you on your unexpected day off," he said suddenly. "If you could ask for anything right now, what would it be?"

Uh, that was a no-brainer. A dark and dangerous man like himself naked in her bed. Basically she was living the dream here.

But he was looking at her expectantly, clearly wanting her to make a request like he was some sort of genie in the bottle.

"What do you want to do?"

"Make you happy."

"I'm serious."

"Me too. Trust me, the idea of putting a smile on your pretty face isn't a hardship. Let me do this."

"Where do you come from?" she asked wonderingly.

"They don't make men like you around here as far as I can tell."

"I haven't always had this philosophy. Guess you're one heck of a muse."

"I have a pretty good bathtub," she said in a flash of inspiration. "It's big enough for two and has amazing jets. One of those eighties wonders."

"Hell yeah." His lighthearted mood returned in a flash. "I don't suppose you have bubble bath."

She snorted. "Is the Pope Catholic?"

"Bath time it is." The corner of his lip curled into a wicked half smile. "The question is are you going to come out of it dirtier than when you get in."

# Chapter Eighteen

W ell, well, well, Ms. Kelly." The doctor strode back into the room with the X-ray in her hand. "Would you prefer the good news or the bad news first?"

Jill gritted her teeth. That didn't sound promising. "Bad." She grabbed the sides of the exam table so tightly that her fingers punctured the thin medical paper.

"You didn't break anything. However, you've given yourself a grade-three ankle sprain: that's a full tear of the ligament."

Her heart sank. "Are you serious?"

"Did you hear a 'pop' when you fell?"

"Not that I remember." Jill shook her head. "I was too busy farewelling the world and wondering how bad it hurts to break your neck."

"My nerves." Linda's mom gasped from the plastic seat in the corner of the urgent care treatment room. "If I had lost you, honey, what would I have done?"

"A couple ibuprofen and I'm sure I'll be fine." She adjusted her weight and winced when her foot knocked against the exam table. "I don't know much about sprains. What's the prognosis, doc?"

"You're going to need a splint to immobilize the ankle, but with rest and regular physical therapy you should be able to resume normal activity within six months."

She flinched. Maybe she'd hit her head in the fall too. "Six . . . days you mean?"

The doctor glanced up with a frown. "Months. This is a serious sprain, Ms. Kelly. The worst in fact."

"But I need to open my store!" Her pulse quickened. How could she have been so careless? "How can I hang paintings if I'm hobbling around on crutches? Plus I jog regularly; it keeps me grounded."

"Guess you'll have to try meditation. Do you have help for your business?"

"I can't afford to hire someone," she muttered, doing the mental calculations. She made a living running Chickadee, but to hire staff would seriously eat into her profit margin.

"Let me pitch in." Linda sat up straighter. "I come free and can get you ready to go. You can sit in a comfy chair and boss me around, honey."

"I can't believe this is happening," Jill muttered, rocking forward and burying her face in her hands. "I thought that putting in the offer on the cottage meant that maybe I was finally moving forward and instead I landed flat on my butt. This is what happens when I don't get enough sleep and then try to take on too much. Or maybe I'm just cursed."

The doctor cleared her throat and she glanced up, unable to keep the glare off her face. "What? I'm not sure I can handle any more news period—good or bad."

"Just a question." The doc sat down on the wheeled stool and gave her a piercing look. "Have you ever been evaluated for depression?"

She gaped. "Huh? Why?" What was going on? She'd come in for an injury, not to talk about her mental health.

"I noticed in the chart that you lost your husband a few years ago. You just mentioned that you have trouble sleeping. Have you ever considered seeing a therapist or trying an antidepressant? It might help."

"I don't want to take a pill that will change who I am. And I'm not sure if you've noticed but there aren't exactly a lot of therapists in this neck of the woods—and even less who are taking new patients. Besides…," she demurred, ducking her chin, her voice dropping to a whisper, "I go to a grief support group."

The doctor nodded. "That can help."

Linda turned to her in surprise. "You do?"

"Well, I went once." She didn't miss the fact that the doctor and her mom gave each other a long, carefully neutral look. "I didn't hate it. But I've been busy. It's not easy running a small business, especially in the art world." She gave an impatient gesture to her foot. "Anyway, the last time I checked, it was my ankle that was in trouble—not my head."

Her mom rose to her feet. "Honey, we are just trying to help."

"Stop." Jill held up a hand. Anger bubbled up in the pit of her stomach and it was easier to give in to that hot surge of emotion than invest an ounce more energy in remaining reasonable. She was at the bottom of her bucket. The idea of losing Chickadee was simply too much. "Don't talk to me about wanting to help me."

Linda's sigh was heavy. "I know I didn't always make the right choices but I'm also tired of being punished over and over for every mistake."

The doctor stood and inched toward the door. This wasn't a conversation to have in front of a stranger, but the horse had left the barn.

"I'm grateful for what you provided. But did you have to work at a bar, leave me alone night after night, when I wasn't even a teenager? It was awful. I know you did your best, but pardon me if maybe your best wasn't quite good enough."

As soon as the words left her mouth, Jill regretted them. But her ankle throbbed terribly, darn it, and her shop was all she had. If the gallery went out of business and she lost her livelihood, she risked losing more than her financial future, she risked her very identity.

Jill buried her face in her hands.

"I'm sorry. I'm just really freaking out here."

"Sounds like you have a family matter to discuss." The doctor cleared her throat, clearly desperate to escape. "I'll give you two a moment. I'll get a splint and crutches and be back in five."

The door clicked shut behind him and the only sound in the exam room was the hum of the air conditioner.

"I won't let you do this," Linda said after a long minute. "I know what you're doing."

"Oh yeah? Fill me in." Jill tensed, ready for her mom to get angry. She couldn't say she blamed her.

But instead her mom walked toward her, arms outstretched. "I won't let you push me away anymore. Trust me, I know better than anyone that your childhood wasn't all sunshine and roses, and that in many ways you had to grow up too fast and shoulder too much responsibility. In hindsight, I'm sorry I didn't make different decisions, but I'm here now and I can see that you're hurting, and you're alone, and afraid."

"I'm not afraid," Jill bit off, but the lie sounded hollow even to her ears.

"I can't imagine how hard it was to lose Simon, but you are not alone. I may not know a lot but I can make anything sparkle. I'll get your gallery in tip-top shape. And I can help you move." She offered a crooked smile. "Goodness knows I've moved houses more than a few times."

Jill's lower lip trembled. She bit it hard with her two front teeth but that only made her eyes spring a leak.

"You're so strong," Linda continued, enveloping her in a tight embrace. "But sometimes even the strongest people need a helping hand."

"I shouldn't have said all those things a minute ago." Jill breathed in deep, the lavender scent of her mom's perfume grounding her. "My words were so incredibly ugly. I hate that I did that."

"It's not like they weren't true."

"No, but you really did try your best. Deep down I've always known that, I don't want to have all these horrible feelings inside me. I don't want the anger." Her voice broke as a hot tear escaped down her cheek. "Most of all, I don't want this sadness."

"I know, I know you don't."

Jill pulled back and ground fists into her eyes so hard that she saw stars behind her eyelids. "It would be so much easier to be numb."

"If you were numb, you wouldn't be you. You have so much heart, baby." Her mom stroked her hair.

Jill grabbed her mom's hand and squeezed it hard. "If you're willing to offer to help me even though I was just so rotten, then I'm willing to accept."

Linda's smile was bright. "I won't let you down. And I won't let you lose Chickadee."

And for once Jill believed her. But the question that still burned in her stomach was—would *she* let everyone down...the craft fair, Simon's memory, the dream of the cottage, her mother's faith...herself?

And then, right there in the doctor's office with her foot propped up on the exam table, Essie's name flashed on the caller ID.

"H-hello?" she stammered.

"Girl, you sitting down?" Essie replied.

"Essie, you have no idea," said Jill, suddenly praying her favorite real estate agent was calling with the news she so desperately wanted to hear.

# Chapter Nineteen

The problem with Chance wasn't the benefits part, it was the *friend* part. He really did seem fascinated with her and she didn't know what to do with that.

As they faced each other in the bath, he cocked a brow. "What song is that?"

She frowned. "I have no idea what you're talking about."

"You were humming just now."

Her eyes widened. "I was?"

His gaze was amused. "You hum all the time."

"I do?" She ducked her head, giving a weak smile. "I mean I guess I sort of know that, but I never really think about it."

"I love it. But that tune was familiar." He snapped his fingers. "'Son of a Preacher Man'!"

She wrinkled her nose. "Oh my god, I *do* do that, don't I? I never really had anyone notice before."

"I notice everything about you," he said softly, nudging her foot with a smile that drizzled through her like melted chocolate. "Don't know how, but it's like I'm on your frequency or something."

"Yeah, I get it. It's easy to be with you." And she meant every word. She didn't know how to explain it but they synced.

"Got an idea." He nudged her with his foot. "Let's play twenty questions. I want to know more about you."

"What?" Bree grimaced. "You know I work at a knitting shop, have a crazy dog, and a home that has been stuck in the eighties for a few decades too long. That's about it." What better way to make him glance at that expensive-looking Apple Watch, declare an urgent appointment, and hit the road?

It wasn't that she found herself that boring—after all, she truly loved her craft, reading, spending time with friends, and Cranberry Cove, of course. But he lived in New York City, for Pete's sake. He was a man who didn't just dream big, he *did* big. He'd designed towering buildings that reached toward the clouds.

He could go to any big city and have his pick of exciting women, yet he wanted to hear about Cranberry Cove, how her great-great-great-grandfather had been a Nova Scotia cod fisherman who brought his boat into the village during a storm, seeking safe harbor. How he met the daughter of the lighthouse keeper and never left.

Chance's eyes went wide. "Your family kept the lighthouse?"

"A long, long time ago, but yeah. They did. And after that for a few generations the men went to sea, while the women stayed home, raised the children, knit sweaters, blankets, scarves—there is a closetful of hand-knits in the spare bedroom so you can say that I came by my obsession honestly."

"I'd love to see all of it."

Her gaze searched his face, trying to root out the subtle tell, the indication that he was mocking her.

"What?" he asked at last.

"I know you're making fun of me, but you have an excellent deadpan."

His lips took a downward turn. "Why would I want to make fun?"

"Uh, because my interests are boring?"

"Passion is sexy as hell."

She furrowed her brow. "But my interests are just so different from yours."

"That's what makes them fascinating."

"Well, I'm glad you think a bunch of antique baby blankets are interesting." She pursed her lips. "Most men would probably run screaming."

"You want kids someday?" He looked genuinely curious.

She tossed up her hands, unsure how to answer that. "I'm thirty-five."

"Your point?"

"Well." She blinked. "I guess I've been single so long that I imagined kids weren't really in my future. If I had the chance, would I want to be a mom? Maybe? I don't know. I love my niece, Tansy. It could be fun. But I also have other dreams."

"Tell me."

"I wish I could buy the Grandview Inn," she whispered, hesitant to give too much volume to her fragile dream. "I know it's an unrealistic fantasy, but I can't help it. For a while now I've dreamed of owning and running a hotel, creating a sanctuary for people to relax and recharge. I've spent my entire life loving that old inn, and it would be amazing to return it to its former glory. It's part of the town, our history."

"Not stupid at all," he said gruffly. "You care about Cranberry Cove's legacy. Historical buildings aren't just a matter of civic pride or beauty, they preserve a community's link to its past."

"Exactly." She leaned forward, excited to share this connection. "Sometimes it feels like life moves so fast these days. I don't want to forget what makes our town special. I love looking at the inn knowing it was there when my own great-grandmother and -father were alive."

"So what are you waiting for?" He clapped his hands. "Do it!"

"I..." Her smile faltered as reality returned. "I don't have a shot. Come on. I can't come up with that kind of money."

"What about investors?"

"Ha! Investors. Listen to you." She gave him a little splash. "You can take the man out of New York, but not New York out of the man. We don't do flashy deals here in Cranberry Cove. We live simply."

"I don't think anything about the woman I saw singing onstage that night was simple." He reached out and clasped her knee, a solid supportive gesture.

"That woman wasn't me."

"Oh yeah." He arched a brow. "You have an evil twin locked in another closet?"

She snorted.

"But if you're serious about the inn..." He slowly looked her up and down. "Maybe I can help you draft a business plan."

She jerked, startled. "You'd do that?"

"Sure. I love that you have a passion. But if you want to make it happen you'll need a road map."

"It just seems so unattainable." She frowned, hating how weak she sounded. How unconfident. If Chance found passion sexy, this would dry up his interest in no time.

"That's why you make the plan." He didn't look put off. If anything, that slight clench to his jaw seemed as if he was determined to convince her. "Once it's all there, step by step, in black and white, you can see what you need to do. Don't call it a dream; call it a plan."

"A plan, not a dream," she repeated softly. "I love that."

And it wasn't as if she didn't have the entire vision mapped out, both in her head and her secret notebooks.

It was just a matter of believing in herself, just like her mom had always said.

All the pieces were there. Heck, she'd even designed labels for her imaginary complimentary breakfasts:

Lemon Elderflower Waffles
Savory Steel-Cut Oats
Bite-sized Eggs Benedict
Cranberry Smoothies

"If you're serious, I'll email you some templates to look at, then once you've read them, we can talk it through."

"I'm serious all right. And I'll try not to be daunted."

"Good, because believing in yourself is the first step to success. Wasn't it Abe Lincoln who said if I have eight hours to cut down a tree, I'd spend six sharpening my ax? That's all a business plan is at the end of the day."

"An ax." She splashed water at him again.

"Yep, chop through all the uncertainty and doubt."

"Okay, Paul Bunyan, if you're offering, I'm in."

"Cool."

His devastating grin got her hot and flustered. She shifted, eager to redirect the attention. "Okay, mister. I think it's your turn in the hot seat. Are you close to your brother?"

"Luke?" He blinked at the pivot, frowning slightly. "Yeah, you can say that. We're different in many ways but he's my kid brother and I love him."

"Different how?"

"I loved math and drawing. Going to college was a no-brainer for me. It's what my dad wanted and I wasn't the kind of guy who wanted to let him down. Luke wasn't a school kind of guy, but he is also one of the smartest people I know. He reads something like three hundred books a year and can build anything."

"Sounds like a cool person."

"He works hard. I've been enjoying helping him out." He broke off, frowning a moment as if debating to say more.

"What is it?" she asked.

"Well, we haven't spent much time together since my parents moved away."

"I'm sorry." His furrowed brow indicated there was a deeper pain there.

"Luke doesn't get along with our father as well as I do, they are different in many ways, but both have a temper. But it is mostly Karen who drove the wedge between us. After my folks left, we saw each other less and less because those two couldn't stand each other."

"Karen?"

"My ex. She never paid attention to what makes Luke amazing. He thought she was a snob and he was right in hindsight. Now that she's out of my life, he's coming back in."

"Maybe a silver lining?"

"Yeah, it is. I can honestly say everything has happened for the best. Now I'm free."

Even though the bath was still warm, Bree went cold. She leaned away, her shoulder blades pressing against the cool tile. Chance was so charming it was easy to forget that he was just here for a bit of fun. Just because he made her feel special didn't mean she *was* special to him.

This was supposed to be an easy fling, and suddenly it felt like it had the potential to be so much more than that. Not only was he offering to help plan a path to make her dreams come true, but he was also getting more and more dreamy every minute she spent near him.

He must have noticed her sit back because he said, "Hey what do you say we get out, dry off, and let me treat you to one of the lobster rolls on Main Street? I can make a list of some good business books to read."

"That sounds like a date." She frowned. "And we're not supposed to be doing that."

"Can't it just be dinner? A cold beer, warm bread, and amazing seafood?"

She wanted to say yes. Be the kind of woman who could have casual sex, friendly bath chats, and a night out with a cute stranger, but the longer she spent with Chance the more tender her heart became. He would leave and she couldn't risk missing him because if she started she might never stop.

"This was a great surprise. And I really love lobster rolls. But I'm going to bow out." She climbed out of the tub and reached for her old bathrobe hanging on the back of the door—her secret weapon to kill sexy times.

"Seriously?" His mouth tightened in concern. "Have I made you mad?"

"I'm fine."

Now he really looked worried. "I won't pretend to be an expert on women, but I know that if a woman says she's fine that she's anything but."

"It's not a big deal." Bree considered pleading a headache or another excuse but why not just be honest? What could it hurt? "You've made it clear that Cranberry Cove is just a summer getaway, but it's my life. I'm trying to be just friends and don't want to get attached." As she ground out the words they felt so silly.

*Get* attached?

Too late for that! Her skin felt like Velcro, wanting to press against him, form a binding seal. Maybe it was too much too soon, but there it was. He offered to support her professional ambitions, he was easy to talk to, and she came alive in his arms. It was already going to hurt like hell when he left.

"I see." His monotone response gave nothing away. He didn't tell her she was being silly. But he didn't reassure her either. Instead he inclined his head slowly. He didn't look like he loved her decision, but he wasn't going to argue.

"I understand." He audibly cleared his throat. "Sorry if I've made anything harder for you. For what it's worth I love your company."

She forced what she hoped was a convincing smile. Mom had been the master of those. No matter how she was feeling: hurt, mad, bad, she always kept people guessing with her enigmatic Mona Lisa smile.

"Are you sure you're feeling all right?" Chance gave her a skeptical once-over. "You look in pain. Headache?"

Guess Bree was less Mona Lisa and more Moaning Myrtle.

Terrific.

"I'm fine. I am enough." She regurgitated some chirpy empowerment post she'd spotted yesterday on Instagram, a graphic in the stories of one of her knitting acquaintances who had a tendency to overshare.

The random blurt didn't seem to do a lot to reassure Chance but it certainly wasn't inspiring him to stick around either. They had enjoyed each other's bodies and she'd appreciated the way he'd listened to her go on and on about the Grandview. No man had ever paid her such careful attention, as if he honestly cared to consider what word might come out of her mouth next. It had been an exhilarating sensation, going to her head like a flute of champagne on New Year's Eve.

But just like those parties hit their zenith at midnight, she too risked pulling a Cinderella and turning back into a regular, boring girl standing next to a pumpkin.

"Sounds like that's my cue," he said, adjusting the low slung towel on his waist. "I'll get out of your hair and just send you the email like I promised. Be sure to read the links. They should help."

"Sounds good." From the corner of her eye she could see his Adonis belt slip into view, those toned V-line muscles.

The old quote "If you love something set it free" popped into her head. A panicked giggle burbled into her throat and she tried to mask it with a cough.

"Sorry, I might be coming down with something. Hope you don't get it," she added, trying to arrange her features into an expression that vaguely resembled a person coming down with a summer cold.

"Gotcha," he said, stalking out of the bathroom. It might be her imagination, but he seemed a little hurt by her sudden shift.

More like he wanted to go another round. That's all she was to him and it would be best to remember that.

He was gone within five minutes but not before placing his flash drive next to her computer. "Also, before I forget, I put together a general plan complete with sample photos of similar spaces and a cost sheet," he said before leaving, his professional tone making it hard to believe he'd ever whispered dirty nothings in her ear as she writhed beneath his touch.

"Sounds great," she chirped. "I'll take a look and report back. And thanks for the business pep talk too."

"Anytime."

She didn't watch him go. Instead she slammed the door shut and braced her back against the wood. Finn stared at her with a quizzical expression.

"Don't you start," she groaned, burying her face in her hands. She breathed for a minute, long and slow, and then gathered up the courage to see how Chance had proposed to redesign her house.

Five minutes later she was trembling and ten minutes later she had to get up from her desk and lie down in the tangled sheets that still smelled like Chance.

He hadn't just looked at her house and stuck in a few styling upgrades like a home-and-garden reality TV show. It was clear that even in their short time together, he really got what made her tick.

Every idea he had shared had been done as if he'd put her at the center of it—the real her—the colors were vibrant dove white, sagebrush green, and dusky blue—

coastal and peaceful, yet natural and unpretentious. The kitchen had a playful bohemian flair down to gleaming wood floors covered by bright Turkish carpets. And best of all was the fact that it would only take a couple of weeks. He wasn't looking to turn her place into the Ritz, just bring it into the twenty-first century. With a few clever shelving units there could be houseplants, a cozy rocking chair next to a shelf of organized wool skeins, and best of all a little napping nook surrounded by built-in bookshelves. He'd also incorporated a plan for surround sound in most living areas so she could be enveloped by music.

She had never felt so seen or considered.

It was clear he had put a great deal of time and thought into this plan. Maybe he just loved his work and it was clear he was really good at it, but this didn't feel like a simple job done well. This felt like an effort from the heart and she didn't know what to make of that.

He said he had to leave. She heard his words. She understood the reality. And yet...

She rolled over and groaned into the pillow. She couldn't deny that despite her best intentions he'd found his way into her heart, and she didn't know what to do with him there.

# Chapter Twenty

Despite being down a functional foot, Jill passed the next few days in a happy, if surreal, blur. The cottage owners had accepted her offer and now in a mere thirty days, the sweet yellow cottage would be truly hers. A bottle of Veuve Clicquot that Essie had dropped off sat on her counter and Linda had been true to her word, whipping the Chickadee Studios into fabulous shape for its reopening.

Life was . . . good.

Paintings were hung. Glass jewelry cases were displayed in enticing ways. All the quirky, stylish home wares and bric-a-brac were positioned to invite customers to linger and explore. Plus the space was so spick-and-span you could eat one of Renee's pies off the sparkling floor.

"And away we go," Linda said, flipping the chalkboard sign on the door from Closed to Open as Jill clapped her hands.

From down the hall wafted the mouthwatering scents of buttery crusts and fruit fillings, the hum of lively conversation, and the click and scrape of satisfied forks gathering the last morsels off ceramic plates.

The only other retail space currently open in the Old Red Mill was Castaway Yarns right across the hall. But the Woods' bookshop was being renovated on the second floor and Essie said she was currently drawing up leases for a yoga space, a pottery studio, a hair salon, and a pet supply boutique. With luck and a sprinkle of pixie dust, by the time the holidays rolled around, this space would be rocking and rolling.

But now it was time to give some gratitude where gratitude was due.

"Hey, Mom," Jill said, pushing herself up to her feet and steadying herself on her crutches.

The word hung in the air.

*Mom.*

Not Linda.

It had slipped out so naturally, something that hadn't happened since she was a kid.

She glanced over shyly, to see if Linda had noticed.

The single tear streaking down her mother's cheek suggested it was heard loud and clear.

Jill swallowed. Hard. "Is it okay calling you that?"

"Yes, please." Her mom sniffled, nodding. "I...I can't tell you how much I like hearing it."

"Okay, good." Now it was Jill's turn for a tear to wet her cheek. "Because I like saying it."

Something shifted between them, an invisible thread stitching them back together. "Mom," Jill repeated the sweet word again, "thank you for having my back and helping get Chickadee open again. This store isn't just my career, it's my life's work." Her throat tightened as her voice cracked. "Today it feels like I'm getting a part of myself back."

"Oh sweetie." Linda placed a hand over her heart, her eyes shining as brightly as the bobs of polished sea glass dangling from her earlobes. "It's been my absolute pleasure."

"I always wanted to...you know...share things with you." Jill thought of all the times she had wanted to bake cookies or read books or play a game and her mom had been too exhausted from her late shifts. This moment felt like a fresh start, a chance to share and connect at last, one step at a time, starting now.

They stared at each other for a long moment and just as they both opened their mouths to speak, Bree bounded in, clutching a bouquet of—

"Here," she said, thrusting it out. "Happy reopening, friend!"

"What's this?" Jill grinned down at the bouquet. "Hand-knit roses?"

"Yup." Bree's cheeks were as pink as the wool petals. "I found the pattern last month and they seemed like the perfect crafty congratulations gift. I'm so happy that Chickadee is back in business."

"Hello, hello!" The door opened up again and Renee

and Sadie entered, a heavenly scent wafting up from the pie tin in Renee's hands.

"Welcome to the mill," Sadie sang out, reaching to give Jill a hug. Her growing belly bounced off Jill's hip causing them both to giggle—even as Jill forced her gaze from Sadie's beautiful glowing shape, pushing away her flash of envy.

Bree's eyes narrowed, concerned, noticing Jill's wince. *Darn it.* Jill forced herself to remain relaxed and light. "What on earth do you have there?"

"A s'mores pie," Renee said proudly, holding it up so everyone could see. "A graham cracker crust, chocolate filling, and toasted marshmallow topping."

"Amazing," Jill breathed, focusing all her attention on this decadent treat.

"Oh stop." Renee waved the compliment away, her ears turning a faint shade of pink. "It's nothing really."

"You stop." Sadie wagged a finger. "What have we been talking about? You need to own your awesome. To hell with modesty. Shine on, you crazy diamond!"

"Fine." Renee rolled her eyes, but her smile widened. "That pie is going to be the best thing you've ever put in your mouth."

"Ever?" Bree arched a brow. "Hmmm. I might need a bite too."

"I should let you get on with it." Linda shuffled toward the table in the corner where her tote bag was propped up next to the register. "See your friends and start your day."

"What! Where are you going?" Jill exclaimed.

"Home." Linda waved her hand. "I don't want to be in the way."

"Mom," Jill said. "Please stay. I really do need an assistant. Maybe that person could be you? We could be a team. I mean, only if you want to."

Linda gathered her close and stroked Jill's hair. "I never thought this chance would come."

"Me neither." Jill was crying openly, but they were good tears, hot and heavy with hope. The long-standing anger and resentment she'd carried regarding her mother ebbed like a low tide, pulling away and revealing a new possibility, a path forward together. "But it's so good that it has."

"I'll just pop the pie here," Renee said, settling the tin on a small wooden table by the window. "I hope you have a great opening day. Sounds like it already is."

"Indeed," Sadie said, resting a hand on her belly. "I love a happy ending."

A familiar old pain crept back into Jill's chest, not quite eclipsing the perfect moment, but darkening the edges.

"Thank you," Jill murmured.

Bree's phone rang. She pulled it out of her pocket, glanced at the screen, made a face, and then put it away.

After Renee and Sadie left Chickadee, Jill turned to her mom. "Hey, do you mind holding the fort for a second? I want to see something over at Castaway with Bree."

"Of course," Linda said as she moved her tote bag into the back closet. "I'm going to finish pricing the watercolor coasters if that's okay by you."

"Sounds great," Jill said. "And I don't expect you to start

full-time with me right out of the gate. You'll need to give the folks you clean for notice."

Linda nodded. "Yes, there are a few bookings that I need to honor but today is wide open. I'll get right to work."

Jill waited to speak until she and Bree walked into the yarn shop. "Is Noreen here?" she said, looking around.

Bree frowned, her gaze wary. "No, this is her day off."

"Okay, good. Then spill." Jill put her hand on her hips. "Who just called you a few seconds ago?"

Bree paled. "No one."

"And by no one you mean Chance." Jill arched a brow.

"What the heck." Bree stared, mouth open. "Are you a mind reader now too?"

"I just have a PhD in Bree Robinson behavior. And right now I can tell that you are head over heels about this guy, but you're keeping this fling under wraps. Why?"

"It's so stupid." Bree groaned, leaning against a rack displaying craft magazines. "I got attached to my fling. I can't anti–bucket list correctly."

"Come on. It can't be all that bad. He has to be crazy for you too, right? I mean who wouldn't be?"

"He's made it clear he's going back to New York City. He has a life there. Cranberry Cove is just a little Podunk town that had a big hurricane and his brother came into town to score work. He isn't going to stay here and I can't just be the good-time girl who is there when he wants some action and will wave to him in the rearview mirror when he eventually drives away."

"Oh dear." Jill reached for her friend's hand and gave it a squeeze. "You've fallen for him. Hard."

"I've done something." Bree dragged her hands through her hair. "Because I'm clearly deranged. And a little bruised."

Wow, she had it bad.

"What was he reaching out to you about?" Jill asked.

"Probably the remodel. Though it looks like he's kind of letting his brother do most of it," she declared, looking close to tears.

Right before Jill could respond, a customer came in, all coiffed hair and pearl stud earrings. "Hi dear. You see this sweater vest I'm wearing? I like how it fits but the color is too summery. My complexion is more of a winter. Do you have patterns for a white sweater?"

Jill did a double take to see if the woman was joking but her expression was the definition of earnest.

Bree always insisted that she was entertained with the odd questions she fielded in the knitting shop:

Do you have any spare yarn?

Where can I buy this yarn online?

Oooooh. I like that scarf you're wearing! Can I buy it?

And right now, true to form, her friend didn't bat an eye, god love her. Instead, she waved Jill off with a smooth gesture and was already listening to the woman's babbling with a patient smile.

When Jill stepped out into the hall, she nearly collided with Ashley Wood.

"Oh, sorry, I'm always in the way," the woman stammered, smoothing back her red hair.

"What? Stop, I'm the one who wasn't looking where I

was going." Jill frowned, hating to see the tension practically wafting off the woman. "Hey, do you want to come into my shop? Hang out for a bit?"

Ashley glanced at the gallery with a wistful expression. "I can't. I have to put in a shipment order. Jack is golfing with Kent."

"And left you to do all the work?"

Ashley glanced around before taking a step forward. "I'm fine. Kent's just in a mood. He is having some sort of business trouble. I think it's with the inn, something stalled. He's trying to get a meeting with the city council."

"Is that a fact? Tell me more: What's going on?"

Ashley's face shuttered as if she realized she'd said too much. "I'm sorry. I don't know more than that. I really do have to go."

And with that she was gone up the stairs, as if the devil himself were on her heels.

Jill shivered to herself as she stepped into her shop, her mom ringing up a middle-aged couple. Looked like her mom could sell too.

After the customers left, Linda beamed, the warmth of her mother's smile cutting through the chill of her encounter with Ashley. "They bought three giclée prints. They were just going to go with two, but I showed how the one with the boat on its mooring really held the look together and they agreed it would be perfect for their second home!"

"Go Mom!" Jill high-fived her. "Look at you being the Upsell Queen!"

"Oh but this is fun." Linda's voice was infused with joy.

The rest of the morning she charmed customers and Jill worked on the Cranberry Cove Art Fair production schedule.

She was still smiling when she noticed the event in her calendar. The monthly bereavement group was tonight.

Oh.

Her stomach tensed. Today had been so easy, bright and happy, an afternoon when death and darkness seemed far away. She wouldn't go to group tonight. It wasn't the right time. She was fine.

But that urgent care doctor who asked her about therapy and antidepressants rose up in her imagination.

A hard truth settled into her heart. She might be good right now but she wasn't always. And lots of change was on the horizon with her getting ready to leave the condo she'd shared with Simon and move to the cottage they'd once dreamed of growing old in together.

It would be smart to be more balanced. The undeniable reality was that everyone needed a support system to help them move through their grief. While her friends were vital, none of them had experienced the close personal loss of a lover, and as a result no one fully "got it." At the bereavement group she could talk to folks who were also living life after loss, people who really understood. And she needed to build more bridges. No one should be their own island.

So a few hours later, when she poured herself a hospice coffee—gosh it really was good—she was genuinely glad to see Andrew arranging the yellow plastic seats into a circle.

On the white board behind him were written three questions in black dry-erase marker.

How Deeply Did You Love?
How Bravely Did You Live?
How Fully Did You Let Go?

All good questions.

She sat, cradling her coffee cup between her palms, and let the magnitude of those potential answers sink into her skin, travel through her tense muscles, and settle in her bones.

"Jill!" Andrew walked over, a kind smile brightening his features. He wore brown corduroy pants, and a pin-striped collared shirt topped by a forest-green sweater. His professorial demeanor immediately put her at ease. "I was hoping to see you here again."

In response, Jill did what she did best. She deflected. "My shop just opened. That talented daughter of yours needs to come in and talk vases with me."

"That's so kind of you."

"I don't feel kind. I feel frazzled. Like it or not...I need to be here," she said, and tasted the truth in every word. "For a long time I felt like I buried my future with my husband. But I didn't. It's just a lot different than I'd planned."

Andrew sat down beside her, took off his glasses, and polished them with a small microfiber cloth. "Such true words. When our spouse dies we lose more than a precious person. We lose our dreams for the future. It doesn't mean we can never dream again—it's just our dreams of life with that person are gone."

Jill thought of the yellow cottage. How she had once imagined a very different life to be lived inside those four walls. She rubbed her chest, her aching heart. No matter the pain, she was still her, still breathing, still alive. What might truly break it would be losing all her dreams.

Simon used to call her his princess.

Maybe she needed to dust off her crown and get busy believing in a brighter future.

# Chapter Twenty-One

Bree plopped her suitcase on the pristine daybed in Renee's guest room and glanced around, taking in the damask wallpaper, the cotton Turkish towels folded just so on the dresser, and jasmine-scented tea lights. It was perfect, just like her big sister.

Chance's brother Luke had called to warn her that there would be some noisy construction for the next week. Between that and the confusing prospect of being around Chance, this retreat seemed like the safest option. She didn't want to risk being in his orbit. His gravitational pull was so strong she was afraid she'd lose her bearings altogether.

Her sister had kindly offered her a refuge as Tansy had gone back to LA, and it seemed like the best option at the time.

A sound traveled up the stairs—one that made Bree cock her head.

Renee was laughing. No…that wasn't just laughing, she was shrieking with merriment.

Unusual. Her sister wasn't one for hysterical laughter.

Her boyfriend Dan's voice rumbled back in low amusement.

Interesting.

Those two were like peas in a pod.

Her sister was always so careful. Measured. Not calculated, just wary. And no surprise given the fact her ex-husband had had an affair with their daughter's kindergarten teacher. Then she'd fallen in love with the handsome pediatrician at the practice where she'd worked and since making it official, Renee's happiness was clear to anyone who saw her.

And as amazing as that was, it currently kind of stunk. Dan had recently moved into Renee's beachside cottage and there wasn't much worse than being a third wheel. But she'd have to suck it up and make the best of it, because at the end of the day, her sister's happiness was far more important.

Giving them some alone time, she curled up on the bed and opened up her laptop, going to the email she'd spotted this morning and rereading the words.

Hey Blondie, **Chance had written.** Here's a bunch of links you'll find useful in making a business. Plan for success. Your dreams can be as big as your bravery, and I believe in you.

God, she didn't even need him in the same room to get off, this guy was able to curl her toes with a simple pep talk.

She clicked through all the information he sent and soon was reaching for a notebook, sketching out the framework of her idea.

Her heart beat a fraction faster. Maybe this was possible.

Maybe she could really own Grandview. Put her degree to work. Live her best life.

"Hey B, dinner!" Renee called.

Bree glanced at the clock and startled. Two hours had passed, and she'd written pages of ideas in between looking up old hotel management class notes from her college courses, ordering a few well-reviewed business management books, and reading step-by-step business plan templates. Setting the notebook on her nightstand she marched down the stairs, making sure to hum loudly just in case the lovebirds were making out. While she was happy that Renee was embarking on what seemed like a wonderful relationship, she didn't want to be in the front row for the ooey-gooey Dr. Dan PDA.

"Hey, you two," she said, gingerly stepping into the kitchen. She suppressed a sigh of relief to find them both seated on opposite sides of the breakfast nook, a delicious-looking dinner set out between them—a mixed green salad, red wine, and a yummy smelling main dish.

"I made us meat loaf," Renee said, gesturing to the third place setting. "Myles had ground beef on sale at Shopper's Corner and I couldn't resist making Mom's recipe."

"That's my favorite." Bree's mouth watered as she took a seat.

"Dan just told me that he loafed me—get it—l-o-a-f." Renee snickered again.

Bree arched a brow at Dan. "Guess you had to be there."

Dan, a handsome silver fox with electric-blue eyes, gave her a wink. "I'm used to getting more groans than giggles with my humor. Guess this means we are meant to be."

"Sounds about right." Bree piled greens on her plate, crisp and fresh, clearly picked from Renee's abundant garden. The idea of eating something heavier like the meat loaf suddenly soured her stomach.

She'd never felt "meant to be" with Ian, her old fiancé. That had been the whole problem. She'd convinced herself that the idea was a clever ruse used to sell animated princess movies. She and Ian had worked, and that had seemed like enough.

Even though she now knew that it really, *really* wasn't.

And as happy as she was for her sister, god, how much did she want to sit in a cozy nook at her place making bedroom eyes at a hot guy.

She glanced out the window at the rain clouds coming into the cove.

What was she doing? Pining away was pointless and she wasn't a masochist. This needed to stop. In fact she hadn't directly communicated with Chance since that wonderful-and-then-awful afternoon. Luke's office had been sending over ideas related to the renovation—it wasn't going to be a major overhaul; she'd use enough from her inheritance to proceed with cosmetic changes and removing a wall or two. Once she'd signed on the dotted line, Luke had come over to do measuring and scheduling.

Finally, the place would be more her own.

She stuffed the mixed greens into her mouth just as a flash of fur outside on the patio caught the corner of her gaze.

She blinked. Blinked again. And nearly screamed.

Finn was leaping around the corner of the yard, knocking over and breaking Renee's collection of potted plants.

She had left him in the fenced yard because she didn't trust her dog inside Renee's perfect home. But now he was gleefully destroying her sister's immaculate yard. And as if to rub salt into the wound, Dr. Dan's dog, Moe, watched the entire canine circus unfold from the doggy bed on the back porch.

"Oh my!" Renee jumped to her feet.

"It's okay, I got this." Bree ran outside, clapping her hands. "Hey, hey you need to stop this instant. No, no, no!"

Broken bits of ceramic were cast about the flagstones, blossoms and soil scattered in disarray. Renee loved her plants, tended over them with care and pride and in one wild bender her dog had broken eight pots.

Bree charged at him but he knew he was in the doghouse and made a run for it, easily leaping over the charming white picket fence that divided Renee's property from her neighbor and business co-owner, Sadie.

And he didn't stop there. Sadie had her side door propped open and in he went without so much as a please or thank-you.

Bree covered her eyes, imagining too easily the damage he could do. Sadie was an interior designer, and while she had a lively toddler, the last thing she needed were muddy prints on her rugs or her stuffed pillows to serve as chew toys. Plus little Lincoln would likely be terrorized.

"Bree?" Renee called from the open door. "Hey, it's fine, really, don't give it a second thought—"

"I'm so sorry." Bree broke into a run. It would be awesome to be the kind of woman who could hurdle over fences but she'd probably knock the whole darn thing down if she tried. Instead she circumnavigated it and tore up the Landrys' driveway just in time to hear Lincoln scream from inside the house.

Her blood went cold. Finn was nothing but loving; he'd never hurt a flea. But she wasn't around little kids that much and if something happened—she'd never forgive herself.

There was zero time for basic niceties so she burst into the Landrys' home.

No immediate signs of carnage evident.

She cupped a hand to the side of her mouth. "Hello? Where are you guys? It's me, Bree!"

"Up here!" Sadie called. She didn't sound angry or terrified. In fact, she sounded...happy?

Bree had never been upstairs in the Landrys' cottage, where the bedrooms were located. Cleverly placed skylights allowed for maximum light and while light gray walls sounded depressing in theory, they were actually calming, like being cocooned in sea fog.

The double doors to the master bedroom were wide open and Bree stepped shyly inside. Sadie was curled up with Lincoln on the massive king-sized bed and right in the middle Finn seemed to smile up at her.

"You rascal," she said, wagging a stern finger.

Lincoln crawled over and leaned against his mother's face. "Mommy? Am I in trouble?"

"No, sweet boy," Bree said. "But Mr. Finn is in deep doo-doo. I'm going to kill him."

Lincoln gasped and grabbed his mother's upper arm. "Mommy, don't let the mean lady take him. I don't want Finn to be dead."

"Oh, I'm so sorry, Lincoln. It was just a silly expression. I love Finn, I just don't love him running into other people's houses. Would you ever go into Miss Renee's home and jump in her bed?"

Lincoln shoved a finger into the corner of his mouth and shook his head.

"Of course not. But that's what Finn did to you, huh?"

"We were reading *Pete the Cat*," Lincoln offered. "Then wham, doggy kisses."

"I'm so sorry," she told Sadie. "He broke a few of my sister's favorite pots before coming over here."

"I'm sure your sister understands and this was a lovely visit. Ethan has been talking about getting a dog."

"Oh? And does that seem to be in the cards?"

"Sure, when this new baby graduates from high school!" She gave her stomach an affectionate pat.

"Where is Ethan? I should apologize to him too."

"Don't be silly. There's no need." Sadie waved her off. "I sent him to Portland to get a few things for the baby.

I need a couple more swaddles and I'm going to try cloth diapers this go around—at least part of the time."

"Dang girl, that's no joke."

"A few months ago I would have agreed with you. But lately I feel more confident. I don't need to be perfect, I just need to be better than I was the day before. And barring that, I just need a cuddle from this little man. Myles is doing a home delivery any second—I'm too pooped to run errands today."

"Since when is Shopper's Corner doing home deliveries?" Bree asked. Myles, and his husband, Nathan, owned the local grocery store and were two of her favorite people in town.

"It's genius, right? Ethan has been talking to them about doing online orders, and they went ahead with it. We're their first customers; figured we'd help them work out any kinks while being extra lazy."

"I love it. Say, I'm also just getting started on another blanket for the baby. Do you have any color requests?" She'd been considering a seafoam green, but right now if Sadie requested yarn dyed with squid ink sourced from the Aegean Sea, she'd seriously consider searching for it just to make amends.

"You are so sweet." Sadie leaned back on her stack of pillows, stroking Finn's back. "I think when it comes to knitting I'll trust the expert."

Bree thanked her lucky stars that Sadie was being so kind about her marauding dog. "Are you sure there isn't something that I could do to make this up to you?"

"Your sweet doggy here is just a little reminder to embrace the daily adventures."

"I like this doggy. Mommy, I want doggy."

"Aw, that's great, sweet pea, I'm sure Auntie Bree would let you play with Finn anytime. He can be like your furry cousin."

"Yay!" Lincoln threw his chubby arms in the air, a cherubic smile on his face.

Boy, she was good.

"Hey, it's funny you're here. I met someone this morning who mentioned you. Ashley Wood—the new owner of the bookshop that is going into the mill."

A mental picture of a gaunt face and brilliant red hair leapt into Bree's mind; Ashley's timid yet restless energy was unforgettable. "I met her briefly. Not sure we hit it off though."

"Really?" Sadie cocked an eyebrow. "Because she invited us all over to her new place for tea tomorrow. She and her husband are renting the sweet, old barn that the Hoopers renovated into a house a few years ago."

"Cool. I've always wanted to peek around in there."

"She said she didn't have your phone number. She seems lonely. You should reach out."

"Text me the details. As for you, dog, you're coming with me. Say goodbye to Lincoln and tell him you will play later."

"He likes to fetch balls?"

"Fetch, yes. Return, that's still a challenge. We should definitely get on that, don't you think?"

Lincoln solemnly nodded and it was all Bree could do not to rush over and pinch his chubby little cheeks.

As she opened the door to let herself out, Myles pulled up in his vintage pickup truck, giving her an enthusiastic wave. "Hey, friend, I haven't seen you around lately."

"I know, I've been busy," Bree answered, tugging an elastic from around her wrist and pulling her hair up into a messy bun. "I'm having some work done on my house."

"I noticed." Myles winked as he walked back to the truck bed. "Nathan and I were taking a walk yesterday and went by your place. There were two guys outside working that looked on the right side of hunky."

"Essie recommended them." Bree blushed. "They're good at what they do."

"Uh-huh. I'm sure." Myles grabbed a box of what looked to be veggies, milk, and whole wheat bread. "And I'll bet you a bottle of wine that you've noticed they look good enough to do. You aren't a nun. Nathan and I want to see you happily settled."

"You and Nathan have set a high bar," Bree said with a wistful giggle. "How can the rest of us compete?"

He flourished a hand. "We want more couples' nights. Renee found her prince, it's your turn next."

"I'll tell my fairy godmother," Bree said in a teasing tone. "And I miss you. I actually need to go to the hardware store soon and pick out some paint and fixtures. Maybe you and Nathan can come along?"

"Sounds good, but remember I'm the one with the better taste." Myles liked to heckle his husband, but they loved each other deeply.

Back outside, Dan and Renee were waiting for her on the porch swing. It seemed like everywhere she went, there was another happy couple.

"Everything okay?" Renee asked as Bree returned holding Finn by the collar.

"Sadie was amazing about her surprise guest." Bree stared hard into her big sister's face, probing for any signs of annoyance. "You're seriously not mad?"

Renee cast Dan a flirty sideways glance. "Do I look angry to you?"

He kissed the end of her upturned nose. "Furious."

"Grrrrrrr," Renee teased.

For Pete's sake could they be any cuter?

"Hey, I'm actually not hungry tonight—late lunch. How would you feel if I cleaned up the mess and took Finn for a walk on the dog beach to burn off his excess energy?"

"I already cleaned up the massacre," Dan said, "while you were in Sadie's house."

Bree shook her head. "That was like five minutes."

Dan shrugged. "Guess I'm a fast worker."

"See why I love having him around?" Renee said as he wrapped his arm around her waist and kissed her neck.

Adorable. And disgusting. And just like that she was desperately missing Chance.

"Let's scram, Finn," she said. She'd send Chance her business plan later to critique along with some of the ideas from her notebooks. That would have to be enough.

Bree walked the quiet neighborhoods until she hit the ten-thousand-step benchmark on her Fitbit, and then she kept right on going. While she daydreamed over the fabulous cowls and hair scarves that she had knitted for the Cranberry Cove Art Fair—and certainly didn't think any more about Chance Elliston—she found herself beneath the rocky cliffs staring up at the white-shingled facade of the Grandview Inn.

"Hello," she said to it. "I don't know what's happening with that Wood guy, but I'm hoping me and you have a date with fate. I'm going to do my best to figure it out."

A couple peered over the railing at her in curiosity, their blond brows furrowed in confusion.

Bet they didn't expect to see a grown woman on the beach jabbering away to thin air. Rather than looking like someone with a few issues, she burst into song, pretending like it was what she had been doing all along.

As she belted up the titular song to *Oklahoma!* she glanced back in the couple's direction. Gone. Presumably for more peaceful surroundings.

Whistling to Finn she decided to escape while the getting was good.

And because the lovebirds would still be awake, she decided that she'd head to Jill's place. Her bestie was packing up the condo and could use Bree's support. Jill was a total pack rat, hoarding her precious junk like she was a dragon brooding over a lair of stolen gold. Except in this case it was things like every yearbook from kindergarten to senior year, or the locker notes that they had passed each other back and forth all through high school.

Bree's heart swelled. Jill had done such an incredible

job looking after her and supporting her through her cancer scare. It would be nice to look after Jill for once rather than the other way around.

Funky acoustic guitar music was blaring out the open sliding glass doors at Jill's condo.

Bree slammed her car door and cupped her hands to her mouth. "Hello?"

She bit the inside of her lower lip to keep her jaw from falling open when Linda stepped outside, drying her hands on a linen dish towel.

"Oh hi, Bree dear. Hang tight and I'll let you in."

Linda appeared, looking radiant with her silver-streaked hair, groovy harem pants, and a jingle-jangle of engraved silver bracelets. "This is a nice surprise," she said, holding the door open so Bree could pass inside.

It felt amazing to see Linda here and to see she and Jill were really mending fences.

"Is it okay to have my dog come in too?" She gestured to Finn, panting happily beside her.

"Of course. I am a huge puppy lover." Linda dropped to a crouch. "And aren't you a handsome boy."

Finn cocked his head, perking up as if accepting the compliment as his due. Both women laughed.

Bree reached out and helped Linda back to standing. "How's it going helping Jill pack up?"

Linda grinned. "She has a lot of stuff. We could use the help."

"Yeah, I thought I'd lend a hand but I don't want to step on your toes."

"Nonsense. I'm in the kitchen wrapping up plates and culling condiments. Did you know my daughter had three kinds of ketchup in the fridge?"

"I did indeed." Bree grimaced. "She likes one kind of ketchup on her homemade French fries, one kind on her burgers, and another kind altogether on her eggs."

"Eggs?" Linda shook her head in mock horror. "Where did I go wrong?"

"I think it's gross too." Bree pushed up her sleeves and put her hands on her hips. "I would love to help out."

"There's a crawl space you can access from the hallway. I hate to ask you to do it because I'm convinced there are spiders up there. But Jill can't go because of her ankle. She went out for a short walk, part of her physical therapy."

"I'm happy to explore the crawl space." Bree smiled, leading Finn to a braided rug beneath a sunny window where he promptly curled up with a contented sigh. "I don't mind spiders. *Charlotte's Web* made sure of that."

Linda shuddered. "I'm afraid I can't say the same."

When Bree climbed up the ladder and peeked into the crawl space, it was empty of spiders, empty full stop, except for one box near the entrance. It wasn't a cardboard box, but an adorable custom-made container with a lid covered in soft gray and pink stripes. She went on tiptoes on the ladder and pulled the box closer. Popping the lid, she frowned.

The box was half filled with adorable baby clothes. Maybe it had been left here by an old tenant?

"Hey, Linda?" she called, carefully carrying it down.

"Do you know what this is all about? I'm sure none of this belongs to Jill but it's a little strange."

Linda opened the lid and picked up a blue cotton onesie with a puffin sewn on the front.

"My. Isn't this sweet?" Linda looked up, a frown line deep between her brows. "This was in the crawl space?"

"Yeah. Weird, right?" Bree took the onesie from her, unsure what to do next.

"What the hell are you doing with that?" A tense voice snapped.

Bree turned slowly, and there was Jill, angrier than she'd ever seen her.

# Chapter Twenty-Two

When Jill had been in middle school, she'd gone down to Cranberry Cove's Whitepoint Beach with a group of friends. A storm had been brewing and the air was scented with that strange pungent zing of ozone and rainwater. The high surf advisory was too easy to ignore as they ran, and laughed, chasing each other with seaweed and bits of slimy flotsam and jetsam.

Growing up by the ocean, Jill knew the old phrase "Never turn your back on the waves," but Ryan Comeau had been there, and he was so cute with his black hair, green eyes, and sarcastic sense of humor. She was watching him and not the breakers when suddenly the world had gone cold and dark, icy seawater flooding into her mouth and ears, as she tumbled about, like a rock being polished.

Luckily, she was only mortified, not injured, but the surge of the water that afternoon was something she never forgot. And she felt a surge of similar power now, except instead of the frigid north Atlantic Ocean, it was a volcanic wave of red-hot anger.

"Where did you get that?" she repeated, louder this time, as if she needed to shout over the cacophony of blood thundering through her ears. Finn whined, nudging her leg with his black nose, agitated by her outburst, and she sank to his side, wrapping her arms around his neck.

"Jilly Beans. What's gotten into you?" Bree asked wonderingly, her cheeks going pale as confusion and guilt warred over her features. "I wanted to help, and your mom said you can't get up in the crawl space and she's afraid of spiders. And I didn't mean to make you mad, but I'm so confused. Whose clothes are these?"

"They're mine, okay? Mine!" Jill flew forward and grabbed the puffin onesie, the one she'd bought from a Portland seamstress when stocking a small line of organic baby clothes for Chickadee three years ago.

It had been right after peeing on that stupid pregnancy test and seeing those two telltale lines that promised to give her and Simon the family they'd dreamed about. And right before Simon and she had had the world's most pointless argument over some of his online spending purchases, and he'd left in a huff, hopped on the bike, and never heard that she carried his baby inside her.

A baby that left her in the weeks following in a quiet flood of blood and cramping in the middle of the night, leaving her emptier than she'd ever been, even emptier than she'd been on the day she learned that Simon would never come home again.

"Honey." Linda stepped forward. "I'm so sorry. I didn't know there was a baby."

Bree was statue still, tears pouring down her cheeks, her nose running. Her hand, pressed over her mouth, was trembling.

This was too much. Jill's throat slammed shut. She'd never talked about her grief, *couldn't* tell anyone, to form the words was a physical impossibility, better to shove that chapter down in the deepest part of herself and forget it had ever happened.

"There was never a baby," she bit out, jumping back to her feet. "At least there was *barely* a baby. I miscarried a few weeks after Simon died. I never even got to tell him, it was so new. Instead, we got into a stupid fight over a credit card bill and then I lost them both. I lost everything."

She didn't cry. This grief was deeper than her aquifer of tears. The sorrow she felt was as bleak and lifeless as the South Pole, a barren, frozen landscape. It was a punishment to be endured, because she had started that stupid fight stressed about finances and being pregnant.

"My fault," she repeated, slumping against the wall, pressing the little onesie to her chest. "My fault. My fault. My fault."

She'd thought her future with Simon would be rock solid, never imagining that she'd be the one to fracture everything, cause the quake that destroyed their lives.

"Oh no, no, no." Bree shook herself back to life, enveloping her in a huge hug as Linda joined in, wrapping her arms around her waist.

"We're here for you," her friend murmured. "Through whatever, whenever. Remember you aren't alone, you've never been alone."

Jill breathed in their perfume, but it didn't comfort her. Instead the scents felt too sweet, too strong. She pushed free, unable to breathe.

"No one knows the whole story," she whispered. "I found out that I was pregnant. And the morning that I wanted to tell Simon, I opened up our credit card bill and saw that he'd ordered expensive new tools for his business without telling me. His work was doing pretty well and he wanted to treat himself. But I was thinking about how the baby was coming, and we didn't have awesome insurance, and I know diapers cost a fortune. He said I was nagging him and that annoyed me. So I decided not to tell him the news, that it was better to wait until our tempers both cooled down. He left angry because *I'd* frustrated him. It's why he was distracted when the deer came on the road. It's why he crashed his bike. It's why he died. And it's why my body got too overwhelmed and couldn't carry the pregnancy. That was my punishment for Simon."

"You've been carrying so much pain inside you." Bree walked into the kitchen and grabbed a glass, filling it with water. "I never in a million years imagined that you were carrying such a heavy load."

She led Jill, limping, to the couch and pressed the water glass into her hand.

Jill let herself be cajoled into sitting, into taking a sip of the tepid liquid that she didn't want.

All she wanted was the life she'd lost.

"It doesn't matter," she said dully. "Talking won't bring them back. I'm sorry I freaked out at you in the hallway." She held up the little onesie, crumpled now by how hard she'd been squeezing it.

"Honey, I'm your best friend," Bree said softly, kneeling before her and taking her hand. "Do you know what that means? When you hurt, I hurt. You know how much Simon loved you. Remember how he always called you his princess. That guy was in love with you from day one. Every couple fights sometimes, but that doesn't mean there isn't love."

"He adored you," Linda said, crouching beside Bree and taking Jill's other hand. Finn curled up at their feet. "We all do."

"I've lost so much," Jill mustered. "Sometimes I feel like I'm just a shadow of a person. Why did this have to happen? How is it possible that Simon is gone forever? That our baby never got a chance to live? Couldn't I have at least been allowed that, just that one little thing? I'm stuck in this waking nightmare and even though I know people want to help, no one can take away this hurt. It's mine, and mine alone. And I hate it. Sometimes I even hate Simon for dying and leaving me here alone. And then I hate myself for thinking that even for a second."

Jill closed her eyes and rocked her head back on the couch and let her mom and Bree anchor her for a moment. No one spoke. Out loud that is. The silence was like the moment before an expensive vase hits a marble floor or the first winter snow begins falling, both fraught and peaceful.

Outside the window, a summer rain began to splatter the panes, and the three women sat, and grieved, and loved, together.

* * *

Jill was still off-kilter the following morning as she turned the Closed sign to Open over at Chickadee Studios. Her mom was due in two hours but for now it was just her, and the store and the familiar surroundings, even in this new location, were exactly what she needed.

She still felt raw after yesterday's unexpected confession, her secret underbelly exposed for the first time. Bree and her mom had both been great, treating her with gentle, tender care and not forcing her to talk any more about that time. But her dreams were troubled, restless, one of those awful nightmares where you are running, and something is coming, you can hear the footsteps, feel the hot blood pounding in your chest, but whenever you crane your neck over one shoulder, trying to see what the heck it is...nothing's there.

As she took a sip of the French roast with vanilla creamer in her travel coffee mug, the bells her mom had hung on the shop door gave a little tinkle.

"Good morning, I wasn't sure if I should have called first, but we were driving by the mill and I know you wanted to talk to my Penny."

It was Andrew, the monthly bereavement group convener, and beside him, Andrew in the female form, if he was born a tall, athletically built young girl with the same wide friendly smile.

"Dad said that you liked my glassblowing?" she asked with no shred of shyness.

"Andrew, great to see you," Jill exclaimed. And she sincerely meant it. "And Penny, yes, please, come in! I have so many questions."

"Go ahead!"

"What makes a young woman like you interested in glassblowing? I'm curious because it's not something that's really taught in schools."

"Oh yeah." Penny gave a little laugh. "That's true. So a couple years ago, we were in Florida. It was after Mom died, and Dad and I needed somewhere warm and sunny during winter. He found us this cool beach house in Florida, right on the water, and this huge thunderstorm started. Our house gave us the perfect view of this totally awesome lightning show. Then there was this crazy flash and we knew the lightning struck the beach, just past our place. When it was safe, we went out and took a look and that's how I first learned about fulgurite."

Jill looked between Andrew and Penny before throwing up her hands. "I have no idea what fulgurite is, please educate me."

"Oh, it's fine," Penny said with a deprecating giggle. "Most of my friends have never heard about it either. Fulgurite is basically when lightning does the glassblowing, the flash of heat can create all sorts of cool, hollowed-out glass shapes from the sand and it got me thinking how I wanted to try it. Later that year, I saw an exhibition at the state fair about glassblowing and I was really into the heat, the ovens, basically how they re-created lightning using such amazing tools and artistry. They held demonstrations every hour and I ended up watching each one."

"That's so cool! And now you want to turn this into a career?"

"Hopefully! That's the plan." Penny laughed. "I've got my heart set on Pilchuck Glass School in Washington State."

"Which last time I checked is on the other side of the country," Andrew said drily.

"But Daddy, they have small classes taught by world-renowned artists. It's a once-in-a-lifetime experience to learn the craft."

They both turned to Jill with imploring faces.

"No way am I taking a side," she said, backing away slowly. On onc hand she understood Penny's wish to chase a dream, even if it took her far away, and on the other side she empathized with Andrew's reluctance to let his daughter go after the loss of his wife.

"I will say this though"—she held up a finger—"if you want to try the best pie you've ever eaten in your life, head on down the hall to Hester's Pie Shop. My friend Renee is the baker and co-owner and her only daughter, Tansy, goes to university in Los Angeles." Jill softened her tone. "She might be able to give more insight. I know they had some growing pains their first year apart, but you'll be hard-pressed to find a mother and daughter who are closer."

"That sounds really cool." Penny practically bounced up and down. "Dad, can we? Please?"

Andrew had the look of a man who'd been beaten, but accepted the defeat with grace. "You know my sweet tooth, I can't turn down blueberry pie."

"Yoo-hoo, it's me," Essie called, sashaying into the shop in a tight leather miniskirt and dangerous heels.

She stumbled, and not because of her five-inch stilettos. "Andrew Weathers?"

At first Jill thought there was something wrong with her hearing. Essie's voice didn't sound right. She usually spoke with sass and snark, with the brash undertones of a ballsy businesswoman who didn't let anyone steamroll her.

But this...this was soft, slow, and tentative—almost girlish.

"You two know each other?" Penny echoed Jill's thoughts exactly.

"We went to college together," Andrew said, shaking his head as if to gather himself. "Bowdoin. Before I met your mother."

"Mother?" Essie turned to Penny and stuck out a hand as if in a dream. "Of course you're Andrew's daughter. The spitting image."

"Hey, I'm Penny. Who're you?"

"Oh. Right." Essie's cheeks were red. Was she blushing? If Jill looked out the window no doubt pigs would be flying by. "I'm Essie Park. I manage the leases here in the mill, and I'm a real estate broker in Cranberry Cove. Andrew, I had heard through the grapevine that you lived nearby, but our paths never crossed. How strange." She gave a forced laugh.

"Strange indeed." Andrew cleared his throat. "We live close to Freeport. I worked for L.L.Bean for years, but now I have my own private law practice."

"That's right, you went out of state for law school."

"Columbia."

"And what brings you to Cranberry Cove?"

"I coordinate a bereavement group. My wife passed five years ago."

Essie's brows shot up beneath her perfectly groomed bangs. "Oh my god, I'm so sorry."

"So are we." Andrew put his arm around his daughter. "Well, we should be going. Penny and Jill, maybe you can keep the conversation going."

"Yes." Jill jolted, having been focused on trying to solve the mysterious tension filling the room. "Here, Penny, let me grab you my business card." She limped over to where she kept the cards in a delicately woven willow basket and pulled out a small creamy card embossed with a bird. "This is my contact information here at Chickadee. I look forward to seeing a portfolio. It would be great to support a young Maine artist."

"Thanks, Jill." Andrew made a show of looking at his watch. "Oh, look at the time. We really do need to leave."

"But what about talking to my friend Renee?" Jill asked, frowning. Why was everyone acting so darn strange?

"Yeah, Dad." Penny practically pouted. "You wanted that pie. Now my stomach's rumbling."

"Another time," Andrew murmured, making a break for the door. "See you around, Jill, and Essie..." He actually paused and cleared his throat. "Yes. Yes. Nice to see you."

And with that they were gone.

Jill folded her arms. "Spill. Now. What the heck was going on there?"

Essie pretended to pluck an invisible piece of lint off her shirt. "I don't know what you mean."

"Spare me, Park. There was so much water beneath the bridge just now that I almost needed a snorkel. Dish."

"We went to college together. No big deal. We were on an exchange program together. Paris."

Jill waggled her eyebrows. "Ooooooh-la-la."

Essie stared at the door with a wistful expression. "I'd never felt right looking him up."

"The plot thickens." Jill steepled her fingers. "It sounds like you were more than exchange students visiting the City of Love."

Essie backed against a wall and pressed her hands to her cheeks. "Andrew, or Drew as I used to call him, used to be very precious to me."

"Hamana-hamana-hamana what?" Of all the ways Jill imagined this day going, learning that Essie Park had once been in love with Andrew Weathers was certainly not one of them.

Essie's face was a mask of wide-eyed panic. "Do you have any wine here?"

Jill snorted. "It's ten o'clock!"

"Don't judge me." Essie wrapped her arms around her slender middle as if trying to hold on to what remained of her dignity. "Not right here. Not right now." She squeezed her eyes shut. "Have you ever fainted? What does it feel like? I need to sit down."

Jill limped forward and clasped her friend's shoulder. She was trembling. Had she ever seen Essie rattled about anything?

"Come sit down by the register," she said gently. "I don't have wine but I have a thermos of lavender mint tea."

"Okay, okay. That'll have to do." Essie allowed herself to be guided over to a stool and perched at the edge, rubbing her temples. "You must think I'm crazy."

"No, but I'd be lying if I said I'm not intensely curious. Andrew Weathers is like Mr. Rogers's cute younger brother, and he's got you feeling some kind of way, and I want to know all the things."

"We had a month in Paris a long time ago. A perfect month. We took French class together every day, then we'd go out and explore the city: the Eiffel Tower, the Luxembourg Gardens, the Latin Quarter, browse through the Bouquinistes along the Seine and browse the vintage books and postcards. We shared ice creams, had picnics, we talked and talked and laughed, and I've never ever been *seen* by anyone before the way Drew saw me. My family loved me of course, but they never wanted to know the real me, they just wanted me to conform to a role, be the perfect daughter with the perfect grades. They didn't care about my thoughts on art or books or life. Drew cared. He listened. He was my friend and my first... my first everything."

"I see." Jill stood still, she didn't want to make any sudden movements or stop Essie's outpouring.

"When we got back I learned that my father had lost his job. He couldn't afford my college tuition and I didn't want to put pressure on him so I dropped out. I went to Boston and worked, and when I was able I put myself through my senior year at Framingham State and got my marketing degree. During everything I lost touch with Drew. There weren't a lot of cellphones then and social media was non-existent. When I came back to Maine I tried to find him but heard he'd moved out of state for law school and that he had a new girlfriend. That was that." Essie's eyes were bright with tears. "But I'd fallen in love with him. And I can honestly say that I've never again met any other man who I've connected with on any meaningful level." She reached for a box of tissues and dabbed her eyes. "It's silly, really. It was probably just all those early twenty-something hormones that made him seem so special. And the fact that I've never been lucky in love just made it easier for me to create a fantasy in my head."

"I don't think it's silly at all." Jill poured the tea from her thermos into a delicate teacup and passed it to her friend. "I had that with Simon. I felt like he got me in a way that no one else did. I don't have a word for what we had, it was just—"

"Magic." They both said it together, exchanging sad smiles of understanding, before reaching for each other, their long hug expressing all the words neither could say.

# Chapter Twenty-Three

"To the telephone pole, to the telephone pole," Bree chanted under her breath, jog-walking as Finn pranced beside her, barely breaking a sweat. Exercise was supposed to clear her head and give her a sense of calm and clarity. Instead she was wanting to simultaneously vomit and eat a double-scoop ice-cream cone. Even if the only reason she stood here today was because fifty thousand years ago, her ancestors had been fleet-footed enough to avoid the jaws of a saber-toothed tiger, she was going to have to let the gene pool down.

With a groan, she paused, bending over, hands on her knees, gasping to catch her breath.

This had been a tumultuous week. First, Chance hadn't responded to her business plan, hotel ideas, or her last questions on the home renovations. What was up? Maybe he'd lost enthusiasm? But second, and far worse, was how

Jill had disclosed the painful secret of her miscarriage, and the fact she blamed herself for Simon's death. It had been devastating to realize how much loss her friend had been keeping, and being unable to help her shoulder any of the burden. It made her feel sick, like she'd been the queen of self-absorption. It had always seemed as if Jill had been holding back, but she had never wanted to push her friend. But now it was clear that Jill had avoided her pain by focusing on being Bree's one-woman cheering section, always happy to organize their trips, their girls' nights, and that arrangement had suited them both. But maybe Bree had been too selfish—never looking the gift horse in the mouth.

Now Jill was AWOL. Linda was left working in the shop, and all she'd share was that Jill had been sleeping a lot, asking for alone time. That was the gist of the texts she'd send to Bree whenever she wrote to see how Jill was doing.

Then came the fact she couldn't even retreat into her comfy bed because Chance and his brother were still working on her house. And she couldn't invite Chance into the comfy bed at her sister's house because one, Renee would never stop asking questions and two, she'd get too attached. Plus, he hadn't even responded to her last email, so she didn't want to look desperate. As easy and breezy as a summer fling sounded, Bree had learned—the hard way—that she just wasn't wired that way. If she cared about someone, she went all in.

And now, despite every effort, she couldn't get Chance's voice out of her head.

"Hey."

She groaned. And now she was having audible hallucinations, his deep voice rumbling in her mind.

"Are you okay?"

"Of course not," she snapped at the hallucination, yelping when two large hands grabbed her shoulders and lifted her to standing.

Not a hallucination.

Chance was here, in a black athletic top that set off his biceps, revealing the thick veins that ran beneath his olive skin, and his shorts exposed the perfect amount of strong, muscular quads. Was he beautiful? Without question, in that way that made her heart skip and her knees turn to Jell-O. But more than his good looks, it was the expression in his eyes.

Here she was, face red from exertion and surprise, messy bun, a sweaty upper lip, wearing old yoga pants that had never seen a downward dog and a T-shirt of a black cat holding a bone that read, "I found this humerus," and those baby blues stared at her like she was Cleopatra coming into Rome.

"Water?" He handed over a plastic bottle and she popped it into her mouth like a baby with a bottle. Easier to hydrate than meditate on the monumentally unfair reality that she'd fallen head over heels for a guy who wasn't only leaving but was also incredibly kind and crush-worthy.

"You okay? You seem a little out of sorts," he asked gently, maintaining the intense eye contact that made her want to open up her arms and ask him for a hug, to breathe him in and forget the world awhile.

It was uncanny how he always seemed to know the exact right thing to say.

"Decided to try running. Decided it's not for me."

"Hey, if life doesn't challenge you, it doesn't change you."

Bree shoved the water bottle back at him and took two steps back. "You sound like my best friend, Jill."

His brow furrowed. "And that's a bad thing?"

"No. She's always got the perfect saying to try to push me in the right direction, even if she doesn't always follow her own advice."

He was silent a beat. "Walk with me?"

"Walk?"

The dimple put in an appearance. "We could run too, but you seem like you could use a cooldown."

She rolled her eyes, hoping that made her look noncommittal rather than as overeager as Finn, who was currently trying to dislodge her arm from her shoulder socket in an effort to slobber all over Chance.

"Where do you want to go?" she asked lightly, reaching up to tuck a flyaway hair into her topknot. The afternoon sun heated her already warm skin.

"Let's check out that hotel of yours."

"The Grandview?" She bristled. "Be realistic. Don't get my hopes up."

He hiked his dark brows. "Humor me?"

She tapped the corner of her mouth, noting that his gaze lingered on her lips with a faintly puzzled expression as if he were working out a particularly diabolical crossword challenge. "Fine."

At least she didn't leave him totally unaffected.

"I read through your business plan," he said after a beat. "I also looked through the concepts you shared."

"Okay."

The ensuing pause made her jittery. What was he going to say? That she was a joke? That dreams could become real, but only if the person doing that dreaming had the ability?

"They were good. More than good. It's clear you spent a great deal of time and energy on visualizing how to bring the Grandview back to life. I've been working on fine-tuning the financial projections. Getting it to the stage you could look at getting a loan."

"Really?" She tripped and he caught her arm, hanging on a beat too long.

"Really. I think when I send it back you'll be happy with the result. Your analysis and marketing and operation ideas were spot on. And you're right, the location really sells itself, especially if we go ahead with your idea to add in luxury breakfasts as part of the package. I tweaked the financials. I know you laugh at the idea of investors, but with limited to no capital to sink in, that's the direction to pursue. Overall, I'd say we make a great team."

"Thank you," she said, flustered. He'd taken her off guard again, but it had been of her own doing. He had read the plan just as he promised. The only reason he hadn't gotten back in touch was because he was working on it.

As her mind reeled, they walked in silence, side by side, Finn trotting between them with a contented smile on his face as if he'd always been a part of their trio.

*No. Stop that.* She frowned inwardly. She and Chance weren't anything except a curious tourist and a friendly local...who were working on a business idea and happened to know what each other looked like naked.

She cringed.

"Why do you keep doing that?" he asked.

"What?" She forced her face into a smooth mask of innocence.

"Your face is like an open book," he said, giving her a sideways glance. "The problem is I can't always read the story."

"Maybe you're not trying hard enough," she teased.

"Hey," he said. "I've been thinking a bit about our last time together. Well, a whole hell of a lot more than a bit if I'm going to be honest. Kind of hard to have you out of my mind when I'm working at your house every day, rifling through your underwear drawer on my lunch break."

She tripped over her own feet, stumbling. "Excuse me."

He steadied her without missing a beat, his hand lingering on her arm a moment too long. "Sorry, that was a joke. The second part. Not a very good one."

"Especially given the fact that I never wear underwear."

It was his turn to trip.

"Sorry, that was a joke. Not a very good one." She glanced up at those now familiar blue eyes and got lost a moment.

"You're something else," he said in a tone that sounded an awful lot like the highest praise. "And you're never far from my mind. While I'm never going to violate your privacy and snoop through your personal things, as we work on the house, I won't pretend that I don't check out all the photos you have on the wall. You look a lot like your mom."

Pleasure flooded her. "Seriously?"

"God yeah. That smile? It lights up a room."

Her throat constricted. "I still miss her every day. She was such a great mom. Renee takes after her in many ways. Sometimes I worry that I'm more the chick that never left the nest. Back in the same house. Never pushed myself to do anything with the degree I got. Never wanted to leave this town. I've played it safe my whole life and I don't think that's what she wanted for me. I worry somewhere she is looking down, disappointed." She bit her lip. "And that's a heck of a lot more than I intended to say."

"Never apologize. I like listening to you."

"It's just…you'll be gone soon. I don't want to lose anyone else important in my life. I can't afford for you to become important because you won't be sticking around."

She heaved a heavy sigh before pointing a finger at a path nearly hidden by the surrounding trees. "Turn here, it's the shortcut that brings you out to the cliff right next to the inn."

"I came to Cranberry Cove to clear my head," Chance muttered, almost to himself. "But I've ended up more confused than ever."

"I'm going to be honest," she said, sucking in a breath, unable to tamp down the impulse to get this off her chest. "I like you. A lot. More than a lot. And I'm scared to be around you because sometimes it feels like at any moment I'm going to hit the point of no retreat and lose my heart to you. Up until this point, I've been doing a pretty good job of convincing myself that I was content, and now you're messing with my illusion."

He reached out and took her hand. "The last thing in this world I'd ever want to do is hurt you. It's just...the reality is that when I leave here I'm going to be so damn busy. I'm afraid that I can't give you the attention you deserve."

"'Too busy' is a myth," Bree surprised herself by blurting. "People make time for what's important to them. I'm not looking to be let down easily. Just be honest."

"Fine. You want the truth, blondie?" He released her hand and rumpled his hair in an agitated manner. "I don't know what the hell is going on here. I got divorced. I left the city to clear my head and hang with my brother doing good, honest work. I met a cute woman at a bar who had a voice like an angel and a body like a goddess, but more important a heart bigger than anything. And I didn't plan for that. And you can see from my obsession with making a business plan, that I'm a planner, Bree. I don't do things unless I can see four to five steps ahead. But with you I keep breaking that rule over and over and over."

She sensed what he was saying was the truth, and even if it wasn't the perfect answer, she couldn't ask for more than honesty. "Well, you can't follow your heart if it's more confused than your head."

They walked in silence a moment, emerging onto a lush green lawn. The white shingled hotel was positioned on the top of the small hill. To the left, cliffs dropped down to Whitepoint Beach. People were all over the stretch of buttery-colored sand, reading books, walking dogs, splashing in the calm water.

A subject change was in order. She was tired of talking in circles with this man. "I can't imagine anyone would come here and want to tear this building down."

He startled. "Shit. That reminds me. I did some digging on the developer. Kent Wood? I know why he sounded so familiar now."

She frowned at his deep brow furrow, her heart clenching. "Uh-oh, why do I get the acute sense that this isn't going to be good news?"

"He did a bunch of shady land speculation deals in New Jersey and has a rep for unscrupulous behavior. He's run a highly profitable business that has left a wake of hurt people behind him. At the same time, he's not dumb. He's been able to fund the reelection campaigns of prominent folks who wield a lot of influence. He plays the game hard, and he plays to win."

"If I didn't feel out of my league before, you are doing a dang good job of convincing me now." Bree walked toward the cliffs. Not that it would really make a difference, but the air felt cleaner there, further removed from the inn and Kent Wood's plans for it. She suddenly had the reckless urge to confide in this man, to share the thing she'd been keeping under wraps, the little flicker of hope in this situation. "Can I...tell you a secret? One I've never told anyone. Not even my sister. Not even my best friend."

"I'd be honored," he said promptly.

"I mentioned I have a degree," she whispered. "No one else knows about it. I did it online through UMass Amherst. It's in hotel management."

"And..." He looked encouraging but puzzled. "I mean that's fantastic. But why would that sort of achievement be a secret?"

"I finished the course two years ago and since then I've done exactly nothing with it. Cranberry Cove isn't exactly bursting with hotel opportunities, but the idea of leaving just isn't an option. This is my home, you know? I love it here." She sat down on the grass, Finn nestling in beside her, and wrapped her arms around her legs, careful not to release his leash. "But I want to do more than work in the yarn shop forever. I want to have my own business. My grades were good. I maintained a three-point-nine average. Now after my cancer scare it feels as if I need to go for my dreams because this is it. This is my life. This is my shot. And I'm so afraid."

"What about?" He sat next to her on the grass, not touching, but his presence was there, real and reassuring.

"Failure I guess. Or looking stupid. I guess both. Failing and looking stupid. I want it all. My professional ambitions realized *and* the ability to stay in my hometown. This hotel is so out of my league. Just like you really. It's fun to imagine having the life of my dreams but the reality is that I'm not Cinderella. There's no fairy godmother. And I'm just a big, fat chicken."

Her last words echoed down to the beach, and she didn't

even realize that she shouted them until a few people turned to glance up, slight frowns on their faces.

Terrific. Now she was making a public spectacle of herself.

"What I need to be is content. I have a great house. And thanks to you and your brother—and my savings—it's getting greater. I have supportive friends. My job is fine. So many people have it so much worse, so why should I complain? I'm alive, right? My parents don't have that luxury. Simon doesn't have that luxury.

"So I'm a small-town gal who keeps notebooks of hotel ideas under her bed. So what?" Her voice shook and she knew she'd said too much. It was time to make a graceful exit.

"I have to go. Now. Just forget about the business plan. You have lots going on I'm sure. You don't need to humor me."

*O-kay.* Maybe not graceful, but definitely to the point. She stood up and dusted off her seat.

"Wait," he said, rising to his feet, hands half extended as if she were a skittish horse.

Bree raised her hands to the sky. The blue, blue sky. "Why am I telling you all of this?" Finn yelped at her high-pitched voice. "None of this is your issue. None of this is your responsibility. I just want and want but... I can't have because my dreams are too big. I need to keep it small. Keep it real. That's just who I am."

She took a step away and then another.

"I'm sorry to lash out. This isn't on you. You've been

supporting my dreams. It's on me. I need to be content with what I have. Being with you is like being in that Greek myth about the boy who flew too close to the sun, what's his name? Whatever. You've been upfront, but I haven't listened because honestly? Being with you made me feel like the person I always wanted to be. Renovating the house, making love in the afternoon, transforming my hotel dreams from ideas in a notebook to a real life. But what if it's all just a pretty dream and it's time for me to wake up?"

He came after her. "Wait!"

"Please don't." Her voice was high and tight with the effort to hold in sobs. "I don't want to cry in front of you. And my house is torn apart so I can't go home and sob in my own bed like I really, really want to. I need to go home and make Renee think that my day was perfectly boring so she has no reason to ask prying questions. Please."

"Why are you doing this?" he half shouted, frustration cutting through his features. "You shouldn't sell yourself short."

"Let's just walk in opposite directions," she said with a sad smile. "We'll be doing that soon enough as it is."

And with that she took off down the path, not letting tears fall until he was out of sight.

Her phone buzzed.

That wasn't him was it?

She forced back the mental image of him chasing her down on a white horse, brandishing roses, pledging to live in Cranberry Cove and be by her side forever.

It was Jill.

Bree huffed a breath, bringing herself back into the present moment.

If there was ever a time she needed her bestie. But wait…Jill needed *her* right now. She had to be the strong friend for once.

"Hey you," she said in a bright voice.

"Want to meet up and grab a wine at Plonk?" Jill asked. It was Friday night, and bottles were half price at their favorite wine bar on Main Street.

"Aye, aye, captain," she sang out, determined to keep the tone upbeat. "I need to drop Finn off at Renee's house and then I can walk over."

"Okay, let's say thirty minutes."

Bree did a quick change in Renee's spare bathroom, stripping from her sweaty jogging clothes, taking the world's fastest shower, and wiggling into a sunflower-yellow sundress that had a tight bodice and straps wide enough to give her support without a bra. A quick spray of dry shampoo and a furious bout of hair brushing and she was as good as she was going to get.

Thank god Renee was at Hester's because she'd have a million questions.

Bree knew it had been silly to keep her online degree a secret, but it had felt in many ways like if people knew what she'd done, they'd expect things, and what if she couldn't deliver?

But after Jill had the courage to share her painful secret, it was time to come clean.

And that's just what she did the minute she sat down in the sun-dappled bistro table on Plonk's rooftop patio.

Jill processed the news and then reached out and took Bree's hand. "I'm so sorry that you didn't feel okay telling me."

"No. Please don't say that." Bree squeezed her friend's hand. "I'm the one who should apologize. My secret was due to my insecurity and the fact that I was scared to face the pressure of actually chasing my dreams. Your secret was...so painful, honey. I don't know how you didn't shatter."

"Oh, I did," Jill said ruefully. "Every damn night. I'm just really good at supergluing myself back together every morning."

"You've always been the strong one in this friendship. Please trust me to be able to hold up my weight. You can count on me to support you."

"I do," Jill said, leaning forward on her elbows. "You are such a good friend. The problem has been me not trusting myself to be vulnerable. I've had to keep everything on lockdown because otherwise I'm afraid that I'd just roll around town like a basket case."

"Girl, if anyone is allowed to fall apart now and again, it's you. I don't care if it's in Shopper's Corner or the town square. You have earned the right to feel however you need to feel whenever you need to feel it."

"Thanks." Jill took a long sip of her rosé. "I really do mean it."

"Can we make a promise that we'll never keep anything from each other ever again?" Bree asked.

"Deal."

And when they clinked their wineglasses, their eyes were both bright with unshed tears.

"And I have to tell you, having Linda work at Chickadee has been incredible, not just professionally, but for our relationship," Jill said, dabbing her eyes with the corner of her cocktail napkin. "She's an excellent employee, but more important the experience is actually bringing us closer together. I feel like I finally have a mom. Plus with the art fair right around the corner, and the fact I'm closing on the cottage in a couple of weeks, there's a lot going on. With Linda stepping up, I'm not as worried that I'm going to lose my mind."

"I'm so happy for you." Bree topped up Jill's glass. "I've always loved Linda, but I know you have so much history there."

"We do. And there is still a little pain. But how can my future be brighter if I don't let go of hurt? Speaking of which..." She flushed. "Can I tell you why I really asked you here?"

Bree fake pouted. "You mean it's not for my sparkling personality?"

"Well, always that. Here, look at this." She dug in her purse and pulled out a magazine—*Maine Today*. "Go to the dog-eared page."

Bree opened it up and there was an article about spinning wheels and looms. Pretty cool, a woodworker from about an hour away was making them, and the article was about the rise in slow crafting, people spinning wool to make their own yarn. "This sounds awesome, but I have to tell you, I'm totally fine buying my wool. Spinning is a whole other level."

"I wanted to ask what you think of *him*." She pointed at the artist's picture. He looked mid-thirties with a riot of blond-brown curls, a trimmed beard, and kind eyes. His well-worn denim shirt was open at the neck and revealed a flash of chest scruff.

"He's cute in that arty sort of way. Looks like a character. Why?" Jill hadn't asked what Bree had thought about a guy since Simon's death. None of the men she'd dated had rated more than a passing conversation.

"His name is Cooper Haynes. He's coming to the Art Fair. I put him next to Castaway."

Bree frowned. "Are you trying to set me up? He's nice looking but not my type." Her type had ice-blue eyes, expressive brows, and a face that looked equally at home in a boardroom or nestled into her pillow.

"He's *my* type." Jill snatched the magazine, staring down at the photo. "We've been emailing about his booth and then I saw this picture this morning. But I don't want to jinx myself. Doesn't it seem like tempting fate to land my dream house and then have a guy I'm actually interested in?"

"Absolutely not." Bree was firm on this. "This is big. You deserve a crush. And he'll be at the fair. Perfect timing."

"Not perfect at all! The fair is in two days." Jill made a horrified face. "Emails and Internet-picture pining are one thing, but it's different to confront an actual artsy hot guy in person. This is stupid. Tell me that I need to let it go and just focus on running the event, okay?"

"Absolutely not." Bree leaned in on her elbows. "You don't have to jump the guy in his booth, but you owe it to yourself to see if this...interest...is there in real life. Don't overthink. Just see how it goes."

"Don't overthink? You know who you're talking to, right?" Jill groaned, about to say more when a shout drew their attention.

They both glanced down at the parking lot below.

"I'm warning you!" It was Jake Wood. He was leaning over Ashley who was pressed against their Honda CR-V, her face white. "Don't do anything stupid."

"Please," she pleaded in a heartbreaking voice, "I want this to be our home. I don't want people to hate us."

"The only opinion you should care about is mine. And right now, you're in danger of losing it. You screw Kent and I'll make sure you pay. Blood is thicker than water."

"Jake, please stop talking like that. I'm your wife!" She was crying now.

Jill and Bree traded uncertain expressions.

"So start acting like it," he yelled. "Now shut up and get in the car before you make an even bigger scene." He scowled up at Jill and Bree before getting in the car and slamming the door.

"What the heck was that all about?" Jill whispered.

"No clue but, my lord, he's an asshole," Bree muttered back. "Did you hear the way he spoke to her?"

"I should have dumped my drink on him."

"That was awful." Bree furrowed her brows. "I'm worried about her. What should we do?"

Jill thought it over. "Let's reach out. See if she wants to come out with us and Essie. We can try to figure out what's going on with her."

"Good idea. That needs to happen sooner rather than later. On my god, Essie! That's right. I meant to tell you. Oh my gosh, so here's what happened…" She filled Bree in on Essie's encounter with Andrew Weathers and there under the summer sun, for just a liquid moment, they were just two friends, gossiping over wine, and even though the world could be hard, it was always a little easier when shared with a best friend.

# Chapter Twenty-Four

Cranberry Cove's Main Street was abuzz with art fair mayhem. White canvas tents had been erected and vendors were bringing in utility vans to unload everything from landscape portraits to ceramics to whimsical garden decorations, to hand-sewn quilts. Linda was working over at Chickadee. Jill's walking cast was up to the challenge and she had her trusty clipboard checking off vendors as they arrived.

So why did it feel as if her heart were ready to break out of her chest like the Kool-Aid Man busting through a brick wall?

*Oh yeah.*

Because one name didn't have a tick next to it.

She glanced at it for the thirty-second time in an hour.

Cooper Haynes.

This was stupid. So stupid. She was being so stupid. She'd been married, for Pete's sake. She wasn't some insecure high schooler trying to figure out a way to say hi to the cute boy.

Except that's exactly how she felt.

That picture in the magazine. She had nothing to go on but that picture. But the moment she saw it, something shifted inside her heart, and when she read the name, she'd had to sit down.

She tried to let out a breath, remember what Bree said about not pressuring herself, just to see how it all played out. But her chest stayed tight.

This wasn't just a random guy who sparked her attraction. This was an artist whose work she admired, and the first guy to give her any sort of zing since she lost Simon.

"It was probably just a good picture," she muttered to herself, turning around and pacing back to Castaway's booth where Bree and Noreen were almost done arranging skeins of yarn. Cooper's booth was still empty.

Maybe he wouldn't come.

Maybe he was sick.

Maybe he forgot.

She huffed up her bangs.

"You okay there, sweetheart?" Noreen asked, grabbing a feather duster and wiping off a shelf of knitting needles displayed in glass mason jars. "You need an energy bar? I have three in my purse. Keep them for low blood sugar moments."

Bree caught her eye, immediately reading her mind.

"Just setup day jitters," Jill called with forced cheer. "Always a lot going on."

"I saw a woman doing dog portraits when I went to use the bathroom," Noreen added. "Bree, sweetheart, you should get that new pup of yours in for a sitting. It would look really nice in your house. How's that renovation going anyway?"

"I was going to check it out this afternoon." Bree got busy tying her shoe. "I haven't been over there in a week. I need to see their progress, they should be getting close to done."

"Excuse me?" A soft low male voice interrupted them. "I'm here to check in and I was told to find the woman with the clipboard."

Jill turned around and her mouth went as dry as the Sahara Desert.

Cooper Haynes's magazine photo wasn't a fluke. If anything, he looked even better in person. Plaid shirt? Check. His brown beard had little flecks of gold. Good lord, it was a gift he gave his face. It looked soft too. So soft.

His brow furrowed. "You are Jill, right?"

She blinked as Bree came out of the tent. "She absolutely is," her friend declared. "Jill's the fabulous brain behind the Cranberry Cove Art Fair. She can help you with anything and everything you need."

Bree's tone sounded perky and innocent but Jill didn't miss the innuendo underneath. But before she could give the woman a subtle elbow in the ribs, Cooper was reaching out his hand.

"Great to meet you. Glad to finally put a face to the name."

A jolt of heat shot up her arm at the contact, tingly with

awareness. His hand was warm and strong, the pads of his fingers tough with calluses. The kind of hands that would feel deliciously rough on her body, even if they were gentle.

"Face? Name," Jill stumbled, shifted uncomfortably, thankful she still clutched the clipboard so she wasn't reduced to slapping her forehead.

Awkward silence.

"From all our emails?" he prompted gently. "I'm glad to meet you in person."

"Of course! Yes. Me too. So good." She tried to gather her composure. "Shall I show you your location?"

"Sounds great."

She turned and walked four feet to the tent. "Um. It's right here." Good lord, what was she doing? Despite her fantasies, she had the sex appeal of a math book right now.

"Oh." He chuckled. "Well at least it wasn't far. Can I pull up my truck and unload?"

"Yes, here's your event parking pass; this will get you past the barriers," she said handing him a laminated yellow card for his dashboard. But as he reached out to grab it, it slipped through her fingers.

"Let me get it." He grabbed it and stood just as she bent over.

*Crack.*

The back of his head connected with her nose as her glasses went flying. A cascade of blue stars tinkled through her vision that faded to a dull shadow before a burst of pain caused her to almost be sick to her stomach.

"Oh my god!" He fumbled in his back pocket, producing

a red bandanna. "You're bleeding. Use this. It's clean. Promise."

As she pressed it to her bloody nose she didn't know what hurt more, her face or her pride.

"Jill!" Bree bustled over from the next booth. "I'm going to find some ice. I'll be right back. Will you help her find a spot to sit down," she asked Cooper. "She sometimes faints around blood."

She did. Which explained why she was getting woozy.

"Easy now, I've got you." He braced her beneath the arms and lowered her onto the curb. "I have a sister who is the same way. Best thing to do is put your head between your legs and breathe."

She complied. "I'm fine," she muttered. "You don't have to sit here."

"What? And miss my chance to play the hero. No way." He didn't sound like he minded one bit.

Bree came back and handed Cooper the ice. Jill heard the short exchange but refused to look up. If she saw pity in her friend's eyes it would be more than she could handle.

"I'm so sorry," she whispered. "Is your head okay?"

"My mom always said I had a thick skull. Guess she's right. I barely felt a thing. I've got your glasses too, by the way."

She glanced over, beneath the bag of ice, and saw him polishing her lenses on his shirtsleeve. The gesture was so small yet so thoughtful that her eyes prickled.

"Thanks."

"You have beautiful eyes." He gave a wry smile. "Sorry, I'm sure you get that all the time."

"What? No? I do? I mean, I don't. Get that. Not for a long time." She bit the inside of her cheek to quit babbling. "It's nice of you to say so though. Most women could use a compliment when they are sitting, bloody, in a gutter."

"I only pay a compliment if I mean it," he said gravely.

And she was grateful for the ice because at least it would hide her blush. Miracles worked in mysterious ways.

"You should get to unloading," she said. "I don't want to keep you."

"You're funny."

"How?"

The corner of his mouth crooked up. "You keep rushin' me off like I have somewhere I'd rather be."

"Well." She realized she was shuffling her feet and forced herself to quit fidgeting. "Don't you?"

"Nope." He kept his calm, steady gaze locked on her. "This is fine right here."

Maybe he had a concussion. No one was this good in real life. But he seemed as if he meant it and so Jill gave up and decided to take him at his word.

"I was looking forward to meeting you." She removed the ice pack and gingerly prodded the side of her nose. Nothing felt broken. "Your work—I've been admiring it for a few years. I didn't imagine that you'd be so young."

That made him laugh. "I'm forty. Not exactly young."

Ah. He looked younger. But still…he wasn't exactly the kindly grandfather she'd pictured.

"I guess it was the spinning wheels."

"I get that a lot. But I was raised on a homestead. My

parents grew what we ate, in the garden and in the barn. They wanted a simple life for my sister and me, close to the land. My mom took to raising sheep and I decided to make her a spinning wheel one Christmas. I found I had an affinity for it. So that's how I started."

"You sound like a really good son."

"Just one who loves his mama." He sat back, bracing himself with his hands.

His forearms were strong, carved with muscle, and deeply tanned.

And those hands.

She couldn't help but notice them, remember how they felt during their fleeting touch.

"Jill? Jill? Oh there you are, thank god." A local ceramicist bustled over, waving her arms in a flustered gesture. "We need you. Someone has backed into a no-parking zone and left their vehicle with the hazards on. They're blocking people trying to get out."

"No rest for the wicked," she said to Cooper, who was up and offering her a hand before she'd even begun to stand.

"Here you go." He eased the glasses onto her nose with gentle care. "I didn't hurt you, did I?"

"No, I promise." She glanced over to where a small crowd was beginning to argue around the mis-parked mini-van. "Yikes. Looks like they really need me."

"Seems so. Guess I'll see you around, Jill Kelly." And the way he said it made it seem like a promise that he intended to keep.

# Chapter Twenty-Five

B ree felt like a creep but she couldn't stop sneaking looks inside Cooper Haynes's tent. She had never seen her friend like this. Jill had met Simon when she was away at college so seeing her so shatterpated was a revelation of sorts. Her confident bestie became a flustered, frazzled ball of nerves when she was interested in a guy? It was comforting, if not disconcerting, to discover the chink to her armor.

And now Bree was busily gathering intel to make snap judgments on the guy like a best friend should.

So far she discovered that he'd packed a sandwich in a brown bag, which to her best guess was peanut butter and jelly on wheat bread.

Verdict: neutral.

He had a water bottle with a craft brewery bumper sticker on it.

Verdict: positive.

He listened to bluegrass.

Verdict: kind of annoying.

He helped not one, not two, but three older women carry goods to their tents.

Verdict: awesome.

And last but not least he came over and introduced himself before clearing his throat and asking Bree for Jill's phone number.

"And why should I give that to a stranger?" Bree asked, arching a brow, feeling like a stereotypical father figure when a boy turns up to date his daughter.

She'd make this Cooper Haynes work for it. Jill deserved that much.

"I thought I should check up on her. See how she's feeling. She got a hard crack on the head."

"It's sweet of you to ask." Bree pursed her lips. "But don't worry, I can check on her. Make sure that she pops an Advil."

"I gotta say." He wrapped a hand around the back of his neck with a slight grimace. "You're not making this easy."

"I'm her best friend; it's my job to look after her."

He gave an approving nod, respecting the statement. "I appreciate that. And your honesty. So let me get right to the point. I want to ask her to have breakfast with me tomorrow."

"Not dinner?"

"I like pancakes." He shrugged. "Is breakfast weird for a first date? I don't . . . do this a lot."

Her heart melted. Oh my gosh, this earnest guy was charming her socks off. "Breakfast is perfect. She loves the old Redmond Diner on the road coming into town. They do killer wild blueberry pancakes and use maple syrup tapped from the trees on the back of the property. Jill always orders the lobster eggs Benedict so don't let her wimp out and settle for toast or fruit salad."

"I won't." His easy confidence was appealing, so was his friendly face. He might be a little too backwoods-hipster for Bree's taste, but she had a gut feeling that the talented woodworker was a good man.

And she couldn't ask for more than that.

After she gave Cooper Jill's number she set out in search of coffee at Morning Joe's, and paused to read their chalkboard, which changed every morning. Today it read, "Roses are red, violets are blue, I can't rhyme...Give me coffee."

She was still giggling as she stepped inside, narrowly colliding with Ashley Wood, who was standing aimlessly in the middle of the shop.

"Sorry, I didn't mean to mow you down," Bree said. "Are you in line to order?"

"Goodness, I blanked out." Ashley shook her head, the dark circles under her eyes nearly matching her black tank top. Her hair was covered by a silk wrap but the tangled tendrils sneaking out didn't appear as if they'd been brushed in the last few days. "I don't know what to do."

"Well...you normally pick a way to get your caffeine fix." Bree strove for a lighthearted tone. "Some folks like lattes. Others prefer mochas. For me I like a nice flat white, extra hot, two percent milk."

"He left me." Ashley sounded like she was underwater, the words muffled as if she were choking on the consonants.

"Who? Your husband?"

"He disappeared and took everything," she continued. "All the money in our joint account is gone. The Honda. My grandmother's silver spoon collection. The only thing left is the bookstore. Somehow my name is the only one on the lease. I let him handle the arrangements." Her voice rose with panic. "I didn't realize. I didn't know what he was doing."

Wow, what a snake. Bree reached out and took Ashley's too-thin arm and gave what she hoped would pass as a reassuring squeeze. "Let me call my friend Essie. She's the real estate agent who leased the properties in the mill. She'll have some ideas on how to help."

"Bree?" Essie picked up on the first ring. "Speak of the devil, I was just about to call you. Figured you'd better hear it from me."

"Uh-oh." Bree gripped the receiver as her heart sank at Essie's grim tone. She held up a finger to Ashley and walked out of hearing distance. "Do I have to sit down?"

"The Grandview Inn." Essie's voice sounded flat. "It sold today. I wasn't the broker but I heard through the real estate grapevine."

"Oh no! That awful Kent." Ugh. His awful, smug face and greasy, combed-back hair flashed in her mind's eye.

"I don't know much. It's a private company. And a cash offer. It could be someone else."

"Come on. Obviously it's him," Bree said flatly. Her sweet dream had popped. Worse still, the person who popped it also wanted to tear it down. It was just too awful for words. And it was all her fault. If she hadn't lashed out at Chance, maybe he would have finished making suggestions on the business plan and she could have moved forward.

Instead she went and let her stupid self-doubt shoot her in the foot. Hadn't her breast cancer scare taught her anything? What was the point of her anti–bucket list if she wasn't going to really commit?

She glanced away in frustration, her gaze landing on the pale, drawn face of the woman twenty feet away. With a shake of the head, she tried to refocus.

"Not to change the subject, but you know Ashley Wood, right?"

"Bookstore Ashley?" Essie's voice went up a decibel. "She's fantastic. Her husband's a tool like his brother," she muttered. "But keep that opinion on the down low."

"Oh, she knows. Can I give you her phone number? She needs to talk to you about her bookshop lease ASAP."

"Of course." Essie had slipped into real estate mode, the voice of calm reassurance. "Also, one last thing."

"Sure. Anything."

"I . . ." Essie sounded hesitant. "I haven't walked through the fair yet. Is there a glassblower there by any chance? One who is young, a teenager, but has a dad who is six feet, sort of a silver fox?"

Bree frowned. "I'm not sure. I haven't seen one but there's a lot of people here. Why?"

"Oh no big reason," Essie said quickly. "I just know this guy Andrew who has a daughter that does that and I wondered if he was there."

Bree remembered what Jill had told her at Plonk and tried to hide the smile in her voice. "Andrew, huh."

"Never mind. I'm being silly."

Was Essie stuttering?

"No you're not! I will call you if I spy anyone fitting that description," she said slyly, half amused and half concerned for Ashley, who was now pacing around the coffee shop. She looked close to a breakdown. "I gotta go. I'll have Ashley call you."

After she hung up, Bree got Ashely nestled into a quiet spot out back where a row of potted plants afforded some privacy.

"Okay, here's the plan. Contact Essie now and explain your situation with the lease and your husband skipping town. She can help you figure out the best next steps. Also"—she pulled out a pen and scrawled her number and address on a cocktail napkin—"here's how to get a hold of me. Please do. And I'll stop by your shop too, and check in. You won't be alone. We look out for each other around here."

"Thanks." Ashley picked up her phone with a shuddering breath. "I'm so grateful. I really don't want to lose the store. I know it's terrible to admit it, but I loved the idea of that shop, and living here in Cranberry Cove, more than my husband."

"I know we don't know each other well, but obviously there was a lot more to your marriage than met the eye. It's not my business but if you need help or a friendly ear, please think of me."

"That means more to me than you can possibly imagine." Her fingers inched to the phone. "I'll feel better once I know what's happening with the bookstore. Then I can think about how to fix the shambles of my life."

"Good luck, I'll leave you to it. I need to run out and check on the contractors at my house."

What she really needed to do was to tell Chance that the Grandview had been sold. Her world had been shaken to its foundations, and like it or not, in the short time she'd gotten to know him, he'd been a rock. Right now she felt adrift and with any luck a single look from him would give her a much needed anchorage. He was one of the only people in the world who knew how serious she was about her dream, and about her secret degree that had been a way to try to attain it.

Once she was reassured Ashley had Essie on the phone, she was off.

When she arrived at her house, her heart fell a little when Chance's black truck wasn't in her driveway. At least there was the whine of machinery coming from inside the house.

Bounding up the steps, she burst through the front door and pulled up short. Was this really her home? The tired, brown carpet was gone, replaced by a gleaming oak floor. Had that glorious floor been hiding under worn-out Berber carpeting the entire time? The window in the living room had been replaced, turned into a wide and cozy window seat complete with a built in bookcase on one side. She walked into the kitchen and her jaw dropped. It wasn't a total renovation by any means but it was a revelation of color and efficiency. The cabinets had been painted a creamy white, the counters were made from recycled glass and the bottom cupboards near the oven had been replaced with deep-set drawers. No longer would she have to hunch over, straining her back, to find a Tupperware or cast-iron pan.

The drill sound grew louder.

"Hello?" She smoothed her shirt as she rounded the corner.

"Oh, shoot, you startled me!" A guy peered down from a ladder next to a barn door he was installing in the hallway bathroom. A guy who looked so much like Chance and yet was so nothing like Chance.

"Hi, Luke."

"Heya, Bree," he said, lowering the drill. "What do you think?"

"This all is looking absolutely amazing. It's still totally my house and yet it's so much more. It feels like you guys gave the place a new lease on life."

"Glad to hear it." Luke grinned, obviously proud of his handiwork. "That was the idea."

"Sorry to barge in but I'm looking for Chance." She shifted her weight. "Is he around? I was hoping to bend his ear about something."

The smile faded from Luke's face as puzzlement took over. "You mean he didn't tell you?"

Her heart sank. "Tell me what?"

"He went back to New York this morning. Guess that's why he worked well past midnight painting the last few nights. And then this morning he told me he had to go. No warning. Sounded like something was going down that was too important to miss."

"Too important," she said vaguely.

Probably one of those skyscrapers that he loved to design.

In their last conversation she had made it perfectly clear that she couldn't meet him halfway, so he was well within his rights to take off. He didn't owe her more than that.

So then why did she feel so sad?

"Shit." Luke came down off the ladder. "Your face. I'm so sorry that you didn't know. That's not cool to do to you."

"Aw." She flapped her hand, offering a lighthearted gesture. "It's fine. Don't give it a second thought. We hardly knew each other." A lie. The time you knew a person didn't correlate to the depth of the connection. But she couldn't say that here, not to his brother, for Pete's sake.

"But Chance was crazy about you." Luke's brow furrowed.

"Me?" she scoffed. "Yeah right."

"Seriously. You're all he talked about. No offense but it got kind of annoying. No basketball. No Patriots. No fishing. Just Bree this and Bree that. You and that hotel. The Grandview."

"Guess he got both of us out of his system." She shrugged, huffing a laugh although none of this felt funny.

"When I talk to him again, want me to pass along a message for you?"

"No! Please don't mention this conversation. It would make me look so awkward—which I am—but if you could keep that fun fact to yourself I'd really appreciate it."

He mimed zipping his lips. "But I'm shocked he didn't say anything. He's been great to work with this summer, don't get me wrong, but what he did to this house, he was working like a guy possessed. He really cared about making the space perfect for you."

She didn't want to hear any more. In fact, how was she going to come back and live in this house knowing that Chance's fingerprints were all over it? He'd left his mark on her home, just as he had on her body. He was everywhere. And nowhere.

"So…" She jerked her thumb over her shoulder. "I'm gonna go then. Stuff to do."

"Want me to ream him out?" Luke gestured to his phone on the ground. "I can call and holler at him if you want."

"No! It's not like that. Seriously. We had some fun, a few laughs, that was all."

Her lie seemed to appease him because he gave a distracted nod, turning his attention back to the barn door. "I'll be wrapped up here by tomorrow if you want to start moving back in during the afternoon; everything should be ready to go."

"Great. I'm going to feel like a princess in here." She started to back up. "Oh, and Luke? It's cool Chance left. Don't tell him that I was rattled, okay?"

His long gaze was just like his brother's, and like Chance, she couldn't BS him. He knew she was fibbing, but then he gave a curt nod, relenting. He wasn't going to rat her out.

"Don't worry. Never saw you."

"Perfect. And thanks again for everything you did here. It's looking so wonderful, like something out of a home and garden design show."

"It's all Chance. Jerk isn't just a hotshot New York City architect but now he's showing me up here on my own turf." Luke's good-natured smile indicated he was kidding. "But he loves what he does. Needs to run his own show. He's got more talent than is fair."

"It's true," she answered quietly. "He's a good guy."

He shot her another inscrutable look. "The best."

She didn't want to break down in front of this man, even if he was kind. It was just a lot to lose the dream of Grandview and then Chance all in one morning. But what she could do was reclaim some dignity.

Straightening her shoulders, she lifted her chin and pasted what hopefully passed for a believable grin. "Well, keep up the good work. I should get back to my yarn, I've got to finish setting up my shop's booth."

"Is that what all the fuss is downtown? I saw the tents while driving over this morning."

"Oh yeah, I forget you aren't from here. It's the Cranberry Cove Art Fair, *the* summer event. My best friend organizes it. You should come down and walk around, tickets are only five bucks to get in and there are artisans

from all over the state, even some that come down from
Canada and from other parts of New England. It's still on
the small side but it's getting a great reputation."

"I'm not really an arty guy, but sure, why not? Thanks."
He grabbed his water bottle and took a long swallow.

"See you down there," she said, and walked back out the
door and into the sunshine.

She'd come close to losing her heart, but it was better
to have nobody than someone who wasn't all in. Chance
wasn't that guy for her and no amount of wishing was
going to make it so. Just like the inn. In real life, you
don't always get the things that you want, and things don't
always go your way.

She found herself walking in the direction of the lighthouse and along the road, made a point to focus on every
step, every breath. No matter what was going wrong, she
was here. She was alive. And that was what she needed to
celebrate. Not that long ago she wasn't sure if she'd have a
future. If, like her mom, she'd have to exit from the earth
before she was ready to say goodbye. The anti–bucket
list had been a way to reclaim her life, and sometimes
living hurt.

She let herself in through the rusty old gate and caressed
the hydrangeas that grew on the other side of the chipped
picket fence. They'd been there for as long as she could
remember. Maybe her ancestors planted them. She liked
to think of a woman who looked like a mix of Renee and
herself, up here on this barren hill, exposed to the rough
turn of the tides. Perhaps these delicate flowers were her

way of marking her place, providing a little bit of pleasure on her uncertain journey.

The wind was whipping up and it tossed tendrils of hair around her face.

On the other side of the cove was the beautiful old hotel, and between them was the town of Cranberry Cove itself. She could see the white tents on Main Street from here, and in the distance the roof of the Old Red Mill rising from the lush, green forest.

She might be lost in so many ways, but in one way, she could never be. This was home. Her home. And one way or another she'd figure out how to make the life here that she knew she deserved.

# Chapter Twenty-Six

Jill frowned in the mirror, holding a jar of foundation. Luckily the smack to her face hadn't resulted in much more than light bruising on either side of her nose, but still, should she try to cover it up, or would that look too forced and artificial? She put the foundation down and glared at her makeup bag.

Cooper had invited her to a breakfast date before the art fair opening, and while she was excited, nerves were going on and off inside her like a tangle of Christmas lights. She had no idea what to wear, how to style her hair, or what kind of makeup to apply.

"Honey?" Her mom let herself in the front door. Jill didn't mind. In fact, she'd been wondering about offering Linda a room in the cottage once she'd moved in. They weren't exactly the *Gilmore Girls* but she had realized once she gave her mom a chance, she really loved her company.

"Ugh, I'm in here," she called out, tightening the towel around her chest. "I'm having a crisis of confidence. Please help."

"I'm here to the rescue." Linda appeared, leaning against the doorway. "What's going on?"

"I...have a date." She cleared her throat. "Sort of."

"Oh?" Her mom looked like she was swallowing back a smile. "What's a 'sort of date'?"

"A man asked me to breakfast. An artist. From the fair."

"Ah. I see." Linda folded her arms, the silver bracelets on her wrist jangling together. "And you like this man?"

"Maybe? I could." She reached over and grabbed a silky scarf, looping it around her neck, then knotting it, then untangling it and tossing it onto the bed. "Getting ready feels impossible. I mean, I'm just not used to caring what another guy aside from Simon thinks about me, you know? But I think, um, maybe it's a crush." She blushed like crazy. "I think I actually like him and that feels good and terrible, you know?"

Linda nodded. "Can I help you primp?"

"Really?" Jill wanted to hug her. "I normally feel like I am all set in the personal grooming department, but I'm overthinking everything."

"We can do this. You blow-dry your hair and put on that nice rose face cream you love. Leave everything else to me."

Jill hesitated—was this a good idea? Time was ticking down. What if Linda made her look like a laughingstock and there was no time to change?

But her mom's expression silently said "Trust me" and so Jill gave up and gave in. "Okay, just please make me look...pretty."

Her mom gave a gentle smile. "That's easy, honey. You're already pretty."

"Thanks but you're my mom. That's what you're supposed to say."

"Maybe, but that doesn't stop it from being true." She clicked her heels and gave a mock salute. "Permission to raid your closet?"

"Aye, aye." Jill giggled as she pulled out the hair dryer and her favorite mousse.

After she had her hair under control, she walked into her room. On her bed her mom had laid out a wrap denim skirt and paired it with a pretty peony sleeveless blouse and her favorite nude-colored summer sandals with the dainty scalloped edges.

"Yes." She clapped her hands. "That's perfect. It's cute and doesn't look like I'm trying too hard. Now I just need to decide if I should wear earrings or not."

"I was wondering if you'd consider these," her mom said, shyly handing her over a small fabric bag.

"What's this?" Jill emptied the contents into her palm. They were adorable boho tassel earrings with fun geometric beading; the pastel colors would complement both the top and her rose-gold hair. "Wow. I love them. Where are they from?"

"My living room," Linda said quietly. "Remember how I told you I made jewelry?"

Jill did. And she remembered how she'd dismissed the

idea out of hand, believing that her mom wouldn't be up to her standards, either for the fair or her store.

Guess she'd need to find a hat and eat it.

"Mom." Jill shook her head, needing to put this right. "I'm so sorry that I didn't ask to see your work. You're amazing and I'm a jerk."

"No, you aren't. When you didn't seem excited about me applying to be at the fair, I didn't push it. I know I bear a lot of the responsibility for why our relationship was strained in the first place. But now it means so much to know that you like them. I have a blast making jewelry."

"You can tell. These are really fantastic. We could sell them in Chickadee and they would go like hotcakes."

Linda's eyes widened. "You really think so?"

"Absolutely." Jill slid her arm around her mom's waist and squeezed. "I hate that I didn't take you seriously when you told me the first time. I want to see everything you've made. There's real talent here."

Linda clapped a hand over her mouth and squealed.

"Are they all this fabulous?"

Her mom nodded proudly.

"Good lord, you are going to make a fortune." Jill couldn't resist hopping on the balls of her feet.

Linda's cheeks flushed as her eyes went bright. "I just want to help your store be successful."

"We are a good team, you know that?"

"Oh honey, my heart is so full." She gave Jill a quick hug and then nudged her to the bed. "Okay, get dressed so you aren't late."

When Jill came out into the living room in her cute outfit and earrings she almost felt confident enough to rock this date.

But her mom was frowning.

"What's wrong?" Jill took a step back.

"You look lovely, but there's something missing." Linda reached into her purse and pulled out a tube of lipstick. "Try this. You used to wear this color all the time. I loved it so much I bought one for myself. It glams up your whole look."

Jill took the lipstick and read the name. Vixen. The shade that Simon used to love. The color that she'd put in her trash can not so long ago believing that she'd never need it again.

"I don't know, Mom."

"What's the harm of putting it on? You have time to wipe it off if it's not for you."

"Okay, okay. Let me see how it looks." She walked to the living room mirror and looked at her reflection, wide-eyed, excited, and scared. She applied the bright color and smacked her lips and there she was, the woman that she hadn't seen in years: sexy, confident, and ready to accept and receive love.

"See what I mean." Her mom laughed. "Now you're ready. Go knock this poor man's socks off."

"I don't even know who I am right now," Jill said in a wondering tone. In many ways she felt like Cinderella getting ready for the ball.

Her mom grabbed her shoulders and pressed her

forehead to hers. "You are a beautiful, talented, smart, funny woman. Everyone you meet glows brighter because of your light. You've gone through hell, but you're finding your way again."

Jill's throat tightened. "Thanks, Mom. And thanks for loving me no matter what."

"Always and forever." Linda kissed her cheek.

Jill got to Redmond Diner ten minutes early, wincing as she glanced at the watch on her Fitbit. So much for being fashionably late, she was more like an eager beaver.

But there Cooper was, in a corner booth, the small, intimate one built for two, and he held up his hand in greeting.

"You're already here," Jill said as she approached.

"I heard they make great blueberry pancakes, and I'm something of a connoisseur." He slid out and to her surprise went in for a hug, nothing gropy, just a quick sweet embrace. "Just kidding. I was excited to see you. Maybe I'm not supposed to admit that but screw it, I am."

"I like honesty." She slid into the bench across from him.

"Good. Me too." He fiddled with his fork, tapping his thumb over each tine. "I have a confession to make."

"Go ahead."

"I looked you up on the Internet before I got to Cranberry Cove." He cleared his throat. "I liked your tone in your emails and I was curious. And when I saw you? Whoa. I just wanted to meet you."

She stared at him. "You're kidding."

He met her gaze. "Not even a little. Honesty, remember?"

"This is going to sound crazy but I did the same thing to *you*."

He dropped his fork. "No."

She started laughing. "Sort of!" She tossed her hair over one shoulder. "I saw your picture in *Maine Today*. The profile piece they just did on you. I recognized your name and then I couldn't stop looking at the photos. I felt so weird doing it but I couldn't help it."

The waitress approached to take their drink order.

"Coffee, black with cinnamon," they both said at the same time.

"Aren't you two the cutest," the waitress muttered, unable to restrain an eye roll as she walked away.

"How did you know how I drink my coffee?" she demanded.

"I didn't. I ordered how I drink mine." They both smiled and it felt like they had known each other for a minute and years all at once.

"So what's the deal? Do you have a dozen ex-wives buried in your backyard? A secret career as an assassin for a nefarious foreign government? Put it out there. Tell me your worst." She was rambling and couldn't stop herself.

He frowned. "I'm not sure what you mean."

"You can't be this perfect." That's it, she needed a muzzle.

"What?" He settled back into his chair with an amused snort. "I'm nowhere close to perfect."

She arched a brow. "Convince me."

"I'm told I snore if I get a cold." He gave his beard a

thoughtful stroke. "I love my work, and sometimes when I'm in the zone I forget to eat or sleep. I get grumpy in the winter, but I love Christmas."

"How is that not perfect?"

"Oh and my sister lives next door to me and my parents live across the street. I've had girlfriends not like how close we all are."

"No ex-wives?"

"Nope." He hesitated. "I know about your husband, Simon. I'm sorry. I read an article about his accident when I was looking you up."

"I loved him." She sighed deeply. "He was a good man."

"I'm glad." He didn't break eye contact. "And I don't want you to feel like I'm coming on too strong."

"I can't pretend that my heart isn't scarred and that the idea of caring deeply for another person doesn't scare me. But maybe my scarred little heart is stronger than I realized, and I have more to give."

He sat back, openly admiring her.

"What?" She touched the side of her cheek with the tips of her fingers.

"You might be the strongest woman that I've ever met."

She winced. "Please don't put me on a pedestal. All I've done is try to survive the hand dealt to me."

"I don't think that's it at all." He gave a small shake of his head. "But I won't sit here and embarrass you either." He pushed a menu at her. "A little bird told me you have a thing for lobster eggs Benedict here."

"Bree." Jill didn't even have to ask.

"That's how I got your number. She's a good friend."

"The best," Jill corrected. "I know people say diamonds are a girl's best friend, but they've got it all wrong. A girl's best friends are the real diamonds."

He grinned and the crackling, no-words-to-explain-it magnetic energy flowing between them threatened to light up the eastern seaboard. As their eyes locked, she was lost, in the sort of way that finally felt like being found. And if she leaned in to that feeling, maybe her whole world would change.

# Chapter Twenty-Seven

Hey, lady, got change for a twenty?" A man wearing a University of Maine Black Bears football jersey waved the bill under Bree's nose.

She frowned at his pushy gesture, as well as Andrew Jackson's windblown hair from her perch inside the art fair entrance ticket booth. *Here we go again*, she thought. *Does no one carry fives anymore?* The small bills in the metal cashbox were starting to run low. She'd volunteered for the morning shift to sell tickets as a favor to Jill, and was happy to do so, but it would be nice if more people said please and thank you. Some of these out-of-towners seemed to be born in a barn.

She gave the man his change and took a sip from her stainless steel travel mug, grimacing at the coffee. Great. It had gone cold and there wasn't even anywhere to heat it up nearby. A bee buzzed by her ear and she swatted it away;

she hated when their little stingers got too close. The sun was just peeking over the buildings, in the perfect position to shoot rays straight into her eyes. A seagull circled overhead and she squinted at it with menace. "Don't even think about it, bub."

She grabbed a marker and made a small sign: "Need small bills please!!" She added the second exclamation mark for good measure.

For Pete's sake, she gave a rueful smile at her grumpiness as she taped the sign to the counter. Might as well admit she'd been in a funk since yesterday, upon learning that Chance had skipped town without saying so much as a "see ya later, alligator," and that no one, not even his brother seemed to know the real story as to why. And then there was the matter of the Grandview getting bought by Evil Kent. It didn't seem fair; it sucked when bad guys won the day, and yet reality was reality. No point crying over spilled milk and no getting around the truth.

But how was she ever going to stomach watching the beautiful old dame of Cranberry Cove be bulldozed to the ground to make way for an ultramodern lighthouse concept? The very idea made her skin crawl.

"Change for a twenty?" a deep voice asked.

It took everything she had not to groan out loud.

"See the sign? I can't break that right now, sorry," she mumbled, focusing on her cute dusky-pink slip-on shoes rather than another guy who apparently thought the rules didn't apply to him. "I really don't have any more change. You are welcome to walk across the street to Shopper's

Corner and make a small purchase. Once they break that twenty, mosey on back, and I'll sell you a ticket."

"Keep it, and consider it a donation to the cause of supporting local artists."

She froze, finally registering the deep voice. But she didn't want to look up in case she was wrong, so she kept her head down, tucking her chin protectively to her chest as she took a long, deep breath and then another.

Chance. He wasn't gone. He was here, just a few feet away.

"I heard you left," she said quietly.

"I did. I had unfinished business down in New York." He slid the crisp bill across the counter. "I'm serious, keep the whole amount. I want to support the art fair."

"I didn't think you were coming back. I...well, I went to my house. I wanted to talk to you but your brother said you had split and weren't coming back."

"Oh, no." Chance's eyes widened in understanding. "I didn't mean to worry anyone. I told him that I had to go; guess I should have been clearer. I did have some unfinished business and my top priority was well...finishing it. I drove to Boston, caught a flight to New York, and got back here as soon as I could. Guess I didn't take the time to properly talk to Luke. To you. To anyone. I've just been in go mode. I'm sorry."

"Go mode, I see." She studied his features, the small nick on his cheekbone where he must have cut himself shaving, the wide set to his shoulders, the slightly crooked incisor. All the little details she loved. "Where are you going?"

"Nowhere now. I want to stay here in Cranberry Cove if you'll have me." He took her hand. "Bree, I have a question to ask you."

Her heart escalated even as she fought back a rising panic. He wasn't going to do some over-the-top public proposal, was he? He couldn't. That wasn't his style. Besides, they weren't ready for that.

"Chance...I don't know what you are doing."

"Please hear me out." He took a deep breath. "Bree Robinson. Will you go into business with me?"

"Huh?" The idea was so far-fetched and unexpected that she offered a little giggle. "What in heavens are you talking about?"

"The Grandview. I bought it. That's why I went to New York, to get my funds together and close the deal. Your business plan convinced me. I might have told a white lie when I said that I was editing it. In reality, it's an incredible investment opportunity and I decided to sell some assets to make it happen."

Her jaw dropped. If someone poked her with a seagull feather she'd collapse right there. Instead she reached back, took hold of the long French braid going down her back, and wrapped it around her shoulder, hanging on as if it were a lifeline.

"*You* bought the inn?" she stammered when she finally found her voice. "I don't get it. Why?"

"You made me fall in love with the place, just like I'm...." He hooked a hand around the back of his neck. "Oh hell, I might as well admit it. I'm falling in love with you too,

Bree. After the divorce, I let my ex buy me out of the business and I've had quite a good nest egg socked away waiting for the right investment. I want it to be the Grandview, and I'm asking you to be my copartner, to serve as the general manager. Together we'll make the perfect team."

"You want to hire me?"

"No." He reached out and laced his fingers with hers. "I'm talking about co-ownership. Fifty-fifty. I've got the cash, but I don't have the time. I'm going to relocate my work here, but I'll still be taking on architecture clients. I want you to be more than a worker. I want you to have a stake. Nothing would give me more pleasure than making all your dreams come true."

Her peripheral vision got fuzzy. "I don't know what to say."

"My lawyers are ready to draft up the arrangement. I'm serious. I want you as my partner."

"I can't believe this is real." She pressed her lips tight and shook her head. "I could kiss you until you can't breathe."

"Sounds good to me." His smile turned wolfish, even as he stroked her cheek. "I didn't come up to Cranberry Cove to find love, but you cracked my heart wide open. If this path isn't for you, I'll walk away right now. No harm, no foul, but I will say this. From the first time I saw you in those hot-as-hell boots at the bar, I tried to keep you at arm's length. I told myself I was being realistic. But I can't deny the truth. I want to be here with you, working side by side, loving side by side, for as long as you'll have me."

Bree pinched her arm, a hard little squeeze, and yelped in pain.

Nope. She wasn't dreaming. This was real. He was here offering to make all of her dreams come true. This was a man who would always encourage her to live out loud, to let her dreams be as big as her imagination.

"I have to read over the agreement, but yes, what you are offering is amazing."

"You'll have complete say in how the hotel is run, and we can agree on designs together for the renovation. We can give Grandview a great update, but one that will keep her bones, will let her retain her character for another generation. I happen to know an architect who can draw up plans to knock your socks off."

She blinked, a slow smile spreading over her face. "Mr. Elliston. Are you telling me that everything I want is within reach?"

"Just like I learned." Chance's own smile was crooked, his delicious dimple waiting to be kissed. "It's all waiting on the other side of fear."

"Yes!" Bree blurted, every molecule of her body certain this was the right step. This was a leap of faith, but one she was ready to go for because at the end of the day, she was alive, and she wanted to. Two great reasons to do anything.

She opened the ticket booth and flew into Chance's arms, not caring who stared as he slanted his warm, soft lips over her own. He tasted like cinnamon gum, coffee, and the future.

"What about Kent Wood?" she asked when they finally

pulled apart, coming up for air. "I thought he'd bought the Grandview for sure."

"He wanted to all right but I suspected he was scrambling to come up with cash. I had liquid assets so was able to make the offer first. But when I was driving back up here this morning, my lawyer called. Guess Kent's fled the country. Looks like he had some real estate investments down in Florida that weren't on the right side of the law. The feds closed in and he skipped off down to South America. Sounds like Cranberry Cove dodged a bullet in more ways than one."

"Oh my gosh, I wonder if his brother went with him," she said. "Jack has skipped town and taken all of the life savings he shared with his wife. It's a terrible story."

"Wouldn't surprise me," Chance said grimly. "Where there's smoke, there's fire. I hope his wife gets some answers soon. And justice."

"Me too, but I have to say, good riddance to the Woods." Bree leaned forward and rested her forehead against Chance's shoulder, closing her eyes and breathing him in. "As for us..."

"Yeah?" His arms went around her waist, giving her a gentle squeeze. "God, I love hearing you say 'us.'"

She smiled into his shirt. "Not as much as I love saying it."

He pressed his lips into the top of her head. "Deep down I knew that I could never just be friends with you, you're too damn wonderful. So then I figured, why not friends with benefits?"

"A summer fling."

"Except what I really want here, blondie, is a forever thing."

She caressed the line of his face, imprinting the contours into her heart. "Me too."

"Bree?" Jill's voice pulled her out of the moment.

They turned to find her bestie, Essie, and Renee gaping at them. She gave him a sideways glance. "If you are serious about forever, there is something else that you need to know."

"Oh yeah?" He slung his arm around her shoulders. "What's that?"

"These three come with me. We are kind of a package deal." She beamed at the women standing there trying to pretend they weren't eavesdropping.

"Ladies," Chance said, pretending to tip his hat.

"You're looking at the new official co-owners of the Grandview Inn," Bree blurted. "He bought it and we're going to run it together. It's really happening. I get to manage the Grandview."

"Girl, that's amazing," Essie shrieked.

"Heck yes," Jill screamed as Renee clapped a hand over her mouth saying, "Oh my," over and over.

Bree stepped forward and opened her arms, laughing as they both came in for the biggest hug of her life. As Renee, Essie, and Jill breathlessly asked a dozen questions all at once, Bree smiled over at Chance, who watched the scene with open amusement.

"I'm so thrilled for you." Renee was practically bouncing up and down.

"Honey," Jill said. "Do you realize that you took that

anti–bucket list by the tail and turned it into a whole new life?"

Bree laughed as her "You Got This" bracelet caught the sun and gleamed. "I guess anything is possible if you have the right people to support you along the way."

"I'm so glad you found love," Essie said wistfully, giving her a tight hug, a surprise as her friend was never a hugger or wistful.

Then Jill was spinning her around. "You haven't just found your wings, you've taken off."

"You've helped me fly hiiiiiiigher than an eagle," Bree belted out in an exaggeratedly off-key voice before squeezing her with all her might.

And together their laughter rose in the warm, salt-kissed breeze.

# *Epilogue*

*Six months later...*

C an you please hand me another one of those cranberry-turkey sandwiches?" Chance eyed the paper plate brimming with the thick-cut baguettes. "I think these need to go on the inn lunch menu next summer, what do you think?"

"Absolutely." Bree nodded. "We should do a whole cranberry theme. Ooooh and we should commission Renee to create us a signature pie."

"You are a genius."

"Sometimes." She passed him another piece of bread and leaned back on her mom's old quilt that they had spread over the sunroom floor in the inn. Behind the canvas drop cloth, Luke and his work crew hammered away. Outside the window, a cold glittery sun made the ocean shine.

Chance had decided to surprise her for Valentine's Day with a sweet picnic here in the inn. Chance had worked over the designs like a man possessed and in the end created a plan that honored Grandview's history as Cranberry Cove's beloved icon, while ensuring the rooms and facilities were up to twenty-first-century standards. They were putting spa baths in all fifteen bedrooms as well as replacing the windows to make sure their future guests would have unobstructed views of the sea. There would also be a small commercial kitchen where they'd hire a cook to make breakfasts and hors d'oeuvres for the wine hour. Ashley Wood, who'd been slowly coming out of her shell as her divorce progressed, had offered to stock a small library too, with an arrangement that Bree would send guests to the Old Red Mill in return—a deal Bree had happily agreed to.

She was just letting her lids close, drifting into a delicious afternoon nap when she heard Chance's startled yell.

Bolting up, she saw Finn, who had been pretending to snooze beside her, sneak the last sandwich and then tear off in a run.

"You little thief!" Chance shouted in good-natured exasperation. "I wanted that."

"Maybe if you didn't always spoil him," Bree pointed out laughing. "You know he hates his dog food so don't think I don't see you sneaking him little treats. Now he's marked you for a sucker."

"I guess he has me pegged." Chance grabbed her by the waist and tickled her until she shrieked. "I'm a sucker for him just like I'm a sucker for his mom."

"That's all right with me."

"I want to give you something." He reached into his pocket and pulled out a brown box tied with a thin ribbon.

She opened it and found a gold bracelet, much like the one she always wore. Except this one read, "She said she would, so she did."

Tears pricked in her eyes. "I love it. And you."

"Me too. So damn much. That's why I have this too." He reached into his other pocket, and pulled out a small, black velvet box.

Her heart stopped as she reached out with trembling hands. She popped the lid and there, sparkling as bright as their future, was a perfect engagement ring, elegant and simple with a white gold band and a single emerald-cut diamond.

"I don't just want you as my girlfriend and business partner, I want you for my life partner, not fifty-fifty, but a hundred-hundred," he said in a gruff voice. "I came to Cranberry Cove thinking I'd lost my way, but really fate was just leading me to you. Please be my wife."

"A thousand times yes," she whispered as he slid it on her ring finger. "It's gorgeous."

"Not even a fraction as gorgeous as you, blondie." And his gentle kiss was sweet with the promise of forever.

* * *

Jill hit the seat warmer in her car. Despite the February sunshine, it was still Maine after all, and she did love her heat. Cooper had invited her to come out for a Valentine's Day dinner at his house and tomorrow she'd finally meet his family. They had been taking things slow; super slow, but that was the perfect pace for her. He was everything she could want, patient, sweet, fabulously creative. For Christmas he'd built her a kitchen table for her new cottage and every morning as she sat and had her coffee, she ran her hands over the lines of the wood, unable to fully believe that she was finally moving forward.

As she rounded the bend, she glanced up the snow-covered hill to the Cranberry Cove cemetery, quiet under the thick snow. While she couldn't see it, Simon's headstone was finally there, with his birth and death dates carved into the simple granite, along with the lines from the famous E. E. Cummings poem they both had loved:

*i carry your heart(i carry it in my heart)*

And she did. And as she let Cooper in, and Linda, she had discovered the most profound truth of all. A heart is a magical organ that can expand to infinite sizes, the harder you love with it, the more it can hold.

"Love ya, babe," she whispered, blowing Simon a kiss. And then she drove past the town limits to where her future was waiting.

Single mom Renee Rhodes is adrift with her daughter away at college. When she unexpectedly bonds with her neighbor Sadie, the two women hatch a plan to open the bakery Renee has always wanted. But can Renee summon the courage to both follow her dreams and explore her attraction to the dreamy Dr. Dan?

Renee's and Sadie's stories are available in the first Cranberry Cove book, *Forever Friends*! Please turn the page for an excerpt.

# Chapter One

Sadie Landry sliced a handful of strawberries to stir into her toddler's Greek yogurt cup, absently humming along to the Pop 4 Kids playlist on the iPhone she'd propped against a stack of picture books. As she peeled back the foil top, the scent of sour dairy roiled her stomach, and she lurched with a gag. Good lord, had it gone bad? She checked the expiration date. Two weeks away.

*Weird.* Since when had the scent of yogurt become so nasty? Lincoln wolfed it down for breakfast every morning and she loved adding it to her strawberry-banana smoothies.

"Mommy! I make the pee-pee!" Lincoln had started stringing sentences together a few weeks ago. His adorable squeak still came as such a surprise that it took an extra second to register that these particular words were the polar opposite of delightful.

She glanced at the "Keep Calm and Carry On" print hanging on the kitchen wall. Was momsanity a diagnosable condition? *Hmmmm.* Something to research during naptime. Right now it was time to refocus on her nearly two-year-old, nearly potty-trained son tugging at the waistband of her leggings, his hazel eyes dead ringers for Ethan's, constantly shifting from green to brown to gold.

"Mommy? You hear me right now?"

It'd be great if her husband was here and not down in Boston, two hundred miles away.

She tossed the yogurt in the trash, just in case it *was* rancid. "You made a pee-pee?"

"Yep!" Then he hunched, crestfallen. "But not in potty."

"Oh." *Shit.* She tried channeling her inner Mary Poppins, despite the headache that had been nagging her since she woke up. "Um, well...mistakes allow thinking to happen."

He wrinkled his nose. "What you say?"

"Never mind." So much for staying up last night studying *Communicating Positively with Your Toddler.* The tips that seemed so practical on the page at ten thirty felt ridiculous in practice today.

"Come see. Come see. Dis way." He bolted from the kitchen.

She shoved her iPhone into her demi-cup bra—thank God she was wearing one—and gave chase. *Please not the sofa. Anywhere but the sofa.* While the midcentury loveseat complemented the cottage's nautical theme, it turned out that white wool wasn't exactly a toddler-friendly choice.

Mom fail.

Or maybe it was karma being a bitch. After all, scrolling through her former design firm's Instagram feed a few minutes ago was in clear violation of her New Year's resolution to live more in the present. But after noticing the foyer's dust bunnies had not only colonized, but were enjoying a population explosion under the shoe storage bench, she'd found herself escaping through the personal account of her replacement at Urban Interior Studios.

In hindsight, a mistake in more ways than one. Emma Finley wasn't just leggy and platinum, but she'd also nabbed a coveted design award for a hot new sushi restaurant concept in Providence. And had that been Emma's Seaport townhome with the wrought-iron fireplace and a Jo Malone candle burning in the background? Good grief— how much was the firm paying her? When Sadie had worked for the group, she'd felt fortunate to afford the rent on a poky South Boston studio.

Her lips crooked up at the memory of her old place with its claw-foot tub and creaky floors. Even after a long day, Sadie would always stroll the three blocks down to M Street Beach to read a few chapters on a park bench.

Ethan had asked her to marry him in that apartment, her back pressed against the Formica countertop while he kneeled on the kitchen rug.

She furrowed her brows.

If Ethan had proposed two and a half years ago, that meant she'd been gone from the firm for how long now? Two years?

Yep. Almost to the day.

Just then, her boob buzzed. Tugging her phone back out, Ethan's name appeared on her screen.

"Honey. Hi." Sadie instinctively smoothed a hand over her messy bun. Down the hall, Lincoln hopped from foot to foot, motioning for her to join him. Was it worth telling her husband that his first-floor office might have sprung a leak? A Lincoln-sized leak.

"How'd your meeting go?"

"Mommy! I say come see this silly pee-pee!" Lincoln called. "I still get M&M?"

She'd gobbled the last of the potty-training treats for breakfast. *Oops.*

"Sore subject," Ethan groaned. "The meeting was a bust."

Her husband was currently splitting time between his remote home office in Maine and his company's corporate headquarters in Boston. The fall and holidays had gone fine with Ethan only making the trip a handful of times. Unfortunately, with January's arrival came a slew of reasons for Ethan to be on-site. At this point he was traveling to Boston every week, often for days at a time. Not the plan they'd made when deciding to relocate.

"What a bummer. You were so excited about the presentation." Sadie racked her brain, unable to recall exactly what he'd been working on this month. He was a hustler, eternally developing new products for his tech company, his can-do attitude the reason why he'd scrambled up the corporate ladder, impressing managers at every level.

That was, until his recent boss.

"Marlow stood me up."

She could hear the exasperation in his voice and clearly pictured the hand he must be raking through his wavy brown hair. "Turns out the bastard ditched our one-on-one to take a client to Palm Beach on the company jet."

Sadie had a mental flash about being whisked away on a Gulfsteam, sipping a mimosa and nibbling a cheese plate, before blinking back to reality.

"That sucks. But he probably acts like this because he's threatened by your talent."

"You think?" Ethan didn't sound so sure.

"I know." She frowned at her Fitbit watch. Ten fifteen already? Seriously? Where had the morning gone? "Look, it's either that, or he has an asshole gene. His ancestors probably burned witches or took part in the Spanish Inquisition."

Ethan chuckled, and Sadie smiled at the receiver. She hadn't made her husband laugh much lately and the infectious rumble swelled her heart.

Unfortunately, they'd have to reconnect tonight. She still had to uncover Lincoln's pee and hightail him to his two-year checkup that was in fifteen minutes at the Coastal Kids Medical Group.

"Hey, tell you what. Let's pick this back up when you get home," she said in her most soothing tone, just as Lincoln crashed into her knees. "Whoa, bud! Crap, that hurt!"

She yanked her toddler back with a gasp. He'd been out of her sight for what? Three minutes? And in that time, he'd managed to unearth her favorite lipstick and cover his chest in red streaks. He'd even pulled off a Jackson Pollock–inspired art scene over the foyer's creamy damask wallpaper.

That's it. They might as well move to a barn.

"Lincoln, no! Bad! Bad, bad, bad!" Her low-grade headache ratcheted up a notch. "Seriously, what the f-f-frog?"

Her last-minute save didn't stop her son from bursting into startled sobs.

It wasn't an official f-bomb, but it came close. The last thing she needed was Lincoln roaming the playground while swearing like a sailor.

"No, no. I'm sorry. I didn't mean you are bad. You're a good boy. The best boy ever. But that's Mommy's nice wall. Drawing is for paper. Drawing on a wall is bad."

"Sade? You two okay over there? Is Lincoln hurt?"

"He's fine. We're fine." She engulfed Lincoln in a hug, pressing her cheek to his soft chestnut curls, willing him to calm down.

"Cool. Cool. So I've gotta jet, but remember what my mom says—they call it the terrible twos for a reason, right?"

Sadie tried to laugh. It came out like a donkey's death rattle.

"Hey, why don't you give her a call? She'd love to give you some advice."

*Oh, wouldn't she?*

Sadie would rather cannonball butt naked into the frigid ocean out her bay window than discuss parenting strategies with her mother-in-law. Yes, Annette Landry had raised three healthy, successful adults, and she'd enjoyed doing it, too. No, she had *loved* it. Staying at home was "such a precious gift." Something she "never dared to take for granted."

She probably mopped up potty accidents in her signature twin-set, too, complete with the pearl earrings and perfectly applied mascara.

Sadie, on the other hand, had found her yoga pants and sweatshirt so comfy yesterday that she'd slept in them...and was still wearing them today.

Underwear included.

A fact that would make Annette's sculpted bob stand on end.

But while Annette might get on her nerves, her mother-in-law had raised the man of her dreams. And that had to count for something.

"Your mother will be here in the morning for Lincoln's party. I'll borrow her ear then." She prayed she sounded halfway chipper. "Drive safe, honey. I'll see you tonight."

They hung up, an absentminded "love you" on both ends.

* * *

Fortunately, the misaimed pee-pee had ended up in the bathtub.

Unfortunately, removing the lipstick from a squirming child's torso was going to have to count as her day's cardio. There really should be an energy drink named "Toddler." In the end, she resorted to pouring makeup remover over a hand towel and rubbing it against Lincoln's baby-soft skin.

As for the wallpaper, well... she'd figure that out when she got back home.

Tugging a superhero shirt over his head, she gave both his dimples a noisy smooch that sent him giggling. "Next time you're curious about one of Mommy's things, you need to come and ask my permission to play with it. Okay, bud?"

He nodded shyly. "Kay."

She helped him into his parka before deciding her hoodie could ward off the spring chill just fine. So much for waltzing into the doctor's office with an insulated mug of coffee and perfectly flat-ironed hair. Popping two ibuprofens and smearing on some deodorant would have to count as a win.

As the idyllic, seaside cottages blurred past her minivan window, she tried to practice gratitude. Cranberry Cove wasn't just a postcard-perfect Maine village, but her hometown. When Ethan had bought the Brewer place—formerly her beloved grandma's home—as a surprise wedding gift, she'd blamed her tears on the fact that she was eight and a half months pregnant and busting out of her bridal gown. She knew she was lucky to raise her son in a place right down the block from where she'd grown up and where he could enjoy some of her happiest childhood memories, like collecting seashells and licking butter off her fingertips during summer lobster bakes.

She glanced at Lincoln in the rearview mirror. He had

a cardboard book about monkeys propped open in his lap and was examining the pages with such focus, she almost believed he could read the words. Like Ethan, he was an overachiever, already learning his ABCs and counting to twenty. He was cranky if he missed a nap, and certainly a handful at times, but what toddler wasn't? He also gave smiles, giggles, and generous hugs.

And sure, maybe he was a budding graffiti artist (he'd really gone wild with that lipstick) and the root cause of her perpetual exhaustion, but he was also the reason she climbed out of bed each morning. She loved him beyond the power of words.

Was she happy? Grateful? Fulfilled?

Of course.

She was beyond lucky. She had everything a person could ever want.

She nabbed the last spot in the town's municipal parking lot. Okay, she had everything except time. Still, she stole a few more seconds to wipe the sleep crusties from the corners of her eyes and apply a quick coat of Burt's Bees lip gloss. No need to tell the world that her last bath was with a handful of baby wipes.

Where was that woman who used to strut into client meetings wearing four-inch, cherry-red heels and deliver design pitches like it was what she'd been born to do?

Stay-at-home motherhood hadn't just knocked her down a peg; it had dumped her off the stool and doused her in finger paint.

As long as she could remember, she'd dreamed of being

a mom. She'd fantasized about cute names, nursery decor, and tiny outfits. She'd dreamed about how the baby's hair would smell after a bath or how they would cling to her pinkie finger while napping on her chest.

Turned out that she'd fallen in love with a Pottery Barn version of parenthood.

The reality was that her pelvic floor had been destroyed by a thirty-six-hour labor of a nine-pound-ten-ounce baby, postpartum depression had hit her like a Mack truck, and she still tinkled when she sneezed. She'd been puked on, pooped on, and every night when her head hit the pillow she'd wonder how the heck she'd crossed only a few to-do items off her list.

Parenting wasn't just work—that she could handle—it was how it was a mirror reflecting all her shortcomings: impatience, selfishness, vanity, and anxiety.

But she'd turn this ship around. She *had* to. Failure wasn't an option. So she straightened her slouch and pasted on a determined smile, ignoring the part of her that screamed, "I don't know what the hell I'm doing and the idea of screwing up terrifies me."

"Okay, lady, get it together."

Who'd gotten accepted into the New York School of Design? Who'd been a successful professional? This was just wrangling one kid—not rocket science, for Pete's sake. Mothers have mothered for millennia. She'd done her fair share of babysitting as a teen. Time to quit worrying and get it together.

"Whaddya say to hitting the 'restart' button?" she said

to Lincoln, unclipping him from his car seat. He relaxed in her arms and she touched the tip of her nose to his, relieved he didn't seem scarred from her earlier freak-out. "Onward and upward, right, love bug?"

Propping Lincoln on her hip, she made her way toward the Coastal Kids Medical Group.

Until Dot Turner stepped into her path after a scant ten feet.

"Sadie, darlin'. How's it going?" she drawled in her thick Maine accent, punctuating each word with a thrust of her five-pound hand weights. Dot was in her seventies now and had been Sadie's middle-school gym teacher. She still wore her signature neon-pink tracksuit and was probably in even better shape than she'd been fifteen years ago. "Heya, Link."

Sadie hid her wince. The nickname always made her think of breakfast sausage. And just now the idea of processed meat made her want to barf.

"Hi, Ms. Turner." Sadie smiled weakly, pretending that her stomach hadn't just randomly decided to exit through her mouth. Had she undercooked the chicken last night? "I know, I know...I should call you Dot. But old habits die hard. How are you?" Running into old teachers was one of the weird but enjoyable side effects of moving back to Cranberry Cove.

"I'm grand," Dot panted. "Just grand. Training to solo hike the Appalachian Trail this June. Ain't that something?"

"Wow," Sadie said breathlessly. "Impressive."

"Ayuh, another one for the bucket list. Say, you should

join me for a jog sometime." Dot winked. "Everyone with a pulse should be able to run three miles. Use it or lose it, kiddo."

Sadie gaped—Dot wasn't insinuating that she was overweight, was she? Sadie had worked hard to shed the baby weight, although she'd slacked in the last few months. She needed twenty-eight hours in a day to fit in all her jobs: nurse, short-order cook, playmate, teacher, housekeeper, babysitter.

Who knew where the hours went. It was like living life stuck on fast-forward.

"Okay, gotta go, kiddo." Dot forever called her students "kiddo." "Need to keep the old ticker over one twenty! See ya around."

Sadie sucked in her stomach and continued her walk. Wave caps broke in the distance and the air had a salty tang. Lincoln closed his eyes and smiled, the breeze tickling his cheeks.

Just as they passed the Cranberry Cove Bank with its emerald-green shutters and orange brick, a police cruiser rolled to a stop.

"Morning, Sadie. Lincoln." Officer Tyler Cox tipped his hat like a movie star from an old western movie. He looked like one, too, with his eternal five-o'clock shadow and whiskey-colored eyes. "You two holding up okay?"

Everyone knew Ethan commuted and the citizens of Cranberry Cove, especially the town's small-but-mighty police force, were constantly checking in on Sadie as if they knew she was barely treading water.

"We are, thanks." *Fake it until you make it.*

"I pee-pee!" Lincoln announced. "I make the silly pee-pee go in the tub!"

Sadie wrinkled her nose. "Not our preferred location obviously, but we'll take what we can get."

"You?" Lincoln pointed to Tyler. "You make the pee-pee, too?"

Tyler cleared his throat and Sadie was willing to bet that her cheeks matched the Lobster Shack sign swinging over her head. "Okay then. Well, on that note, we're really running late to see Dr. Hanlon. See you around."

At this rate, they were going to be twenty minutes past their appointment time. It would take a miracle for Dr. Hanlon to still see them, but rescheduling would be yet another item on her ever-growing to-do list.

She only made it a few more steps before another interruption.

"Where's the fire?" Essie Park called from a bistro table in front of Morning Joe's Coffee Shop, the *Cove Herald* opened next to her delicious-looking latte. Even though Essie was forty-something, she looked a decade younger with her light peach skin, jet-black hair, and chocolate-brown eyes. While the town's number-one real estate agent always attributed her good looks to her Korean genes, Sadie couldn't help but wonder if Botox played a helping hand.

"Can't chat." Sadie refused to stop a third time. "We're so freaking late."

"Well don't slow down on my account. I only wanted to

pass along the latest bit of real estate news—the Old Red Mill finally sold. Isn't that something?"

"For sure!" *Why in the world would that interest me?* The question vanished as she *finally* barged through the front door of the Coastal Kids Medical Group. The walls were a calming shade of marine blue, and a saltwater fish tank lined an entire wall. Two children were standing in front of it, their breath fogging the glass while they inspected the clown fish and anemones.

As usual, Renee Rhodes was perched at the reception desk in her high-backed ergonomic chair and she smiled brightly in greeting.

"Hey, neighbor." Sadie straightened her posture. "I know being fashionably late doesn't apply to doctor visits, but it's been a morning. Is there any chance we can still be seen?"

Her next-door neighbor, Renee, would never be late to an appointment. Sadie used to babysit her daughter, Tansy, and she'd always arrived to an impeccably clean home that smelled of peonies and fresh-baked snickerdoodles. Renee would leave something delicious for dinner and have checked out the latest cartoon from the library for the girls to watch. The perfect mother. The kind of "together" woman Sadie had always imagined that she'd be.

"It's late," Renee admitted, after a glance at the clock. "But don't worry, I'm sure Dr. Hanlon can squeeze you—"

Before Renee could finish her sentence, another wave of nausea hit. This one meant serious business.

"I'm sorry, can you take him for a sec? Please?" Sadie shoved Lincoln at Renee, bolting to the restroom.

Before the door latched shut, she fell to her knees, vomited into the toilet, then slumped against the tile wall. Pressing a clammy, cold hand against her forehead, she gasped. "Stupid chicken thighs."

It was last night's chicken, right? Yes, of course. It had to be.

Because the alternative was simply too terrifying.

# Chapter Two

"C an you spy the orange-and-white fishy?" Renee Rhodes asked Lincoln, pointing to the saltwater tank. "You have to look hard because he swims fast!"

The toddler nodded, fixing his gaze on the clown fish with nose-scrunched determination.

"Great! Now see if you can spot the crab."

He clapped his hands and wiggled his little butt.

God, kids were so sweet at this age.

After ensuring Lincoln was hypnotized by the underwater world, Renee made her way to the watercooler to fetch his poor mama a drink. Sadie looked rotten, her freckled cheeks sallow and dark circles bruising the skin beneath her eyes. A far cry from the perky babysitter who would bring her daughter *Baby-Sitters Club* books and Popsicle-stick craft projects.

She smiled as she held the glass under the tap. For nearly

eighteen years, Renee's calendar had been scribbled with bake sale reminders, PTA meeting times, and school performance dates. Her nights had been spent sneaking veggies into sauces, helping Tansy with homework assignments, and reading *In the Night Kitchen* a hundred times.

Some might find it boring, but she had loved every second.

Sadie was just starting that journey; a notion Renee sheepishly admitted made her a little green with envy.

The Landrys had bought the one-hundred-year-old cottage next to her two years ago, when the Brewers relocated to North Carolina. Prior to the Brewers, Sadie's grandparents had lived in the home. While the Brewers had been great neighbors, Renee loved the fact that the cottage was back with the original family.

Before moving in, Sadie had had the house renovated. And, as an interior designer, she'd done an exceptional job. From the refinished hardwood floors to the recycled glass kitchen countertops and curated New England artwork, the Landrys' cottage looked like something out of the pages of a home design magazine.

And in addition to their gorgeous home, they had the best gift of all: little Lincoln, so curious and sweet. The early years weren't easy, of course, but the happy memories eventually won out: watching your child take their first steps on the beach or getting a lick of ice cream.

Her gaze strayed to the framed photo of Tansy on her desk. It was from her graduation last June. Her smile was big (and straight, thanks to a small fortune spent on braces) but her eyes were narrowed, the sun shining in her face. Her yellow National Honors Society cords hung around her neck and Renee's mother's diamond studs glinted from her ears.

*My beautiful, smart girl.*

Tansy was a freshman at the University of Southern California, worlds away from their little New England town.

"I'm telling you, Mom, I love it here," she'd declared only two weeks into the term, a time when most students struggle with the first pangs of homesickness. "I never want to leave. It's like I was always meant to be in SoCal."

"Yeah? That must feel so...exciting," Renee had said, trying to force a smile into her voice. "I guess California *is* the perfect place for the next Nora Ephron."

"Uh-huh. Sure, Mom." Tansy had sounded strangely self-conscious at the comment.

"What?" The two of them had swooned over Nora Ephron films for years, gushing over favorites like *When Harry Met Sally*. Tansy was an aspiring screenwriter, and they loved to dream she would be the next queen of romantic comedies.

Tansy sighed. "I've gotta run to class. Chat tomorrow?"

Except they never did. Not the next day, or the day after that. It was left to Renee to reach out and more often than not, her calls were sent to voicemail. Texting had become Tansy's preferred method of communication and Renee was eternally trying to decipher the subtext of animated gifs.

Sadie stumbled out of the bathroom and Lincoln ran

toward her, nestling his head against her thighs as if he couldn't get close enough.

"Here you go." Renee handed her the glass. "Sip this. It should help."

"Thanks." Sadie's eyes didn't match her smile. "Sorry about that whole production. I probably undercooked dinner. Or maybe I'm coming down with some spring flu...?"

She stared at Renee for some sort of answer, like she was the designated adult in the room.

"Also I've been having these crappy headaches. And mood swings. Crazy mood swings. And on top of that? I'm so wiped out all the time. Like I could pass out by two in the afternoon. Is that normal? You know, for life with a toddler? I mean I sound like I'm falling apart, don't I?"

There was no polite way to ask the obvious question, so Renee blazed ahead.

"Is there any chance you could be pregnant?"

The frazzled young mom shook her head with such force that she risked giving herself whiplash.

"Oh, God, no. Not a chance." She tried to laugh, though what came out sounded like a gasp or sob. "That's impossible."

"Okay." Renee nodded, understanding this was not a path she wished to travel down. "I'm sure it's just a little virus then."

"Well if it isn't Lincoln Landry!" Renee's boss, Dr. Dan Hanlon, called, entering the waiting room, ending the awkward moment. He held up one of his big hands and Lincoln high-fived it with gusto. "Whoa there. You've gotten stronger since I last saw you! What's your favorite green vegetable?"

Lincoln clapped a hand over his mouth and giggled. "Broccoli."

"Sorry we're so late," Sadie apologized, her cheeks splotchy. "I don't want to mess up your schedule, and completely understand if you don't have time to—"

"It's no worry at all. Life with a toddler is the definition of 'unpredictable.'" Dr. Dan smiled kindly. "Why don't you and Lincoln head back to room three?"

Sadie nodded gratefully, tucking a stray lock of brown hair behind her ear before marching off. Dr. Dan's arm grazed Renee's as he walked by, shooting her a conspiratorial "what can you do" shrug before following the pair down the hall.

Her arm tingled from the contact and Renee bit her lower lip as she contemplated yet again just how well Dr. Dan's ocean-blue eyes matched his tie, a tie she'd given him last Christmas.

Not that it meant anything. It was just a tie. A tie she'd researched during a three-hour online shopping mission and a gift she'd wrapped three times before she got the bow exactly perfect.

A simple tie. A boss gift. No big deal.

Nothing to see here.

Every morning, Dr. Dan passed along the tear-off from his word-of-the-day desk calendar. Today's word? "Chary," which meant careful, cautious. How appropriate. Best to be *chary* in this situation. She had no business crushing on her boss or his dead-sexy baby blues.

Intensely private in some ways yet incredibly warm in others, Dr. Dan was a widower who knew his way around his forty-foot sloop moored down at the harbor. And lord, did he have the tan, craggy good looks to prove it—not to mention a darn near perfect shoulder-to-hip ratio.

"I wanted to see all the fall foliage," Dr. Dan had once given as a vague explanation for his move. "Not to mention a low cost of living and high quality of life." Though according to Essie Park, who had sold him his log cabin out in the willy wacks, he'd come from away, seeking a change of scenery following the death of his wife.

"Sounds like Sam Baldwin to me," she could hear Tansy saying with her impish grin, referencing her favorite movie, *Sleepless in Seattle*. "Maybe he's ready to find his Annie Reed?"

Renee cleared her throat and her mind.

Though Essie was well intentioned, she never met a story that she didn't embellish. For all Renee knew, Dr. Dan had been a widower for years and was no stranger to the dating scene. He probably had a new fascinating woman on his boat each weekend.

All that added up to mean that Dr. Dan's bare left hand was a whole lot of none of her business.

And even if he *was* available, he was her employer—a no-go zone, venture into that territory and there be dragons. Besides, why would he ever look twice at her, a homebody receptionist who hadn't gotten any in a decade?

If he wanted a catch there were plenty of fish with perkier boobs and sexier underwear.

\* \* \*

At five fifteen, Renee checked out the final patient of the day, Eloise Collins with a double ear infection. The little girl clutched a stuffed rabbit to her chest, sucking her thumb.

"Thanks again for squeezing us in." Jack Collins signed his credit card receipt with a flourish. "I know the office closes at four thirty, but I've never seen Ellie like this."

"Don't give it a second thought." Renee smiled in understanding. "We couldn't have Miss Eloise going all night in pain. The prescription Dr. Hanlon gave you will kick the infection fast. It always worked for my daughter. She was on the swim team, and if there was a single germ in the pool, I swear it found its way into her ear canal."

Jack nodded absently, helping his daughter into her bright pink jacket and waving goodbye. Renee watched them go, thinking of all the times she had to give Tansy eardrops. Tansy hated the sensation, so she'd always pop on the Disney Channel as her daughter relaxed her head into her lap. Working quickly and humming softly, Renee would drip in the antifungal medication, massaging her tiny earlobes after each dosage.

She gave a wistful smile as she locked the front door and slid into her windbreaker.

Kids—the reason parents lost it, *and* the reason they kept it together.

Just then, a hand clasped her shoulder, the touch so unexpected and unfamiliar that she yelped.

"Shoot! Didn't mean to scare you." Dr. Dan flashed an apologetic grin and took three brisk steps back, leaving ample personal space. "I just came out to say thanks for sticking around late. I'd have hated to send the Collinses to urgent care."

Renee nodded, barely able to process his words. How could she think of anything else when the warm sensation of his palm remained branded on her skin? "Thirty miles would feel like three hundred to a sick kid."

"You've got such a good heart." He looked down at her with such intensity that it was either transfer her gaze to the carpeted floor or combust into flames.

"You can count on me," she muttered lamely, repeating the silly line her entire drive home.

*You can count on me?*

What was she, a loyal golden retriever?

Renee parked her silver sedan on Seashell Lane and clicked the automatic lock button—always twice for extra measure, despite the fact that Cranberry Cove had to be the safest town in America—before opening the gate to her picket fence. A cobblestone path led to her gray-shingled cottage. This house, her home for the past twenty years, was the second-best treasure from her marriage to Russell Rhodes, the first being Tansy, of course.

Oh, Russ. They'd moved here at twenty-two—such babies!

Did her ex ever think about their days here in the

cottage? Did he ever regret the life he tossed away like a used tissue?

When they first moved in here, she'd had a perfect picture of how her married life would turn out. Long walks together on the beach at dusk, skipping stones into the water. Four to six noisy kids. A house filled with love and laughter.

Renee's sigh felt loud in the silence. It wasn't all doom and gloom. She had Tansy. And her garden: the phlox, forsythia, and lilacs, the blueberries and sweet fern—everything slowly waking from a long winter's nap. She hugged herself close. The world was coming alive. It seemed so monumentally unfair to feel this empty inside.

"Hey there, mister!" Sadie was laughing next door. Renee could see them across the fence in their little kitchen, the window above the sink propped open. Lincoln was setting dish soap bubbles on his mother's nose and cheeks, finding the effect hilarious. "What is Daddy going to say when he gets home? Think he'll recognize me?"

Lincoln broke into helpless giggles. "Mommy! Mommy! You look like Santy Claus!"

"Ho! Ho! Ho!"

Tears welled up in Renee's eyes as she plopped on the wooden bench in her side yard and picked up a tiny stone bridge from the ground. It was part of Tansy's childhood fairy garden, which Renee still tended to with such devotion, one would have thought she was caring for Versailles.

She fished around in her purse until she located her cellphone.

The phone rang four times before Tansy picked up with a breathless "Hey." Music thumped in the background.

"What's up?" Tansy shouted. "Whatcha need?"

"Hello to you, too." Renee arched a brow. "I was just checking to see what you were up to." Clearly not hitting the books.

"It's the Final Four tonight!" Tansy's voice muffled as she pressed her lips too close to the mic. "Um, sorry it's sort of loud! We're getting ready to watch the game."

Renee flipped through her limited sports knowledge. Final Four, so that meant...

"Basketball?"

"Ding! Ding! Ding!"

Renee bit her thumbnail, an awful habit she'd carried all the way from girlhood into middle age. "Since when are you into basketball?"

"Whatever. It's fun." Tansy sounded a little loopy, a little too carefree. A distinctly male voice murmured in the background, right as her daughter gave a coy giggle. "Hey look, I've gotta run! Doing anything fun tonight?"

"You bet," Renee lied. "Off to Bree's. We're...um, making Italian. Lasagna, in fact. And we're going to check out that new Rebel Wilson movie."

"Oh, haven't heard of it, but sounds awesome!" Tansy accepted the fib easily, readily. "Give Aunt B a squeeze for me!"

The subsequent silence was somehow even worse than before. A caterpillar crawled near the toe of her shoe. She watched its painstaking journey with a small frown. What would it be like to encase herself in a cocoon and emerge as a beautiful, bold butterfly?

She lingered on the bench long after the caterpillar disappeared into the undergrowth, not quite sure what to do with herself. She didn't even jump when a clap of thunder erupted in the sky. Not until the first raindrops started to hit her cheeks did she finally stir, gathering her purse to head inside her empty house, where she would eat leftover chicken pot pie and binge Netflix until it was late enough for bed.

Tansy was off tailgating. Sadie was soon to be snuggled up with her handsome husband and sweet toddler as they read one final bedtime story. Bree was undoubtedly knitting while gossiping with her bestie, Jill. And Dr. Dan was definitely sharing a bottle of red with a gorgeous, fascinating woman.

God she was lonely.

# About the Author

Sarah Mackenzie lives and writes in New England.

### THE SUMMER COTTAGE
### by Annie Rains

Somerset Lake is the perfect place for Trisha Langly and her son to start over. As the new manager for the Somerset Cottages, she's instantly charmed by her firecracker of a boss, Vi—but less enchanted by Vi's protective grandson, attorney Jake Fletcher. If Jake discovers her past, she'll lose this perfect second chance. However, as they spend summer days renovating the property and nights enjoying the town's charm, Trisha may realize she must trust Jake with her secrets…and her heart. Includes a bonus story!

### FALLING IN LOVE
### ON WILLOW CREEK
### by Debbie Mason

FBI agent Chase Roberts has come to Highland Falls to work undercover as a park ranger to track down an on-the-run informant. But when he befriends the suspect's sister to get nearer to his target, Chase finds that he's growing closer to the warm-hearted, beautiful Sadie Gray and her little girl. When he arrests her brother, Elijah, Chase risks losing Sadie forever. Can he convince her that the feelings between them are real once Sadie discovers the truth? Includes a bonus story!

## A WEDDING ON LILAC LANE
### by Hope Ramsay

After returning home from her country music career, Ella McMillan is shocked to find her mother is engaged. Worse, she asks Ella to plan the event with her fiancé's straitlaced son, Dr. Dylan Killough. While Ella wants to create the perfect day, Dylan is determined the two shouldn't get married at all. Somehow amid all their arguing, sparks start flying. And soon everyone in Magnolia Harbor is wondering if Dylan and Ella will be joining their parents in a trip down the aisle.

## FRIENDS LIKE US
### by Sarah Mackenzie

When a cancer scare compels Bree Robinson to form an *anti*-bucket list, she decides to start with a steamy fling. Only her one-night stand is Chance Elliston, the architect she's just hired to renovate her house. Bree agrees to a friends-with-benefits relationship with Chance before he returns to the city at the end of the summer. But as their feelings for each other grow, can she convince him to risk it all on a new life together?

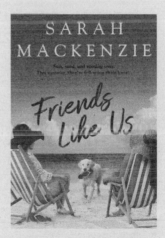

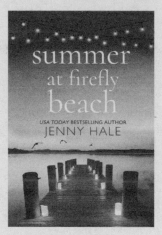

### SUMMER AT FIREFLY BEACH
### by Jenny Hale

Hallie Flynn adores her aunt Clara's beautiful beachside house, yet a busy job and heartbreak over the years have kept her away. But when her beloved aunt passes, Hallie returns to fulfill her final wish: to complete the bucket list Hallie wrote as a teenager. With the help of her childhood friend Ben Murray, she remembers her forgotten dreams ... and finds herself falling for the man who's always been by her side. But to have a future with Ben, can Hallie face the truths buried deep in her heart?

### ONCE UPON A PUPPY
### by Lizzie Shane

Lawyer Connor Wyeth has a plan for everything—except training his unruly mutt, Maximus. The only person Max ever obeyed was animal shelter volunteer Deenie Mitchell. But with a day job hosting princess parties for kids, the upbeat Deenie isn't thrilled to co-parent with Max's uptight owner ... until she realizes he's perfect for impressing her type-A family. As they play the perfect couple, it begins to feel all too real. Can one rambunctious dog bring together two complete opposites?

"Holiday is a consummate master of witty banter."
—ENTERTAINMENT WEEKLY

### SANDCASTLE BEACH
### by Jenny Holiday

What Maya Mehta really needs to save her beloved community theater is Matchmaker Bay's new business grant. She's got some serious competition, though: Benjamin Lawson, local bar owner, Jerk Extraordinaire, and Maya's annoyingly hot archnemesis. Turns out there's a thin line between hate and irresistible desire, and Maya and Law are really good at crossing it. But when things heat up, will they allow their long-standing feud to get in the way of their growing feelings? Includes the bonus story *Once Upon a Bride*, for the first time in print!

### DREAM SPINNER
### by Kristen Ashley

There's no doubt that former soldier Axl Pantera is the man of Hattie Yates's dreams. Yet years of abuse from her demanding father have left her terrified of disappointment. Axl is slowly wooing Hattie into letting down her walls—until a dangerous stalker sets their sights on her. Now he's facing more than her wary and bruised heart. Axl will do anything to prove that they're meant to be— but first, he'll need to keep Hattie safe.